VALOR

HIDDEN NATURE

S. M. SAVOY

Published by
Ace Lyon Books
January
2021

Published by
Ace Lyon Books LLC
Acelyonbooks.com
First Edition
Cover Design by S. M. Savoy
S. M. Savoy *Hidden Nature*
ISBN
eBook:978-1-947122-42-0
Paperback:978-1-947122-43-7

BOOKS BY

S. M. SAVOY

Valor

A Warrior's Fury

A Sun Priest's Magic

Beyond Valor

A Rogue's Passion

RELATED SERIES

Return of the Fae

Enter the Frey

Danu's Children

COMING SOON

Forged by Lightning

Essence of the Storm

Storm Wrought

COMING SOON

Dusted

TABLE OF CONTENTS

HIDDEN NATURE

-1-

ATTACK AT THE SKI LODGE

Charlie's life at the naval academy was almost back to normal— or as normal as he got. Sara was on the road to recovery and slowly but surely regaining her strength. The fight for dominance with the magic had taken all her reserves. Not an ounce of excess flesh remained on her bones. The week-long struggle, on top of the week she'd spent unconscious from the stasis chamber, had left the magic no choice but to use muscle-mass to provide energy. But given time, Sara would recover completely.

Her work at the lab had come to a complete standstill. Oz stayed busy working on all their myriad projects and teaching classes. *A mage's mind never stilled*, Charlie thought, grinning ruefully.

A priest's mind was just as active. Sara had insisted on returning to teaching, promising Liz she'd nap before and after, and quit work in the lab until she'd built up more stamina. The tanning bed helped. Food and rest helped more.

One crisis at a time, Charlie reminded himself before his circling thoughts could generate enough anger and worry for her to feel.

Before the new magic wielders could meet her, she needed to build up some reserves. Another struggle for dominance with her magic in her condition would kill her.

No one mentioned the new warriors to either of them. Everyone tried to project normalcy in the hopes that faking it would make it true. The death and resurrection of Joy was neither spoken of nor alluded to. No one wanted to upset Sara's balance, least of all him.

Joy was likely headed there now, he thought as he spied her near Sara's door, and he picked up his pace to join her.

Joy saw him coming and waited for him to catch up. Charlie gave her a quick hug. His magic hummed happily as it always did when he saw her. He wondered for a moment if this was how his magic would've responded to Sara if he hadn't made that vow and connected them like he had. But sharing Sara's sparkling happiness at her first sight of them convinced him that he was glad he could sense her like he could.

Joy kissed Sara's cheek as the magic swirled about them, looping and flowing in thick skeins and tight spirals.

Joy said, "Keep greeting me like this and my head will swell."

Sara recalled her magic, smiling ruefully as it immediately left Joy and reabsorbed. Her magic was being very obedient.

"I'm trying to work out a balance with the magic, letting it have what it wants whenever I can, and it loves you. We both love you. Letting it touch you is easy. Neither of us mind that you feel our love."

"I love you too," Joy said.

Sara smiled and closed her eyes, drifting to sleep.

Charlie knew they'd both meant it as they knew he loved them too without him having to say a thing. A lie was impossible surrounded by magic. The magic made feelings clear, reveling in them and magnifying them. Joy kissed Charlie's cheek and tiptoed out, leaving Sara sleeping.

Charlie smoothed Sara's hair before going to find Liz to look over Sara's latest test results again. Her lack of energy was really worrying him.

He found Liz in her office and knocked lightly on the open door.

"Come in."

She rose to hug him and gestured him to a seat when she broke from the hug.

"Sara is doing very well."

"She's so tired," he said.

"That's to be expected until the muscles can regrow. She's completely cured from the Paraneoplastic Syndrome, and if the magic will let her hormones alone, I don't foresee her relapsing, but I'll be running weekly tests and if her high levels fluctuate at all, we'll know it."

"And then what?" Charlie asked bitterly.

"We'll cross that bridge when we come to it but, Charlie, the magic has no need to try this again."

"She can't fight it again." Saying the words made him slightly breathless as if he'd run for miles.

Liz winced. "She has no need to. It's behaving. I don't recommend she goes without contact with other magic wielders. Her magic has evolved, and I doubt it will ever become completely quiescent again, but it seems happy enough with the contact she allows it with others of its kind."

Charlie stood. "I really hate this." He more than hated it. Worry and guilt were making his bones ache.

"I know and I'm so sorry."

"It's my own fault. I know that."

"None of this is your fault. It isn't wrong to want things for yourself, Charlie."

"I'll take better care of her, of all of them. Call me if there are any changes."

Charlie closed the door behind himself and leaned against it a moment, reigning in his anger.

Sara had never blamed him for leaving her behind to go the *Truman,* no one had blamed him. But he knew if he'd never gone, her magic would never have woken like it had.

"Being angry won't help any of us," he muttered as he began to jog to the gym. He'd burn off some of his rage and maybe he'd be calm enough not to worry anyone by the time she woke.

A week later Charlie grabbed his math book and headed to the door, holding it for his roommates to exit.

"Paul, I was hoping you could find some time to walk with Sara today? She wanted to talk over some of your game designs, and she could really use the exercise."

"Sure. I can't believe how much better she's doing already."

Charlie hid his wince, He hated lying about her illness, especially to Paul.

He said, "She *is* doing better. She can walk a few laps now without needing to rest. Stasia is meeting her this morning for some light sparing, and Hawk will take her for a walk for me tonight while I stand my watch, but she'll have some free time right after lunch. Don't tell her I sent you though. I don't want her to know that I'm worried—and go slow."

"You're sure all this exercise is okay?"

"Doctor's orders. Liz has proscribed frequent light exercise. If we leave Sara to her own devices though she'd sit at her desk thinking all day. But she'll happily join us as long as she believes she isn't bothering us."

He grimaced ruefully because there was no way to fool her. She was getting seriously annoyed by their worried hovering, and far as he was concerned, she was much too obsessed with finding out who'd orchestrated the abduction of the president last fall. Both she and Oz spent every free minute investigating. She stayed up late almost every night and it was much too worrying. But Paul had no magic for her to sense and he loved talking about his game ideas. He was the perfect companion for her.

The guards at the door greeted Paul with smiles and waved him right in.

Sara was in her classroom and grinned when she saw him.

He said, "Charlie said you wanted to talk over some of my game ideas?"

"Yeah, we were —"

Paul interrupted, "Can we talk outside? I've been inside all day and could use some fresh air."

She rolled her eyes but joined him where she grabbed her coat from a hook by the door and donned it, making an extravagant gesture.

Paul laughed to himself as he led her to the track. She knew he'd been sent and told to bring her outside, but she seemed genuinely interested in talking about his games. When he described his newest idea, she laughed so hard she had to sit for a few minutes to catch her breath. Still snickering she lay in the grass wiping tears of laughter from her cheeks.

Paul sat beside her.

She sat up, leaning on one elbow, and said, "I've been meaning to speak with you about your games. Charlie and I spoke to Mr. Martin, our lawyer, and we want to offer you financing to get your company up and running so that your games will be ready for the release of Virtual Imagery."

"I don't have the kind of money it will take to produce them. I'll need to get investors and hire a business manager. I'm sure I can do that, but not for the release. Once the game is going, I'll have investors coming out of the woodwork."

"You don't need to wait. I'll be your investor and supply all financing and you retain full control of your company. Charlie's dad will get your games ready for distribution until you're ready to take over. Mr. Martin drew up the papers already. Take them to your own lawyer."

She sat, looking a bit anxious. "This isn't charity; it's good business for us. If we don't want our product to tank, we need good games available at the launch. You'd be doing us a huge favor. I emailed you my lawyer's info. Please talk to him soon. We really need to start production to make our deadlines."

Paul jumped up and offered her a hand to rise. She accepted the help, giving him a quick hug.

Charlie was a lucky son of bitch, he thought wistfully as he tucked a strand of golden blonde hair behind her ear. The blue of her eyes exactly matched the blue of her parka. She looked more like her mother all the time, but she had her father's genius for design. He wondered again why she didn't work with him.

He said, "It's good to see you looking so well. Almost back to normal."

"Thanks, it's good to be back to normal, or as normal as I get anyway." A small snort of laughter was quickly smothered as she waved a hand, dismissing his inquisitive look.

Paul escorted her back to the VI building, handing her off to a guard at the door.

She waved and headed inside.

The guard nodded a friendly greeting, but her attention was on Sara, not him.

They both headed to the private elevator that led to the lower level he'd never been in, and he wonder again what they were working on so diligently in the basement.

A fluttering four-inch Valkyrie appeared when Charlie sat down at his desk. His Valory held out a sheet of paper. Charlie reached for the paper and heaved a deep sigh, knowing it would be a request from Major Nelson to attend this week's practice session.

Valory disappeared. The paper fluttered into the air morphing into a computer screen displaying his messages.

His roommates glanced over but they were used to the small figure appearing and quickly turned back to their own desks.

The tone of the note told him the major was losing patience. He hadn't issued a direct order, but he was clearly annoyed.

Charlie sent a denial to the requested meeting for a practice, putting off meeting the new magic wielders again. He hated to avoid his brother, but Sara was still weak and tired easily. The thought of her fighting with her magic again sickened him. The thought of her wanting another warrior made him flush with rage. He put it out of his mind as best he could, which wasn't very well at all. Her anxiety, a direct reaction to his anger, thrummed along his nerves like a toothache.

"Paul, does the invitation to come skiing stand?" Charlie asked.

"Sure, anytime you want. You can stay with us or there's a great lodge nearby. They have a huge fireplace and cozy chairs big enough for two. It's a great spot to bring a date— or find one."

Paul winked at him and Charlie laughed and rolled his eyes.

He said, "How about this weekend? Sara could use some fun."

"Is she well enough to ski?" Paul asked doubtfully.

"Well, not all day, but a bunny slope—sure."

Paul said, "My little brother, Andy, could teach her. He works there part-time when demand is high. You can come over and meet my family. They've been dying to meet you. If Sara likes Andy, he can show her."

Friday, after class, the three of them headed to Vermont in the VI jet.

They had a late dinner at Paul's house and met Paul's family. His sister Abby, his little brother, Andy, and his older brother Trevor were home. Trevor had attended the academy ten years before and told stories of his time there that had everyone laughing. Sara and Andy hit it off right away. He took her to the bunny slope Saturday morning and taught her the rudiments while Paul, Abby, Trevor, and Charlie raced down from the top.

Sara was red-faced and laughing when they met for lunch. She went to the room to nap while the five of them skied. That evening they had dinner again at Paul's parent's house.

On Sunday, Andy gave Sara more lessons until she tired and returned to the lodge.

Charlie came in after his run and kissed her, happy to see her aura so bright.

"Where's Paul?" she asked.

"He says he's packing." He winked and she giggled.

He said, "I'm just glad it wasn't Hannah."

"Me too!" She shuddered dramatically, and he laughed.

"One more run and we'll head home. This was fun. We'll have to come again."

The smile on her face was more than skin deep.

Firelight flickered across her blond hair and flushed her cheeks. *I should've put Hawk in our group for his buff*, he thought as he tucked a plaid blanket about her legs. She grinned up at him. Her teeth were chattering even though she still wore her ski suit, gloves and all, but she was happy, and she'd warm soon before the fire beneath the wool blanket.

She said, "Have fun. I'm going to drink hot chocolate and admire the scenery. Maybe I'll go to our room and take a nap to be rested for tonight."

Anticipation echoed between them. The magic amplified the desire they shared. It had been a month since they'd made love. She'd been too weak and afraid of her magic's response. He loved that she was confident in her control now.

"I love you too." He traced her brow with a fingertip as he closed his eyes and kissed her. The constant ache had eased and for the first time in weeks the weak hollow feeling in his gut dissipated.

Please, God, let us get out of this loop, he prayed earnestly. He knew that he was the cause of the loop, that it was his guilt and anger making them both feel bad but maybe now that he felt her contentment he'd be able to forgive himself or at least not dwell on it.

Soon, he promised his magic as it pushed for contact. Content with how he felt, it didn't push hard.

The bartender eyed the two women sitting alone in the lounge as he mixed their drinks. *Either would do.* One had ordered a margarita, the other hot chocolate. The blond was exactly his type though, curvy and weak. Her boyfriend was a big strong guy. She'd never give a man like him a second glance. He could tell she was in love, her eyes lit whenever the boyfriend came near her.

He laughed to himself. A few drops in her drink and she'd be his. The boyfriend would never know. While he was out showing off to his friends, he'd be doing whatever he wanted to his girlfriend and she wouldn't remember a thing. The bartender glanced at his watch. Her boyfriend had just left, he had a good forty-five minutes.

He added the drops to the cocoa.

The blond smiled as she took the drink in her gloved hands. He smirked back.

Charlie tipped his head back, enjoying the winter sun on his face. One more run and they'd head home. *Maybe she could meet the warriors she'd made soon.* While he wasn't looking forward to it, it had to be done and maybe the doing of it would kill his guilt for good.

Beside him on the chairlift, Andy pointed out deer tracks on the edge of the slope.

Charlie sighed happily and closed his eyes, enjoying the feel of Sara's contentment. This was exactly what she'd needed; time away doing something completely normal. He was tempted to put off their return but knew she'd worry about him missing school.

Her sudden fear buffeted him with a shock like ice water to the face, startling an oath from him. She was suddenly terrified and wanted him desperately.

"Help." Slurred and weak, her voice was barely audible from his wristcomp.

"Sara?" He didn't wait for her response, her terror goaded him to action. He jumped from the lift, ignoring the shocked cries of the others riding it up.

"I'm coming!"

"He just jumped thirty-feet!" A man in the lift chair behind him exclaimed in disbelief. Charlie knew he was taking dangerous chances with exposing his cover— and he didn't care.

- 2 -

CAN'T CHANGE THE PAST

The bartender grinned as she dropped the cup. He plucked a damp rag from the bar top and sauntered over. He was surprised to find her unconscious. Usually, they were just woozy for longer than that. Another patron glanced over, and he waved him away.

"Just a bit too much to drink. I'll see her to her room." The patron turned back to his book, and the bartender grinned. *Like shooting fish in a barrel.*

Excitement lit a fire in his stomach. His hands practically itched to undress her, and he grabbed her a bit more eagerly than he ought to with so many witnesses present.

The blond hardly weighed a thing. The bulky red sweater and down jacket she wore made her look bigger than she was. The dose he'd given her was probably a bit too much. Nothing he hadn't dealt with in the past. The boyfriend would come back and find her still out with an empty bottle of cheap wine beside her.

He threw one of her arms around his neck while he supported her weight with an arm around her waist and dragged her from the room. Sweat trickled down his brow, a combination of nerves and anticipation. No one appeared to be giving them a second glance and he had to bite back his giddy laughter.

The service elevator was empty, and he let her fall to the floor. Her room key was in her pocket and she was in the room right beside the elevator. Humming happily to himself, he let himself into her room.

Charlie called Paul as he skied down the mountain. "Something's wrong with Sara. Get to her right now. She was in the lounge." He glanced at his wristcomp to verify her position. "She's moving, but not responding to me. I think someone has her. Hurry, Paul. They could be armed. If they are armed, stay back, but keep her in sight if you can. I'm calling our security right now. Don't risk yourself. Her security can get to her in ten minutes.

"I'm linking you her whereabouts. She's the white dot. The red dot is who has her. I'm on my way." He hit his panic button and said, "No one summon her. I want to catch these bastards!"

"Valory, give me access to Sara's wristcomp! Show me a three-sixty view!" he snapped.

A screen sprang up in front of Charlie's left shoulder showing a man in jeans and white sneakers dragging her. Rage tightened all of his muscles and the screen gained clarity. He knew his eyes had begun to glow and he welcomed the surge of adrenaline that left him feeling invincible.

A harsh laugh escaped him. He *was* invincible. Is all it would take was a flick of his fingers and nothing -and no one— could harm him. His laugh changed to a snarl. They could harm her though.

The angle from her wristcomp was bad, and he couldn't see the man's face. He debated telling whoever it was he could see him and decided not to. He was still at least five minutes away and didn't want to panic the man into killing her.

The man dropped her to the floor of the elevator and took her room key from her pocket. Charlie didn't know if he'd dropped her before her shocks could hit him or just because he was on the elevator.

The man entered their room and put Sara on the bed, blocking the view with his body now. There was something lecherous in the way he touched her, the slide of his hand against her bright hair, the finger that traced her bottom lip, and fresh rage infused him.

But his behavior made Charlie think the man had no idea what Sara was.

"I'm on my way to you, Sara," Charlie said loudly over her wristcomp.

The man started violently, jumping back, revealing her lifted shirt and undone pants. Her face was bright red, and she was sweating profusely.

The chubby, red-faced man, who Charlie recognized as the bartender, was reaching into his pocket when the door was kicked open and Paul ran into the room.

"Get away from her!" Paul shouted as he tapped his wristcomp.

The bartender straightened and lifted his hands to show they were empty, smiling and licking his lips. "I was just helping her to her room."

Paul braced himself and gestured with a clenched fist. "Get down on the floor!"

"Look, man, I was just helping her," the bartender repeated. "She said she wasn't feeling well."

"Is he armed?" Charlie asked anxiously as he fumbled for his sunglasses. He was tempted to summon her away now that he knew the identity of the man but how would he explain her disappearance?

Paul said, "Doesn't appear to be. I see no gun or knife. Both of his hands are visible."

"He's lying. Sara called me. Don't let him leave, Paul."

"He won't leave. Get down on the floor right now or I'll put you down!" Paul sidled closer.

The bartender dropped slowly to his knees, then lay on the carpeted floor.

Paul slid Sara's sleeve up to feel her pulse. "She's really sick, Chief." He shook her shoulder lightly and got no response. "I can't wake her."

Charlie forced his magic back, an effort of will that made him angrier. The magic fought him, but rage empowered him, and he was able to keep it beneath his skin. Normally, the magic and he were in accord. So much so that he seldom thought of it as a separate entity, but it was making its individual needs crystal clear now, pressing hard for release. A feeling of pins and needles rapidly progressed to a burning ache, but he was a warrior and pain empowered him. He ignored the magic, holding it in an iron grip, embracing the pain for the power it gave him.

He said, "Don't touch her. She'll freak if she wakes and you're touching her. I'm almost there."

"This is Major Elizabeth Harris. What's her condition?" Liz asked.

A small screen showing Liz sitting behind her desk appeared, hanging in the air over

Paul's left shoulder. Charlie's Valory had appeared the instant he glanced at the settings icon. He flicked the icon to mute everyone before saying, "Valory, mute everyone except me and Liz from Paul. Discreet mode," he finished, hoping the program to edit out any mentions of magic would work in the event they forgot that Paul was in the channel. It worked well in testing, but it did mean transmissions had a slight delay. Not that he thought the delay in speaking with Paul would make any difference whatsoever. She didn't need Paul. She needed him.

"Yes, sir," Valory said crisply, saluting and fading back into the screen that now showed small red Xs beside the raid identifier icons.

No one spoke in the public channel.

Every raid member had entered the call and he could see by the flickers in the coms bar that some were speaking, likely giving orders or asking for them. If he wanted to, he could listen in, but he didn't really care what they were doing. He swiped the screen, making it disappear.

"Valory, give me access to Paul's wristcomp. Three-sixty view. I want to see what he's looking at."

The screen shimmered and reformed to a three-dimensional image of Sara as seen from Paul's perspective. He was leaning over her.

Paul said, "Her pulse is fast and irregular and she's unresponsive. Her face is bright red. She's sweating heavily and there's a rash growing on her neck. Should I remove her coat and gloves?"

Charlie could see that for himself. Valory was also displaying a graph of her vitals that was growing brighter by the second.

"Audio alerts off," he said before the screen could begin to warn him that a raid member was in acute distress.

Liz said, "She's having an allergic reaction to whatever sedative he gave her. I'm calling the paramedics and ordering medicine for her. Give her Benadryl.

"Charlie, you'll have to give her an IV. I'm calling Doctor Gotlieb and Doctor Elliot now. Beta is on the way to you. Paul, right?" Liz asked.

"Yes."

"Don't let anyone touch her. Don't touch her yourself. Leave her as she is until Charlie gets there. That's an order."

"Yes, ma'am."

"Get some cloths in cold water. Charlie will need them. What's your ETA, Charlie?"

"I'm less than two minutes away. I can see the lodge." Charlie replied. He flicked off the image to read Liz's graphs, his pulse jumping at the information displayed.

She said, "Paramedics are in route to you. They're a good five minutes away. Keep her cool. She'll likely spike a temperature. Take a blood sample for me. We need to know what this is. Agent Lewis is on his way there. Both of you, no one touches her except Charlie, am I clear?"

Paul said yes again.

Charlie was trying to think of a reason to explain the pain from touching her. Sara's magic would be panicked and need him. Anyone else near her would cause it to react very badly.

Before he could say anything, Liz spoke. "She'll react violently to anyone else and might hurt herself trying to get away. I'm contacting both the police and paramedics right now, but if someone still tries to touch her, stop them."

The patrons outside the lodge exclaimed and hurried away as Charlie skied up. The ones inside mostly stared in shock although two women screamed. The patrons at the door scrambled out of his way, dropping their glasses, and rushing for the door. He ignored the effects of his aura and bounded up the stairs to their room.

"Have you touched her at all?"

"Her wrist for a few seconds checking her pulse." Paul ran into the bathroom and the water began to run.

Charlie kicked the bartender. "You, sick bastard!"

"I was trying to help her. I'm going to sue you!" he bawled through his sobs. He was cowering as far from Charlie as he could get.

"You're a lying sack of shit is what you are! I recorded everything!" Charlie leaned over Sara and smoothed her hair. One of her diamond studs was missing. He spell-stole her heal and used it on her, not caring if the man saw it or what he thought.

Paul returned and handed the wet cloths to him. "Should you take her sweater and snow pants off? She's sweating like a pig."

He said, "The pants are evidence. I'm sure his prints are on them."

Charlie grinned a hard smile when the bartender moaned piteously. He debated and decided to leave her gloves on. The magic might not shock anyone while she wore them.

He frowned as he removed her jacket, wishing now he hadn't made the magic react when she was touched but he couldn't change the past. If he could, he'd change more than that mistake. Her defensive shocks were making life harder for her and wasn't the protection he'd hoped, but he had no idea how'd they'd done it or how to undo it.

The magic was too literal. Because she'd donned the gloves willingly, the man had been able to touch her. Charlie knew removing them would make the magic shock anyone else, his mere presence might make it shock anyone else. He wasn't certain how it would react and that was the problem.

"Leave her alone," he muttered as he removed her coat. He tried to think hard at the magic, begging it to retreat and stop whatever it was doing.

Under her T-shirt, a rash went over her chest, up her neck, and down across her stomach.

He placed the cold washcloths on the reddest splotches, and he sent Paul for more for her wrists. While Paul was out of the room, he spell stole her heal and used it again.

The bartender screamed at the flash of light that burst from Charlie's hands

"Shut the fuck up!" he snapped, turning to glare at the man, who shrieked and huddled away. Charlie turned away before magical pressure made him do something unfortunate.

He removed her boots and threw them into a corner, but he slid her pants off, being careful not to touch the top waistband himself. She wore long johns under her ski pants, which he left on.

Her exposed skin appeared red and swollen. Sweat still streamed from her, dampening her hair and clothes.

The man on the floor cried, whining threats to sue between sobs as he huddled in the corner, clutching his knees and rocking.

Charlie kicked him in the leg. "One more fucking word and I'll rip your head off."

He immediately regretted saying it. Not because it further terrified the man, he was glad the man was terrified, but because his magic began to push harder for him to kill him.

Sara convulsed and began to vomit. Charlie rolled her onto her side and rubbed her back, glaring at the bartender. He really wanted to kill him, and it must have shown on his face or empowered his aura because the man began to scream.

Paul ran back into the room.

"Take him downstairs," Charlie said as he grabbed the wet towels from Paul. "Have the police search him; she's missing an earring and I want to know what the hell he used on her. Send the paramedics up."

Paul ran from the room.

"She's vomiting, Liz," he said worriedly as soon as Paul left. "I healed her and she's still unconscious."

"It's the sedative, Charlie," Liz said calmly. "Her body is trying to get rid of it. I don't know if it's something she was always allergic to or if her magic is trying to help her in its usual inept way. Paul, tell them it's a priority to find out what he used. I'm guessing he used something fast acting but with a short duration. She could wake any minute now."

Charlie cast Spell-Steal on her again as soon as it was up and healed her. "Jesus, Liz, her fever is going up quick. Heals aren't helping her."

His anger was quickly sliding into fear and his magic oozed from his skin. He didn't bother try to call it— or force it back. He didn't care if it showed. He really didn't think he could stand much more of this. Just contemplating her loss tore a moan of anguish from him. It felt as if he'd just gotten her back, and here she was again on the brink of death. His heart stuttered erratically, the magic's panic in perfect accord with his own.

Sara was the magic— not only in his life but literally. He wasn't sure what would happen to it if one of them were to die but he thought it would be a catastrophe beyond recovering from. The five of them held the magic inside themselves and he didn't think those pieces could be retrieved if lost. He was certain the magic was as concerned as he that Sara would be unrevivable. Just thinking it brought the magic to all new highs of panic, and his voice was strident as he said, "What do I do?"

"Get her into a tub of cool water. I'm pretty sure this is her magic. She'll probably wake panicked. Beta will find you a spot and summon you. Doctor Gotlieb says don't leave her alone, not for one minute."

Charlie picked her up and put her in the tub, clothes and all. "She's starting to shiver. The rash is horrible." The red had spread and formed large blisters that wept yellowish fluid. Charlie removed her long johns, getting soaked himself in the process. She vomited again and started to convulse.

"What do I do, Liz?" he asked again piteously as he climbed into the tub to hold her.

"She needs antihistamines." Liz opened the phone line to Paul. "Paul, see if you can locate any Benadryl or allergy medicine from anyone there. The ambulance will be there in two more minutes. Get an EPI pen and use it on her immediately."

Liz cut the audio feed to Paul.

Charlie made his screen bigger and positioned it above him. Oz stood beside Liz now, looking grim.

Liz said, "Anyone else would've died by now, and she still might. Charlie could rez her, but if he rezs her with the poison still inside her, she'll just die again. Using her cure poison won't work for a sedative. He'll reach the rez timer and be unable to save her."

Charlie knew that but hearing her say it tore a moan from him.

"Keep healing her," Oz said needlessly. Charlie was using both his spell-bracelet and Spell-Steal to heal her.

Liz said, "You need to control yourself too and not just to hide the magic but it's going to scare hers more."

Charlie forced himself to take three slow deep breaths. Liz was right but it was easier said than done. He needed something else to concentrate on. Hopefully, something that would calm the magic that was spinning around them.

"Report positions," he said as authoritatively as he could.

The raid began checking in. His pulse jumped when he saw his brother's icon light.

Marcus said, "We're in sight. I can see the police have the fucking bastard surrounded now."

Rage infused Charlie, more for the sound of his voice then the content of his sentence, but he embraced it, using his anger to pull the magic inside himself.

"Don't kill the fucker," he said although he wanted to order them too.

Brenda laughed a harsh bark of laughter.

Charlie said, "That's a direct order!"

Major Nelson said, "No one is killing anyone! Am I understood?"

In unison, except for the three warriors, the raid icons flicked green. He wasn't sure if Oz had put in a protocol for their responses to be last or if they were debating breaking their orders. He made a mental note to check and then put it out of his mind. He didn't care if they broke them. In fact, he almost hoped they would although that would likely lead to more trouble than it was really worth.

He was angry enough now to hold the magic in and he let himself imagine killing the man. Sara's magic would like his rage over that. She herself wasn't aware enough to worry over how angry he was. It was both a relief and aggravating to let himself be angry.

If one of his team began to fight he wouldn't be able to stop himself from joining in. He could barely stop himself now. If it had been anyone except Sara, he'd have run from the room to fight the man, but she needed him. Whether the magic knew that too or was just listening to him, he didn't know, but he was able to remain in the room, calmly for the most part although his hands shook with the need to strike out.

He growled with frustration and repeated, "Don't kill the fucker!"

Nelson wisely said nothing.

A paramedic ran into the room a minute later and handed Charlie a bag. "You're sure you don't want help?"

The man's anxious gaze scanned Sara's convulsing body. He took a step forward then retreated to the open door, rising a hand to wipe his sweating brow.

Charlie was glad it had been a paramedic who ran in as they were neutral to him. He'd feel his aura as evidenced by his hurried retreat but unless Charlie focused on him, he shouldn't run away in terror. The police on the other hand were likely to react strongly because Charlie didn't trust them, and his magic would know that.

Not that he disliked cops. He respected them but they were a threat, and as much as he tried to tell himself they were all on the same team, the magic knew it was a lie. In his heart he knew that police were a danger to him.

"I need the EPI pen and to take blood samples. Give Paul the stuff."

Paul took the bag the paramedic handed him and ran to Charlie. Charlie gave Sara the shot in her thigh and then took a blood sample. She stopped convulsing but didn't wake.

Paul said, "My sister has studied first aid. She volunteers in the hospital and with our local volunteer ambulance. Maybe she wouldn't scare her. She likes Abby."

"I've got this, thanks. I need her other medicine in her blue bag," he said, lying through his teeth. He needed them to leave so he could throw a heal on her.

The paramedic stepped into the hallway and Paul retreated to the other room, returning a few moments later to hand Charlie the small box containing Sara's vitamins.

The magic's panic was easing, the burn beneath his skin lessening, and Charlie was daring to hope.

He said, "See if they found out anything."

Paul nodded and joined the paramedic. The two men spoke quietly but Charlie's attention was on his wife.

He spell stole Sara's heal again. To his immense relief, her temperature began dropping.

"Get the IV in, Charlie," Liz said. "She might need more antihistamines. Get another pen. They won't want to give you one; it would normally kill someone. If you have to steal one, do so."

"I heard her," the paramedic said. "I'll get you one. Carry a pen at all times if her allergies are this bad."

"We didn't know she had any. Whatever he gave her is causing this. Can you go find out what it was?"

Charlie grinned wryly as the paramedic nodded and raced away. *Fearful Presence was a blessing and a curse*, he thought for the millionth time. He wished he could control his aura, but he was grateful Paul at least didn't feel it.

Paul said, "I'll be back in a few minutes with the pen. While I'm down there, I'll ask."

As soon as they were alone, Charlie let his magic loose. It sank into Sara, and he sighed in relief.

Her eyes opened but didn't see him and his breath caught in his throat. She wouldn't survive another fight for dominance with her magic.

"Please, Sara, fight it." He closed his teary eyes, leaning his forehead against hers, trying to project his need of her.

Her eyes closed again. She lay perfectly still under the cold water. The paramedic returned with two more epi pens. He sidled into the room and laid them on the bed. "They found a vial of something, but they don't know what it is. He isn't talking. Your friend told the policeman the FBI would be here and would want it at their lab. She looks a bit better," he finished doubtfully.

Charlie nodded and lied. "She is. Her fever is down to one-o-six and still dropping, her pulse is more regular too. She's taking experimental medicine and might need another shot if it spikes again."

The normal body temperature of a sun-priest was one-oh-six. Right now, her temperature was a hundred and fifteen. No normal human could survive that.

"Cancer?" the paramedic's gaze traveled Sara's wasted frame.

Charlie nodded agreement. Cancer and experimental medicine were as good an excuse as any for what was happening.

"Want us to take her to the hospital now?"

Charlie smoothed Sara's hair back. "I promised her I'd never send her to one. There's a clinic I can take her to. I have a helicopter coming for her. She needs the cold water anyway."

"Charlie, her temp is rising, and her heart rate is up. Give her the second shot," Liz said.

Charlie glanced at Liz and his heartrate accelerated. Liz was biting her bottom lip and looking scared, not an expression he'd seen much from her. It scared him to see her like that. His fear was now stronger than his anger and the paramedic relaxed slightly as the pressure of Charlie's aura faded.

Charlie gave Sara the shot in her arm. "Can we have some privacy here? I'll call if I need you, and thank you, you saved her life."

The paramedic nodded and left the bathroom, closing the door behind himself, grateful to leave the room. The man hadn't done a thing to warrant his reaction and it embarrassed him how afraid he was.

The man's friend stood beside the door, making sure no one tried to enter uninvited. The paramedic's partner joined him there with a stretcher and more emergency gear. He lifted a questioning eyebrow.

"Not good." He shook his head. "One hundred and six-degree fever and he said that was better than it was."

His partner winced. "Brain damage."

"Likely, and it's a damn shame too. She was very smart."

"You know her?" his partner asked in surprise.

"Not personally, no. I saw the interview on TV. She had two doctorates at eighteen."

"They should hang the bastard."

"How many times do you think he's done this?"

His partner shook his head, his lips tightening.

The man guarding the door clenched his hands.

The paramedic eyed him uneasily, but he didn't inspire the same level of terror as his friend. The guy in that room was clearly on a short fuse for mayhem. He hoped the police had searched him for weapons because he'd been called in on the aftermath of enough fights to see that the guy wasn't going to just let this go.

A light flickered and he turned in time to see a fluttering Winged woman appeared. The three-inch figure gestured and appeared to break into black smoke that solidified into a screen that looked perfectly ordinary expect for the fact that it hung in the air.

"You have one of the new Val thingies? I thought they weren't available yet?"

"It's a prototype we're testing." The kid held out his arm to show him the watch he wore. "She helped design it."

"It's much cooler than I thought it'd be."

His partner said, "I thought they'd doctored those images, but the screen really does look solid."

"It's a crying shame," the paramedic said again, shaking his head. He wasn't surprised to see four officers and three men in black combat gear approach. "I bet he was trying to kill her."

Charlie sat in the tub holding Sara's limp body under the cool water and casting her heal every time his Spell Steal was up. The cold water soothed his temper or perhaps it was just holding her close, but whatever the cause, the effect was his rage settled enough that he no longer had to fight the urge to run from the room to kill the bartender. His magic was calming too and no longer pressing for release. Her rash faded and the redness receded as her fever dropped.

"Turn the water off, Charlie. Get her dry and make her comfortable." Liz turned to Oz, holding up her crossed fingers. "Let her wake as calmly as we can."

Charlie lifted her from the tub and wrapped the towel around her. He grabbed the IV that hung from the shower rod and carried it and her into the other room. The paramedics and Paul waited in the hallway while he dressed her. He left his shirt off so she could feel his skin. Her cold wet hair dampened the pillowcase, but he left it as he hung the IV from the light fixture. In her sweatpants and tank top she looked small and defenseless. He had to take a minute to fight his rage.

A police officer knocked on the broken door and entered without waiting for a reply. "We should move her to the hospital."

Paul followed the officer in, frowning anxiously.

Charlie backed as far from the officer as the room allowed, not liking the way man's hand hovered over his gun.

He said, “Paul, show him Sara’s vitals on your wristcomp. A helicopter is coming for her. She’s doing better. The clinic where she receives treatment is preparing for her arrival.” He pointed to Sara’s snow pants in the corner of the room. “I’m sure his prints will be on them. He had her partly undressed before Paul got here.”

“This is Major Harris and I’m in charge of her medical care,” Liz said from Paul’s wristcomp. “She stays there undisturbed.”

The policeman hesitated a minute, staring with narrowed eyes at Charlie, then shrugged, bagged the pants, and headed back out the door.

Charlie heaved a relieved sigh that Liz echoed.

Paul said, “There’s an FBI team here already going through the lodge, questioning everyone and taking statements. State troopers are on the scene as well as local law enforcement and two news vans.”

Charlie could hear sirens and see the red and blue flickers of police light in the window. He knew the place must already be surrounded by law enforcement, and while he was glad of the turnout, it would make their disappearance hard to explain if they used a summons to leave— if he didn't cause a riot first.

- 3 -

NOW OR NEVER

The bartender sweated in the back of the police car. He'd never been so scared in his life and he couldn't believe the turnout for this. Agents and officers from every branch of law enforcement scurried around the building. That scrawny little nobody was someone important, or maybe the boyfriend was someone important. They'd found her earring in his pocket and were sure to find his other trophies.

Nausea roiled in his gut. He thought he might've killed her. *It wasn't murder. She was only supposed to go to sleep*, he told himself, but his mouth was dry and his hands sweaty.

A helicopter that had been circling slowly slowed even more to hover almost directly over the police car he was in. Black-suited figures jumped straight down from twenty feet up. Heavily armed, wearing face masks and headsets, only their eyes showed. A group of three approached the police car he sat in while others ran off. His eyes widened and he bit lip so hard it bled as they got closer. He'd have peed himself, but her boyfriend had already emptied his bladder.

The Marines had shown up in force in less than ten minutes. *Who the hell were these people*? he wondered with dread. *I picked the wrong girl. I should've picked the brunette.*

One of the black clad men opened the door and leaned in. The bartender shrieked and pressed against the far door. The Marine's blue-eyed stare was cold, hard, and very intense. "You better hope you spend a long time in jail because the day you're released is the day you die." The door slammed, and the men turned away and entered the lodge.

He believed them.

Paul stationed himself outside the door of Charlie's room and stopped the FBI agent from entering. He stuck his head inside the door. "Want to use our room, Charlie? The FBI wants to come in yours."

Liz spoke from Paul's wristcomp again, "This is Major Harris, and I don't want my patient disturbed. Clear the hallway please and we'll clear the room for you."

Charlie waited anxiously as the two agents conferred.

Liz said, "They'll go and if they don't, I can stall them for the few minutes it will take to get the raid there to force them back. Under no circumstances leave that room while agents are in the hall. I want you as far away as we can keep you."

"Yes ma'am," Charlie said tightly.

Liz sighed hard. "I'm sorry, Charlie. I don't mean to worry you more, but we really can't afford for them to attack you. I'm tempted to summon you out but…" she took another deep breath, frowning and chewing her bottom lip. She was opening her mouth to speak when the two agents retreated and both Charlie and Liz heaved relieved sighs.

Sara moaned when Charlie picked her up to bring her to Paul's room. "Oh, thank god," he said sincerely. "I'm right here, sweetheart. Come back— you fight, you hear me!" He grabbed the IV and followed Paul, who let him in. "No one comes in."

"I'll make sure." Paul planted himself in front of the door.

Charlie kicked it closed as he said, "I'm here. You're okay, just a bad reaction to a sedative. You're safe, completely safe. No one is hurt." A fresh surge of anger rolled over him. It was a surprisingly liquid sensation as if the anger had form and mass. He could feel it like thick honey coating his body, heating to a hot sticky mass as if it could both help him slid off attacks and pull them in, entrapping them in his rage.

The strength of his anger blocked whatever she might be feeling. The magic wanted the threat to her dead. It pushed him to become Chief and destroy their enemies. It took a real effort of will to remain in the room beside her instead of breaking the bartender in half and ripping him apart.

Logically, he knew the man wasn't a threat to her now— the police had him in custody. Killing him would do nothing, it would be murder. The magic didn't care about any of that. It wanted the threat eliminated.

Sara moaned and retched as she struggled to sit. Charlie tried to calm himself, she needed peace, not anger. He rubbed her back and hair and thought about how much he loved her, which did nothing much to calm his anger because his thoughts kept circling back to how close that asshole had been to taking her from him.

She threw a heal on herself and tried to sit again. Charlie pulled her more upright. "You're okay, just a bad reaction to a drug. You're perfectly safe now."

"I feel awful. I don't think I'm okay," she said weakly.

He sagged in relief that she was speaking to him, that her magic hadn't taken her.

"If I'm okay, why are you so upset? Are you okay?" Her voice rose as her worry grew.

"Everyone is fine. I'm upset because you were so sick. You had an allergic reaction to a sedative.

Sara lifted a trembling hand to her brow and licked her lips. “I feel terrible. Did you take some blood work?”

“Yes, it’s on its way to Liz now. Paul is watching the door. No one will come in. We’re safe and private here.”

He called his magic out and offered a glowing hand. The hand she held to him trembled badly. His magic was absorbed into her. He stole her heal and used it on her again.

“I’m so tired,” she murmured as she slumped against him. “You caught who did this?”

“Paul did. I don’t think it was about you in particular. I think he was just a random pervert. Paul stopped him right away. Nothing bad happened to you except the sedative.”

“Can I sleep now? We can talk later. I’m so tired...”

“Yes sleep, I’m here. I’ll be with you.” Charlie tried to concentrate on his love for her, not his worry or anger. Relief made him slightly dizzy or maybe that was just the result of his absorbing so much rage. The hot sticky feel stayed with him even though he knew she was safe now, asleep in his arms.

Andy and Abby found Paul still guarding the door.

Andy said, "What the hell is going on? Charlie jumped from the ski lift like twenty feet straight down. There's police and FBI everywhere."

"Sara was poisoned and they're investigating."

Abby bit a thumbnail and glanced away as her eyes filled with tears. "Is she dead?"

Paul put an arm around his sister's shoulders. "No, but she's very sick. She was weak to begin with… I'm worried."

"She's in your room?"

"Yeah, I have orders to see no one goes in except Charlie."

Andy said, "Damn, she was just getting better too. He must be freaking out."

Paul shrugged helplessly. His wristcomp beeped, notifying him of an incoming call from Charlie.

"Paul, she woke and her temp is normal again. She's still sick, but I think she'll be okay in time. She's sleeping now. Can you send someone for some bottled water for her?"

"I'll get it," Abby whispered.

Paul nodded and waved his sister away.

Charlie said, "I'll need to take more blood for testing as well. I'll need a cooler and some supplies to do it."

"Andy will get you what you need; I'm staying at the door."

A big man approached. He was dressed in black from head-to-toe, including black sunglasses and he carried a rifle.

He said, "Beta is here, Chief. I'll be right outside. The helicopter is ready to move her when you are."

Charlie said, "Paul, Harrison is part of our security. He can watch the door. Get the supplies, please."

Charlie turned off the call to Paul and spoke in the open raid channel. "She's sleeping now. She woke and was calm. Should I move her, Liz?"

"This is Doctor Gotlieb; I'm following the call. Stay there, Charlie. If she isn't panicked to leave, let her stay. She worked very hard to make her magic listen to her, let's see if it is. Beta can summon you out instantly if it's a problem."

"What are her symptoms?" Liz asked.

"She said she feels horrible, but you heard that. She's weak, unable to sit on her own, and her hands shook badly. I've given her magic twice. She hasn't tried to give me any. She's sound asleep and feels cool to the touch."

"I'm watching her vitals from here and her temperature is still dropping. If it goes below ninety-five degrees, get her in a warm bath. I'm calling for a heating blanket right now. Doctor Elliot is on his way to you, but it'll be two hours before he arrives."

Liz tapped the line displaying Sara's blood pressure. "She needs fluids. If she wakes again, see if she can drink anything. I'm ordering another IV." Liz paused. "Don't let anyone inject her with anything. Only you touch her. Her magic could perceive it as a threat and cause another reaction."

Charlie's pulse jumped. "Can I use a regular blanket on her?"

"Yes, we want her warm, not hot. Let her feel your skin. Try to remain as calm as you can." Liz frowned at the monitor showing Charlie's vitals. "Should I order you a mild sedative?"

"Honestly, I want to say yes, but if this is our magic's new way of dealing with sedatives, I better not."

"I proscribe a shot of brandy," Doctor Gotlieb said. "I'm serious, get him a drink. It should calm him."

"I'll bring you something to give him, Harrison," Lee said.

Charlie checked his HUD for the Scout's positions.

Lee and Manny were inside. Marcus, Joy, Brenda, and Mike were outside. He debated sending them away, grimacing as he flicked his wrist to close the screen. Marcus and Mike were protection warriors too and likely as concerned as he over their healer. Sending them away might be a bad idea.

He flicked the icon to speak privately to Liz. “I don’t want to cause problems. Is it safe for me to be here?”

Oz grinned and shook his head. “Scaredy cat.”

Charlie rolled his eyes.

Liz huffed a small laugh. “You tell me? How …*um*… in control are you?”

“I’m pissed as hell!”

Oz winced and pinched the bridge of his nose. Liz patted his hand absently as she reached past him to open a cabinet beside her desk.

She withdrew a blue pill bottle and Oz murmured, “It isn’t quite ready yet.”

Liz shrugged, her lips curving in an irritated smile. “Better than nothing. We need trials anyway if we’re going to perfect it.”

“What is it?” Charlie asked, not liking the expression on Oz’s face at all.”

“A tranquilizer.”

Before he could say no way, Liz said, “It’s really mild. Likely too mild, but when Doctor Elliot gets there, take what he gives you.”

Oz said, “Take it.” He opened his mouth then snapped it closed, gave Liz an annoyed worried glance and said, “I get you’re worried it will knock you out. I doubt it will. We've been testing on the other warriors but if it does, you know we'll keep her safe."

He didn't say it, but Charlie knew Oz meant the other warriors would be there and their magic would ensure that Sara was kept safe

The conflict he felt over that must have been clear on his face because Oz said softly, "She's the priority here and you causing a riot will endanger her."

"I'll take the damned pill," he said gruffly and flicked the screen off. He hated the idea of it. His wife's magic needed a warrior's rage and if he couldn't give her what she needed, it would force her to another. But Oz was right too. This wasn't about his personal feelings. Exposure might kill them all.

Paul returned with his brother and the requested supplies and found a woman wearing the Scout uniform already there.

"I better call the school and report we'll be late returning," Paul said as he handed Harrison the supplies.

"Master Sergeant Guthrie will handle that." Harrison took the supplies and opened the door after knocking once. "The police and FBI will need to question both of you. Assume you aren't going back today."

Paul shrugged. "I don't really know anything, but I'm glad to help. How is she?"

"Not clear yet. Her doctor is on the way here. Her psychiatrist recommends not moving her while she's unaware. Charlie is doing everything possible. A hospital wouldn't help her, so we'll leave her here for now."

Two more Scouts approached and stopped and spoke with the paramedics. Everyone shook hands and the paramedics left.

"The supplies Liz ordered."

A Scout handed a medium size cooler to Harrison. He smiled briefly at Paul but didn't introduce himself. He and his partner left.

"Do you know what happened yet?" Paul asked.

"Yes, they think he's a serial rapist. The FBI found his trophies. He had no idea who Sara is, and he's denying he was trying to do anything to her. He claims she asked him for help to her room. Charlie's recordings disprove that. His fingerprints are on her pants; both the button and zipper pull have clear prints. Her earring was in his pocket. Sara was just at the wrong place at the wrong time."

"He wasn't trying to kill her then?"

"We don't think so. We think he drugged his victims and they remained unaware of the entire episode. She was allergic. If you hadn't been close, he would've raped her and left her to die there."

Paul glowered and spun away. "Jesus, does Charlie know? He must be furious."

"No, don't tell him either. We want them both calm for Sara's sake—" Harrison paused.

Paul narrowed his eyes and nodded slowly. "I know she gets sick from stress. I know she's recovering from a serious illness and is weak."

"This could be a major setback for her. Too much stress will make her sick again. If Charlie is upset, she will be too."

"How can I help?"

"Just be a friend." Harrison slapped him on the shoulder. "I'm sure she'll want this kept quiet." He sighed heavily. "I doubt it can be. That man had a lot of trophies. He has a lot of victims out there."

Harrison was right. The arrest made the national evening news. Paul was watching the late news in the lodge's lobby with some of the Scouts, his brother, sister, and Hawk.

Hysterical women were calling the police station in droves. The police had confirmed thirty-three victims by eleven p.m. All the women reported the same thing; all had been traveling with a man and waiting in the lodge for the man to do one last run. While waiting, they'd ordered a drink and were woken later by their boyfriends. On waking, most of the women recalled bad headaches. The bartender's trophies were used to confirm cases.

"And this is just the first day." Paul curled his lip, gesturing at the television where the news played. "Sara should get a medal. Think how many women she saved from him."

- 4 -

WHAT PRICE FEAR

Lee called Charlie and repeated what Paul had said. “That outlook might help her, Charlie.”

“Couldn’t hurt.” Charlie agreed. “Paul’s the one who should get a medal though. He ran in the room unarmed to stop him.”

Sara was still sleeping. She’d woken once and vomited but had fallen right back to sleep. Charlie had cleaned her up and reported to Liz.

Doctor Elliot arrived and handed him two small white tablets.

Charlie swallowed them dry, hovering anxiously as Doctor Elliot examined her. He took blood samples and skin scrapings, neither of which woke her, causing Charlie to worry more.

Doctor Elliot said, "I think she'll be fine in time. Keep an eye on her temperature and stay close to pacify her magic."

"Why isn't she waking?"

"She's recovering, Charlie. She just needs time to get it all out of her system," Liz said reassuringly. "Because she was so weak, it will take her longer than usual to recover. Keep doing what you're doing. Hawk is there if you need his aura."

"I don't know what she needs," Charlie said worriedly. "She hasn't said anything. She just got sick and went back to sleep."

Doctor Elliot said, "Her temperature is normal now and her heartbeat and pulse are fine. Keep the IV in for fluids until her blood pressure is normal and she'll be better soon."

Elliot slapped his shoulder and left the room.

Charlie sat beside her bed, holding her hand, waiting for the pills to take effect.

Sara woke again thirty minutes later. "I need to use the bathroom."

Charlie had to help her sit, she couldn't stand or balance herself.

He lifted her and set her on the toilet. "You don't need to be embarrassed; you'd help me if I needed it." He held her steady as she used the toilet and carried her back to bed. "Liz says you need fluids. Can you drink some water?"

The water he handed her soaked her shirt. Both hands shook so badly she wore more than she drank. Charlie called Paul to see if he could get her a straw.

He took her hands in his and kissed them as he gave her more of his magic. It was seriously starting to concern him that she hadn't given him any of hers. "Are you holding your magic in?"

"Always," she replied tiredly.

"Let me have some, please."

A weak blue glow came from the hand she held to him. The magic felt different, but he couldn't put his finger on it. He wasn't sure if it was the pills making him muzzy, although he felt normal if more tired than he should be, or that the contact had been so fast.

"Are you magically depleted?"

"No," she laughed semi-hysterically. "No," she repeated more calmly. "I can't let it out, Charlie. Do you need more?"

She held her glowing hand to his face. This time he recognized the difference. Her magic was no longer eager, it was afraid.

"Your magic is afraid." Charlie released his completely, letting it surround her in the hopes of comforting her magic. Never before had her magic been afraid like this of him.

"It had better be afraid! I'm in control of me, not it! I'll destroy it utterly if it tries again."

Charlie jerked back and grabbed her shoulders. "Okay... Sara, sweetheart, we need to live with it. Both of you need to be happy. Don't terrify it until it panics—"

"It didn't mind terrifying me into a panic, or killing our child, or taking half of Alpha while killing me. Let it be afraid!" Sara said viciously.

The magic surrounding him began to whirl faster. His magic was becoming uneasy. Charlie withdrew his magic. They'd have to work this out, but now wasn't the time.

"Can we go home?" Sara asked plaintively.

"Yes, we can go anywhere you want. There's a large crowd outside. Do you want a port out?"

"No. We can take the jet. I'm okay. Is Paul mad we ruined his trip?"

"Not at all. He's worried about you—about us. He says you're a hero for stopping that man."

Sara snorted. "He stopped him. That man couldn't have done anything to me; your magic protects me. All I did was get sick."

Charlie was surprised by how calm she was. She was angry and unhappy, but not afraid.

"Our Scouts are here. We'll go back in the copter with them. One or two can stay here to go back with Paul."

Sara tried to sit up again and couldn't manage it. "I hate this," she murmured.

Her frustration and building anger transmitted to his magic, making a cold sweat spring up on his brow. It wanted him to go to her but was afraid. His magic was confused enough to make him slightly nauseous or maybe that was the damned pills.

"You just need time and more water, and you'll get better." He stroked her hair, closing his eyes and taking slow deep breaths to quell his nausea.

"I'll be okay." Sara patted his hand. "Can you get me my socks and coat? This is so annoying," she finished bitterly.

Charlie grimaced as her embarrassed frustration morphed to anger.

He let Harrison in, signing for Harrison to stay with her. He said, "I'll wrap her in a blanket and carry her out. She can wear my socks."

His magic was calming, and he hoped it meant hers was too.

He said, "Don't worry about our gear here or checking out or the police or anything. We're going straight to the helicopter. They know you need medical care. Nobody will stop us."

Charlie threw on a sweatshirt and put his boots on as quickly as he could. A pair of his wool socks came to Sara's knees.

"Do you need to use the bathroom or anything?" he whispered.

She flushed and shook her head.

He wrapped the blanket from the bed around her and handed her to Harrison so he could put his parka on. Once in his arms again, he kissed her temple and put his face against hers, letting his magic touch her a moment.

"It's going to be crowded and noisy out there," Harrison warned as they headed to the door. "Beta is here, and we won't let anyone touch either of you." He held the IV bag over his head and followed Charlie.

The small effort of holding her head up was exhausting her. A sympathetic yawn escaped him.

"Go to sleep, I've got you." He shifted his grip as she tucked her face into his chest more and curled her arms on her chest, letting him take care of her, not holding on at all. She wasn't asleep, but she was more comfortable and her trust in him soothed his magic enough to calm it completely or maybe it was just reacting to his relief to be leaving— or maybe it was the pills, but whatever the reason it had stopped pressing and he was too tired to be angry. He just wanted them gone from here. He wanted to hold her and feel her breath and know she was safe, that they were all safe.

He yawned again, hard enough to make his jaw click.

Liz said, "Charlie, I want a blood sample from you when you get in the copter."

Oz said, "How's the anger?"

"Good, I guess. I just want out of here— and a nap."

"We'll work on it but drowsy is better than riots."

Charlie snorted and nodded at Harrison who opened the door.

Flashbulbs lit in a blinding display when he exited the building. Police held reporters back and cleared a perimeter around the helicopter while the reporters hollered questions. The Scouts surrounded them. News crews followed their progress with cameras from the tops of vans as they made their way to the helicopter in the lower parking lot. Hawk, Paul, Andy, and Abby trailed them.

"Harrison, stay here and make sure Paul gets back okay, please," Sara said as they reached the helicopter.

"Thank you, Paul," she said sincerely.

Paul stood in the doorway of the helicopter, biting his lip and still clearly worried. "You're welcome— feel better."

Charlie said, "Thanks, Paul. I owe you one."

Sara closed her eyes, relaxing in arms. Hawk climbed aboard after them and buckled Charlie's seatbelt for him.

She was handling this well, and he felt better now that they were leaving, but he was worried about how angry she was with her magic.

"Stop worrying. I'm fine. Well, not fine, but I will be." Sara kissed his neck.

He let himself be angry, glad he could finally release it.

"I'm not fine. I'm so angry. What he did... God, I hope he rots in prison forever!" Charlie clutched her, his magic surrounding them both. Her hand traced his clenched jaw, a light blue mist of magic on it. He wanted all of it, a cloud to match his own. Angry, sad, and confused, he recalled his magic.

She shivered in his arms. "I can't."

She cried, not over what had happened, but because she was afraid to share her magic like he needed.

- 5 -

MEETING ON THE MOUNTAIN

Charlie was deep in thought on the flight back to Maryland. It was clear to him that Sara's wild fear and panic were the magic. Harnessed tightly she remained calmer but at what cost? She'd live in fear of it getting free— or terrify it into a rash action.

"Don't take us home." Charlie told Drew who flew the helicopter. "Take us where we made Joy and bring the raid to us. All of them."

He framed her face with his hands and stared into her teary blue eyes. The wild fear that had filled her in the past was gone. This wasn't her magic's fear, but hers and it was all the more gut wrenching to know it.

"You're the bravest person I know. We'll face them all together and let our magic mingle with theirs. We can't go on like this, afraid of touching them, of seeing them. What will be, will be. We can't be worried every moment of what the magic will do. Whatever happens, I love you. That'll never change, not ever. If we need to leave them and move away, it's better to find that out now than worry." He kissed her cold lips. "Be strong for me now. There'll be no better time to do this than now while you have control of it."

She shivered in his grasp but didn't object.

The helicopter landed on the empty mountainside. He jumped easily to the ground holding her. The fuzziness had faded and he felt alert and well rested.

Hawk followed.

"Hawk, summon them all." Charlie walked away with her, whispering, "Release it. Let me take care of you. I swear on my soul, I won't let it keep you."

With a sob, she did.

The power of her magic pushed him to his knees and flattened the grass in a fifty-foot circle around him. Tingles raced through him. Somehow, he always forgot how powerful her magic was. She kept it so tightly leashed that the strength of it when she let go always surprised him.

A dense blue cloud lit with sparks surrounded him. Her magic greeted him with joy and fear, swopping and twirling around him in thick blue streamers. His magic joined it eagerly. A hum built, felt under the skin more than heard, and he knew the magic was communicating.

He lost track of time sitting with his eyes closed in a cloud of their magic. When he opened them, the raid had gathered. They were watching from the hillside by the treeline ten feet away. Light snow lit by the starlight covered the hilltop. Cold and crisp, the mountain air smelled fresh and clean. Sara's body was warm against him wrapped in the quilt, but she shivered when he called Joy.

Joy came hesitantly. Their magic loved her.

Charlie took her hand and kissed it. "Release your magic."

She hesitated, glancing back at Drew. Charlie knew she was worried their magic would change how she felt. He knew what he was asking. But he also knew they couldn't afford to be afraid.

"Please, Joy, we can't live like this."

Joy bit her lip, and then with a determined look at Sara, she released her magic. Charlie beckoned Drew over. Joy took his hand and pulled him into their magic. The magic rejoiced, magnifying their love and sharing it. Bright sparks bloomed and the hum increased. Drew grinned and kissed Joy on the mouth then leaned down and kissed Sara lightly. He kissed Charlie on the cheek, and then backed away. Charlie knew Drew was worried but his love for Joy was clear as was his affection for he and Sara.

Joy lingered with Charlie and Sara a moment then followed Drew, but her magic remained, darting between them in small swirls.

"Rick!" Charlie called his brother.

Sara tensed in his arms. Stasia eyes flared blue and her hands clenched around Rick's.

"Please, Stasia, try to control it just for a moment, then you come to us too."

She nodded unhappily and released Rick's hand. Rick crouched in front of them, surrounded by a cloud of his magic. Sara lifted a hand and placed it against his cheek. Her relief was as strong as Charlie's that the magic didn't respond. Rick gave them both a quick kiss on the cheek, and Charlie sagged with relief. The magic loved Rick but not as much as it loved Joy. With his eyes closed he could see the light that was Sara, and it was clear to him that neither his brother or his wife had a connection beyond the affection they shared for each other. The light that was her was firmly fixed on himself and it made him almost lightheaded with relief.

Suddenly Stasia stood beside them.

Rick took her hand. "Let your magic out, honey. It's okay. Can't you feel their love?"

Tears trailed unheeded across Stasia's cheeks as her magic mingled with theirs. She sank to the snow to kneel before Charlie. Magic eddy about them in gentle swirls.

He didn't have to ask; he knew she was overwhelmed with emotion. He closed his eyes and lifted his face to the starlight. Gentle radiance bathed him; a trickle of energy that grew stronger as if the night itself was sustaining him.

Imagination? Reality? He didn't care. He was just happy that the tight knot of his muscles was finally unwinding.

Rick finally stood and pulled Stasia up, wiping the tears from her pale cheek with his thumbs. He led her to the side, and sat, pulling her into his lap while she cried quietly. Too low to hear, he whispered to her, and Charlie turned away to give them privacy.

He called Toric next. Toric stepped forward hesitantly to stand in their magic. The magic twirled up and surrounded him in a tornado of sparks before resuming its lazy movement. Charlie eyed it dispassionately. It was probably as conflicted as he and Sara were. She liked him and he didn't.

Toric met his eye and nodded slowly. Charlie offered him his hand. He didn't particularly like him, but he did respect him, and the magic made his feelings clear. Sara liked him, but in a friendly way. She was embarrassed and dismayed to feel Toric's jealousy. Toric shook Charlie's hand then kissed Sara's cheek before moving to the back of the crowd where he stood with his arms crossed.

Charlie called Major Nelson.

Nelson marched into the magic. The magic receded from him after a bare moment. *It didn't like the major's fear of them,* Charlie thought in amusement.

Sara was confused and saddened by the major's reaction and it surprised Charlie that she hadn't realized Nelson was afraid of them before this. He'd always known it, but then again, Sarah was a healer and didn't weigh threats like he did. Not that he thought Nelson was a threat, but he knew the major was always watching and weighing their actions and if he thought they were becoming a threat, he'd report it to Campbell. Which, as far as Charlie was concerned, was fair because he'd do the same.

The major pursed his lips, opening his mouth as if he might say something but he scurried away before speaking.

One-by-one Charlie called the Scouts to their side. The magic greeted them with dips and twirls and bright displays of static and sparks, causing smiles laughter and tears as it shared Charlie's and Sara's feelings.

It was both awkward and exhilarating to feel their admiration and respect. He was a bit surprised that they all felt such friendly feelings, not only for himself and Sara, but for each other. And he was certain it was their feelings he sensed because they had no magic of their own to influence them.

He did wonder if his, or more likely Sara's, magic was influencing their affection but decided it wasn't anything to worry about as there was no way to prove or disprove it. Besides, he liked them all too and didn't feel manipulated to do so. They were good honorable people and it humbled him a bit to think they'd accepted him so readily as their leader.

Finally, the only three left were the ones she'd changed last. The ones he was most worried about. He called Marcus.

Marcus hesitated. A blush grew on his cheeks visible even in the dim light. "You know I love her too."

"I know. I know she loves you as well." Charlie held his glowing hand to Marcus. The clearing was bright in his senses and he knew his eyes glowed.

A fight between them wouldn't be pretty but he doubted it would come to that. He had no doubt he'd win, and not just because Sara would support him, but because he was a better warrior. And he liked Marcus. He respected him and hoped that Marcus felt the same, but he braced himself to feel hatred.

Marcus took his hand with his glowing one and knelt beside them and Charlie heaved a sigh of relief. Marcus was jealous but more worried than angry. He was embarrassed too but it faded to love or maybe that was Sara's love he was sensing. She was sorry and sad and so protective it rung a surprised laugh from Charlie.

Marcus released Charlie's hand to touch Sara's cheek. They stayed together for a few minutes, no one speaking. Marcus stood fifteen minutes later and backed away.

"Come back. Sara wants you and she's too weak to go to you," Charlie said gruffly.

Marcus glanced at him apologetically before going to Sara and hugging her tightly.

Sara kissed his cheek. "We're here for you always," she said with a catch in her voice as Marcus walked away.

Charlie felt badly that she hurt for Marcus. It worried him that the magic would push her to ease his hurt, but it didn't make Marcus feel better to hug Sara, it made him unhappy, and he hoped the magic realized it and wouldn't press either of them.

"Mike," Charlie called, and Mike came to them.

When Mike's magic touched them, Sara sat straighter and reached for him. Mike smiled and took her hand, holding it easily.

Charlie closed his eyes and tried to run spell timers in his head. He was the jealous one now and he knew it was worrying everyone.

Sara wanted Mike. None of the others affected her like this. She wanted to touch him, and her magic was letting her. There were no painful tingles for Mike.

Mike made a surprised sound and pulled her away.

"He feels like you, like safety and love," Sara said as she hugged Mike.

Mike placed her back in his lap. "That love was what she felt for you, not me."

Sara reached for Mike again and held his hand, turning worried eyes to Charlie. "The magic thinks it's you."

"Call Brenda over," Liz said. "His magic likes priest magic. Let it feel both of you."

Brenda joined them and touched Charlie's hand with her glowing blue one. Her magic felt familiar enough that with his eyes closed he wouldn't be certain if he was touching Sara or her. Her response when he touched her wasn't at all the same though and it relieved him enough that he could say calmly, "Yes, she does feel like you."

Brenda took Mike's hand and Sara took Charlie's. The power of it would have made him yell in surprise if he could have moved but he was trapped, as locked in place as the very first time that magic had touched him.

Liz watched anxiously as the magic wielders greeted each other. She kept an eye on her screens, monitoring their vitals. Although they all appeared calm, everyone had elevated heartrates, even the watching Scouts.

She stifled her nervous laugh and wiped her sweaty palms on her pants. Her heartrate was up too.

"*Ahh*," Sara exclaimed as the circle was complete. Mike, Brenda, and Charlie remained unnaturally still.

The magic lit with a deep purple glow. Arcs of lightning flickered between them and the smell of ozone filled the air. Liz jumped and ran farther away. Thunder sounded and warm wind ruffled their hair as Saint Elmo's fire appeared and covered everyone. Another clap of thunder sounded, and the purplish-blue fire spread from them in waves, coating the raid then leaping to the trees where it dissipated. The small hairs rose on her arms, each a small antenna that waved toward the glowing cloud.

Mike and Brenda leaned forward until their knees touched. The magic settled down into a dense blue cloud around them.

"Valory, notify me immediately if their vitals fluctuate more than two percent from current readings."

"Acknowledged," Liz's Valory said.

Nelson said, "Should we stop them?"

"No. They're in no distress."

“But is that safe…”

Liz shrugged. She doubted it. Anyone with eyes could see something powerful was happening here, but she didn’t need him getting all antsy either.

He wrinkled his nose and crossed his arms, and she held in her annoyed sigh with effort.

“Valory, compare exercise graphs, casting and physical, to currently displayed readouts.”

Nelson relaxed enough to lean over her shoulder to examine the displayed information.

“It’s science,” she said as reassuringly as she could and he scoffed, but his lips were lifted now in a slight, if rueful, smile.

Feeling gradually returned but with weight that was like pushing through concrete. Charlie thought it had been about ten minutes or so but speaking felt like a herculean effort that wasn’t worth making to get the time. He released Brenda’s hand and took Mike's in both of his while Sara held Brenda's.

A hum built beneath Charlie's skin and he felt the magic straining for understanding.

"Sara?"

"I'm trying," she said, and he could feel her intense concentration. That one word had loosened the magic's hold on him even more. He flexed his fingers and wriggled his toes while twisting his neck to release the tension there.

He said without effort, "Give me your hand, Brenda, and concentrate hard on what you feel for me. Show it the difference in what you feel for Mike."

For minutes they traded hands. The magic's concentration was a wave of heat that flowed between their clasped hands.

Mike gave Charlie a small apologetic shrug, leaning in to kiss Sara. He sat back, took her hands again, and kissed Brenda. The magic swirled excitedly and the heat in Charlie's hands broke into specs that flicked over them in static that he could see.

Charlie laughed and kissed Sara. The magic started throwing off sparks of static electricity. He kissed her as passionately as he knew how. The heat he felt from her lips on his filled him with lust, and he deepened the kiss. She wanted him as much as he wanted her.

He kissed her neck in her favorite spot, making her moan. The magic leaped. He moved Sara to his side, reached for Brenda and kissed her on the mouth. Still holding her hand, he kissed Sara again. The magic swirled in dizzying circles around he and Sara.

"It's learning," he said huskily.

Sara was embarrassed as were Mike and Brenda.

He released Brenda and kissed Sara like he meant it, running his hand up her back under her shirt. She made a small, aroused sound and put both hands on his chest, then ran them down his arms. Her embarrassment was subsumed by lust and he wished they were alone.

She was breathing harder when he stopped. He rested his forehead on hers. "I love you." His eyes intent on hers, he drew back and framed her face with his hands. "Only you— just us." He kissed her again as if they were alone. The magic swirled faster, echoing her lust to him until it was all he could do to pull away from her.

Charlie laughed as he released her and noticed Mike's expression, which was torn between embarrassment and heat when he looked at Brenda.

"Spell timers," he said and winked at Mike as he began to mutter them.

Mike laughed and Brenda snickered. They all repeated their timers until they were laughing and no longer lustful.

"This is awkward as hell," Mike said.

"It's trying to learn," Brenda said reassuringly.

"I think it needs all of us," Sara said.

Charlie held out his hands as he called Rick. Rick came to them holding Stasia's hand.

Sara called Joy. With a worried look at Drew she went to them.

"Marcus, Oz, Hawk, it needs all of us," Charlie said.

Sara sat in the circle of Charlie's arms holding his and Mike's hands. As soon as they all joined hands, the magic went wild. He was braced for it this time and the impact didn't surprise him. Once again, he was locked in place. Heat built in his hands.

Lightning flickered and thunder sounded in ringing peals. Above them the night sky was lit with bolt after bolt of lightning. The lightning hovered in the air, not touching down, flickering in scintillating patterns. Instead of landing it rose higher and higher, flowing south until it disappeared.

He closed his eyes to concentrate and was surprised to see not only Sara but everyone near them as shining tendrils of light. He had the barest moment to think, *uh oh*, as the light yanked him in, smothering him in a blinding white flash.

-6-

MAGIC IS BORN

Liz's attention was captured from the display in the sky by the people in the circle when they moved as one, sitting as closely as they could.

"Stay back," they said in unison, making goosebumps appear on her arms.

The magic settled around them, outlining their bodies. An arc of electricity circled, going faster and faster until it appeared to be a solid line of light.

The hair on Liz's arm rose. She checked her recorder to make sure it was still on. They shifted hands again in no pattern Liz could make out. For minutes they sat unspeaking, randomly changing hands.

"The magic is communicating," she whispered to Nelson.

He nodded, intent on the display in front of him.

The Scouts without magic of their own were watching just as intently, sitting in the snow behind Nelson and Liz.

The brilliant light continued to circle the wielders. It slowed and flickered, disappearing and reappearing as it careened among them.

Two hours later the magic wielders released hands. Sara kissed Charlie, and he kissed Brenda, Brenda kissed Rick and he kissed Stasia, she kissed Oz, and the kiss continued around the circle until Mike kissed Sara. They leaned forward and stacked their hands in the center of the circle. Lightning bloomed with a crack of thunder that made Liz's ears ring. Small scintillating strands of light wove around them.

Nelson grimaced and unbuckled his tranquilizer gun. Liz clasped his hand, pressing the gun back into the holster.

"We'll trust them. They're good people. Let's not panic until we have to."

The major withdrew his hand and stepped back. "I'm worried; Sara can't take much more physically."

"Eight minutes." Drew tapped his wristcomp and made the health monitor larger.

Liz nodded.

No one in the circle moved. Tendrils arced into the air, reaching for the Scouts.

Sara removed her hand from the group. "No," she said clearly.

"No," they all echoed, and the hair rose again on Liz's arms.

"This is enough for now," Sara said.

"Enough," they all repeated.

"Charlie is mine alone," Sara said.

"Alone," they repeated one after the other.

"I'm his alone," Sara said.

"Alone," they repeated again. This time they kept saying it.

"No," Sara said, and they stopped saying alone.

Sara reached down and joined Rick and Stasia's hands together.

"Yes," they all said together.

She put Mike and Brenda's hands together.

"Yes," they all said again.

She took Charlie's hand in hers.

"Yes," they all said again.

She put Charlie's hand down and picked up Mike's. "No," she said.

"Yes," They all said.

"No!" She repeated louder. She took Charlie's hand and said, "Yes."

"She's trying to teach it," Nelson said and Liz nodded agreement.

Liz watched Sara move their hands around for another hour, telling the magic yes and no.

"It doesn't want to listen." Nelson frowned at his wristcomp. "How long can they sit in the lightning?"

Sara stopped moving hands around. Grimacing, she casted dispel on herself and screamed.

"Pain" she said in a gasping voice.

"Pain, pain, pain," they echoed. They kept repeating it until she held Charlie's hand and kissed him. "Yes," she said. She leaned over and kissed Mike. "No— pain."

They were silent.

Finally, they said "No pain?"

It sounded questioning to Liz, like they wanted to understand but couldn't.

Sara kissed Mike again quickly. "No! Pain!" She kissed Charlie. "Yes!" She hugged him tightly. "Yes!"

They were silent again and withdrew their hands from each other. The lightning faded slowly. That sat silently in the circle again. One-by-one they fell over and the magic disappeared.

"No," Liz said as the Scouts behind her began to stand. "Let them be. Their vitals are fine. I think they're still communing or whatever we're calling it."

"Do you think it learned?" Nelson gestured to the small arcs of electricity leaping between them.

"We'll find out. If it didn't, they can try again."

Small flickers of static electricity still passed between them. The blue glow returned, and they lay unmoving for another hour while the magic darted over them. On top of the mountain an unnatural stillness prevailed with only the wind to break the silence. No animals moved; no birds called and even the wind was still. The blue glow thickened over Marcus. He crawled away from them.

"The magic is moving them," Liz whispered

Nelson nodded. Deep lines had etched his forehead and grooved his mouth. The magic hovered over each of them and moved them away. It settled over Sara and Charlie. The others moaned and tried to move on their own.

"Stay where you are!" Liz called. "We'll help you when it's finished."

Liz waited anxiously for it to move either Sara or Charlie, but it didn't, it just settled on them.

Her Valory said, "Vital signs have—"

"Cancel audio," Liz said as she examined the graphs being displayed. Sara and Charlie were fine but the rest of them were in distress now. "Stay here," she ordered and walked slowly to Marcus and felt his pulse. His skin was ice cold. His pulse was slow. She checked Joy next then Oz. They were all the same. The magic took no notice of her.

"Make a fire to warm them up." Liz ordered the Scouts. She debated moving them and decided to wait until the fire was built.

"I'll go get supplies." Nelson gestured for Sam to accompany him. The two men headed to the helicopter. He returned two hours later with food, water, blankets, sleeping bags, tents, IVs, and heating packs.

The Scouts set the tents up after they had covered their friends and placed heating packs around them. Liz checked everyone again. They were doing better. She left Sara and Charlie alone in the magic. They sat in the magic another hour and thirty-six minutes. It finally trailed away from them in lazy swirls, coating the other users and growing smaller and smaller until it disappeared.

Charlie slumped over still holding Sara. Liz approached them cautiously and covered them with blankets and the heating packs. "I think we can safely move them now. Get them off the cold ground."

The Scouts carried them into the tents and set them on the sleeping bags.

Liz examined Sara. "Sara is the only one who needs an IV, but I don't think we should give her one. The magic might think it's an attack of some kind. Charlie can do it when he wakes or maybe Mike. We'll have to do some experiments when she's feeling better."

The Scouts set a watch and settled down to sleep as well. Everyone was alert by morning except for Sara and Charlie. Stasia and Rick disappeared into their own tent as did Brenda and Mike. Joy and Drew disappeared into the forest.

Marcus, Oz, and Hawk huddled by the fire with blankets over them. Liz handed them hot tea and toast, checking the vitals of all three. Physically they were fine.

"Want to talk about it?" she asked as she sat beside them.

"That was the worst and best experience of my life," Marcus said bitterly. He glanced toward the tent Charlie and Sara were in. "To be loved like that, that's amazing. I don't have words to describe how they love each other." He smiled slightly. "She loves me too. Not like she loves him, but she does love me. He doesn't. He likes me, I guess; I mean as much as he can. It's so weird knowing what someone really feels for you. She doesn't love Mike at all even though her magic loves him best. I mean besides Charlie of course. The magic loves how she feels for Charlie."

"It likes your feelings?" Liz handed him a fresh cup of tea.

"More than likes them, it craves them. The good ones anyways." He grimaced in distaste. "The bad ones scare it. Pain terrifies it, not physical pain. I don't think it can feel that really— mental pain." He was quiet a minute. "I feel more alone now than I ever have before in my life." He closed his eyes and turned his face away. Oz reached out to him and a flicker of magic passed between them.

"It's lonely being separated from them all. I think we'll feel better about it in a day or so." Oz laid a hand on Marcus's shoulder. "They'll share their magic when we need it."

Hawk snorted softly. "This is going to suck big time. No offense, Marcus, but I really don't want to come to you when I'm lonely."

Oz laughed. "I'm going to one of the girls. I don't mind hugging any of them."

"You'll mind it when Rick kills you for hugging Stasia," Hawk said dryly.

"He won't mind. I know how he feels about me and he knows how I feel about her." Oz leaned back on his elbows and crossed his legs.

Hawk glanced away as a red flush climbed his cheeks. "Do you know how I feel about people?"

"No, just how you feel about me." Oz leaned over and whispered, "I don't need the magic to know how you feel about Sara. Charlie didn't either. I'm sure Sara was surprised, but she does love you too, Hawk."

Hawk's eyes filled with tears. "It's not Sara exactly— I mean, I do love her, but I don't want her, well I do, but... What I'm trying to say is I envy Charlie. I want what he has. Sara is amazing in so many ways, I want that too. I want a beautiful, kind, smart girl to love me like that."

Marcus laughed a bitter laugh. "We all want that."

Liz cleared her throat. "To get that you have to love like that in return. It isn't a one-way street. It's a gigantic risk to put yourself out there like that— to love with all your heart and soul."

Hawk frowned thoughtfully. Oz placed a hand on each of theirs and magic arced through them. Marcus rose, punched Oz lightly on the arm, and headed to Lee.

Charlie woke before Sara. Liz gave him the IV, which he used on her. He stole her heal and used that as well. “I feel like I got hit by a bus.” He groaned as he tried to stretch out.

Liz stood behind him and massaged his shoulders. “Hours of lightning, not a bus. Did you learn anything?”

“That Sara is the stubbornest person on Earth.” He groaned again as he stretched his neck to the side. “I only caught snatches of what they were talking about, well talking is an overstatement. Feeling— yes, what they were feeling about.” He sat beside Hawk and put his arm around his shoulders. His magic went to Hawk in little sparks like static electricity. “Could you do me a favor and sit with Sara a while? I don’t want her to wake alone.”

Hawk nodded and headed to Sara. Charlie stretched his legs out toward the fire. “I wish I could help him more,” he said softly to Liz.

“It’s a hard age.” She sighed unhappily. “I’m not sure that’s wise.” She nodded toward the tent where Hawk was with Sara.

"His magic is lonely, and hers will comfort him best. It's the best I can do for my friend." Charlie stared sadly after Hawk. "He's so lonely and Sara is afraid. Her magic will be comforted too."

"Did it work? What she was trying to do?" Liz handed him a sandwich and a soda.

"I'm not sure how well. I guess time will tell. She did get it to understand that she doesn't want Mike, but it still does. It wants contact with all of them. The magic doesn't like to be separated." Charlie drew his knees up and rested his head on them. "This is just the beginning, Liz. It wants the entire raid. It's willing to wait for now. Sara convinced it that it hurts her to make them, and it doesn't like pain. Her mental pain when it tries to get what it wants confuses it. I think it thinks Sara and it are one, it doesn't understand they have different needs and wants. It wants what she wants and doesn't understand why she doesn't want what it wants."

"It won't just take us?" Liz asked worriedly. She'd always known it was a possibility, of course, but the thought of it made her palms sweat. She had no desire whatsoever to be invaded by an alien.

Charlie sat up straighter and shrugged. "I don't think so. I think we'll have warning, but I can't guarantee it. We need to drop everyone who doesn't want to be changed." He took a deep breath. "Then we need to recruit to fill the spaces. It thinks to be complete it needs thirty. I'm sure we did that by forming the raid when we did. I don't know if she can change its perception."

"Did you try to communicate with it?"

"We all did. Only Sara can. Well, we all can, but she can do it much clearer. Brenda can understand it better than me but not as well as Sara. They both have spells to manipulate magic and understanding languages is a passive ability for both of them." Charlie shrugged again. "I'm just guessing, maybe it just likes her more or fears her more. She can hurt it and it knows that."

Liz waited a few minutes while Charlie ate. "We saw it didn't particularly like Rick or Marcus, but what about Mike? I'm sorry, Charlie, I'm not trying to butt into your personal life, but I need to know what to expect— what to do for all of you."

Charlie laughed bitterly. "It does like Mike. If she wasn't as weak as she was it might leave him alone. I'd be enough." He sighed in frustration. "Not me, my magic would be enough company for hers. It isn't right now; it wants contact with the others. Her magic is desperate right now. It wants to be whole, to be complete. Her fear terrifies it, and it seeks protection. Maybe if it was whole it wouldn't be so afraid.... I feel the magic's need even with her asleep. Hawk is helping. Mike will help more. I'll ask him to go hold her hand awhile. I hate that. I'm trying not to, but I do." He turned away from Liz and they were both quiet again.

Finally, Liz said, "If Hawk helps her, have the others go and give her magic briefly as well. Let it know they're close and will help. Don't let it depend on just you and Mike."

Charlie nodded, but he didn't speak or turn to face her. "Make sure Major Nelson doesn't send them out on any missions, please. Not until we have this better figured out." He rose and headed back to Sara.

He stopped in front of the tent Mike and Brenda were sharing and asked them to come see her for a few minutes. Liz saw him pause before entering his own tent; he squared his shoulders and went in like it was hard to do.

Liz watched in concern. He'd always gone eagerly to her before. There was so much going on with them she could only guess at what was troubling him about returning to her. Brenda and Mike came out together and entered Charlie's tent and it occurred to Liz he'd known exactly where they were without anyone saying a thing. She made a mental note to research that.

Everyone stayed on the mountainside for three days. Sara was quiet and subdued when she woke and extremely weak.

Liz wanted her in the lab where she could be fed intravenously and monitored better, but the thought of leaving the mountain scared the magic. Sara's face got tight and pinched when asked if she could leave. Not her fear, the magic's. It took another day to convince it.

All the Scouts who had magic took turns sitting with her. They were all able to touch her and Charlie now without pain. Sara spent two hours with Liz convincing the magic that Liz could touch her too. The effort exhausted her, and she slept for six hours afterward.

"It's a good idea to teach it that others can touch you guys, but not right now," Liz said to Charlie as she checked Sara again. She sat back on her heels and looked at him squarely. "I hesitate to say this because I know you'll worry, but I think you should be worried. This..." She gestured to Sara sleeping. "This is bad. She's getting worse. She needs food and sunlight. I need to get her to the lab. Harrison went for supplies for me. I'll help her as much as I can but, Charlie, don't let her do anything else magically. It's taking too much out of her. I know you all want to communicate better with it, and you're worried this might be the only chance you have before it makes connections you don't want, but if you keep trying, she'll die. The magic has no real concept of physical limits and she has no reserves. It's damaging her muscles using her like it is. A human body can't supply the energy it's using and if her m-nerves are damaged beyond repair…" Liz stood and hugged Charlie. "I know you both aren't happy yet about how it wants the others, but please let it go for now. There's no reason to think you can't talk to it later when she's stronger."

"She won't want to stop. God, you have no idea how stubborn she is..." He heaved a heavy sigh and rubbed his forehead. "But she will for me. I'll tell her what you said. She doesn't want to die. She'll be reasonable," he said it firmly, but he looked very worried.

- 7 -

WORLD CHANGER

Charlie relaxed when they returned to the lab and Liz had her hooked up to all her equipment and was nodding happily. Liz's relief eased some of the stiffness in his shoulders.

Sara was sleeping again. The effort of traveling had exhausted her. Liz had sun lamps on her and was feeding her intravenously. The room they were in was warm enough to make him sweat; Sara's body temperature was very low.

"When she wakes, give her the orange juice or Oz's conjured water, whichever she prefers," Liz said to the Scouts gathered around her door.

Every magic wielder had crammed into the room.

"One of you stay in here at all times, never let her wake alone."

Charlie said, "She'll be embarrassed needing to pacify the magic like this, so let's make it easier by acting as normal about it as we can. Ask about work or for help on your personal projects or just watch TV with her or something."

They all nodded, and he hid his grimace. She'd know if they were worried and embarrassed or annoyed to be with her, but it was the best he could do.

Charlie stayed with her as much as he could between classes and Liz had wrangled him permission to stay with her at night. The others all came every day. Their magic swirled around everyone; it would settle on Sara then return to its host. She'd usually wake for that. Sometimes she reached for the person to touch their hands, sometimes she just smiled and went back to sleep. She slept almost twenty hours a day.

He wasn't certain if his presence was helping her, but it was surely helping him to be with her. Leaving her side made him twitchy and uncomfortable. He and his magic were in perfect accord that he should be guarding her while she was injured. Not that he thought there was a thing he could do to help, and he believed Liz when she said Sara was recovering, but it felt as if he left part of his soul behind when he left her side.

He needed her well. He needed her.

Paul and Amy came daily to the lab and asked about her.

Charlie met with them in Sara's classroom. "She sleeps almost all the time still. As soon as she's awake more, I'm sure she'd like to see you both. Our security is sure it wasn't a deliberate attack. He's singing like a bird now. I guess he decided to embrace his celebrity status. He's sure to be in prison a very long time."

Speaking of the bartender made him angry and he was sure they could see it in his face, which had heated in what he was certain in a red flush.

Paul was angry too, or maybe embarrassed. His face was flushed with anger too and he was scowling.

Paul said, "It's too good for him. All those women, not to mention almost killing Sara."

"Thank god you stopped him, Paul." Amy glanced at Paul with shining eyes.

"Sara said the same thing. She thinks you're a hero. I have to agree." Charlie grinned at his friend. His anger was fading with the show of solidarity.

"No, just lucky I was close," Paul demurred.

Amy said, "It wasn't lucky, it was brave. You didn't know if he was armed or what he intended. He might have attacked you too. You *are* a hero." Amy went to hug him, glanced down at her uniform, and stepped back. Blushing, she shrugged and touched his hand with her fingertips for a moment before turning to Charlie. "Give Sara my love. Tell her I've been working on all the changes we wanted to make and they'll all be ready." She squeezed Charlie's shoulder, smiled at Paul, and hurried from the room.

Paul stared after her with a small smile on his face.

Charlie laughed at his expression.

"What?" Paul said in feigned innocence, "I was thinking I could use her for some of my game designs."

Charlie chortled. "I'm sure you have designs for her, but if you poach my w—," he quickly changed the word wife to Sara, "Sara's design artist, I'll never hear the end of it."

He couldn't wait to be able to call her his wife in public. He felt Sara's response to his love and knew she'd woken. "I have to go, Paul. Thanks for everything. Not just for saving her life, for being such a good friend." He hugged him quickly, despite the uniform, and ran back to Sara.

By Sunday Sara was doing better, able to stay awake for longer periods. She was still too weak to stand, but managed sitting on her own as long as she didn't try to move too much. Charlie was beyond relieved that she was getting better.

"This will take a while, Charlie." Liz sat on the corner of her desk and opened a flatscreen. "She'll need therapy to recover muscle tone. It's nothing we can't handle, but you should be prepared. I expect her to make rapid progress over the next week now that she can feed herself, then it will appear that the progress has stopped, it hasn't, it just takes time to build back up. So don't worry if she still isn't walking in a week. I'm positive I can help her regain everything she's lost. Medically, she's perfectly fine, there's no damage to her muscles. They're just very shrunken." Liz pointed to the flatscreen hovering by them. "Do you want the medical details of what happened to her?"

"Not now, maybe someday." He hugged Liz. "Thanks, Liz, I'm so thankful we met you."

Liz kissed his cheek. "I'm thankful I met you too. I love Sara like a daughter. You're both my family. We'll take good care of her, and she'll be good as new."

Charlie nodded gratefully and returned to his wife's bedside. He found her video chatting Amy and they were both laughing. She grinned at him, letting her magic free to dart about the room. Oz's program would edit it out and it was cooperating, instantly returning to her without demure when she wished. He kissed her, then sat beside her and talked with Amy too, wishing they'd given in to the magic earlier it was so much happier now that it was mingling with the other magic.

He hadn't realized how tense Sara had been. Her state of unhappiness had been so constant that he'd thought it normal but now with her relaxing her hold, he felt the difference and it made him angry with himself that he'd done nothing to help her earlier. She glanced at him with worried eyes. The magic continued to swirl happily. It liked his anger. She didn't. He made a dismissive gesture and she continued to speak with Amy, but the small worry remained. It would remain until his anger faded.

But he was okay with her small worry. He'd be more worried if she didn't give a shit what he felt, and she knew he'd be angry that she was hurt. He just wished he could help her keep her own magic under control.

The thought distracted him from his anger. He was pondering his options, which were frustratingly limited, until the call ended.

He handed her an orange juice with a straw. "Want some fruit?" Without waiting for a reply, he handed her a small cup of melon.

The open screen by her knee showed images of her game level. “You’re sure you’re up to working?”

“My mind isn’t tired, just my body. And it isn’t really work either. We’re doing this for fun, remember? Amy and I are just finishing our game design. Our level is completely finished and in the hands of the programmers. Amy will oversee it for me.”

“Okay, just don’t overdo it.” He kissed her neck lightly. “I want you better soon.”

She smiled and reached for him. A matching smile on his face, he lifted her into his lap and cuddled her close, enjoying her happy contentment. His head resting on hers, they both dozed off.

Charlie returned to the academy to sleep in his room on Sunday. He’d been nervous leaving her, but she remained content with Joy’s company.

The commandant called Charlie into his office Monday morning. “I was sorry to hear your fiancé is so ill. I'm relieved it wasn't another purposeful attempt to harm her. The panic attacks she suffers from are more understandable. This is the third attack I know of. Have there been others?"

Charlie hesitated.

"Never mind, it's classified, I'm sure." The commandant rose from his chair and paced. "I've requested more armed guards at your lab whenever she's on campus. I have a responsibility to ensure the safety of the midshipmen and I've requested better security for all of you." He paused a moment. "Sealed records, special orders, the privileges you receive here all indicate more goes on with you three than I'm told. Without revealing classified secrets, can you tell me how much of a danger you three pose to the rest of the student body?"

Charlie lifted his hands and bit his lip. Guilt was a ball of ice in his stomach.

The commandant nodded. "Is the threat to Doctor Mitchel and Doctor Simmons, and you're all targets because you're close friends, or are you yourselves targets individually?"

"We're targets for ourselves," Charlie said and offered no explanation, telling himself it was stupid to feel guilty. Telling the commander would make no difference at all. It could endanger them, but logic didn't break apart that hunk of cold.

The commandant paced to his window and spoke with his back turned. "I'm aware, of course, that the three of you do exceedingly well in your classes and that you work in their lab with them. Are you holding back academically to fit in better here?"

"No, we aren't as academically gifted as Oz and Sara are."

"We can supply you with private classes and instruction if you need it," the commandant persisted.

"We receive that at the lab," Charlie assured him. "Our classes here suit us very well. Sara and Oz teach us too. We don't have the..." He paused, looking for the right word. "Vision they do, but we can understand when they explain it to us." Charlie paused again. "I can understand their equations and logic when they explain it to me, but I can't envision it on my own. I doubt anyone but they could. They spend a lot of their time just thinking."

The commandant turned to him smiling. "The great minds of their generation."

"The great minds of this century. The things they think of are amazing. The things they make are incredible. What they're trying to do is world changing."

The commandant frowned and returned to his desk. "I'm aware of their security devices and their game. The computer Doctor Simmons makes is amazing, but not world changing."

"I wish I could tell you what my, *um*, Sara does, but it's classified. What she does— what she thinks— how she thinks, will change the world. I guarantee it."

"If she lives long enough." The commandant rose an eyebrow.

Charlie winced. "Yes. She's learning as fast as she can, trying as hard as she can to bring her thoughts to practical use. The more success she has, the more danger she's in, and she's been pretty successful."

The commandant sighed. "I'll admit, I'll be glad when you're all someone else's problem. Curiosity is killing me. I look out my window and see this new building bustling with activity. My midshipmen talk about the game and what Doctor Simmons can do with his computers, and I wonder what else you're doing in there."

Charlie lowered his gaze to his feet. "As soon as circumstances permit, and clearance is given, you'll be the first person we tell. Sara would be thrilled to show you the game whenever you like. I'm sure we could get clearance to go over our security projects with you as well."

The commandant laughed. "I'll take you up on that. Is she well enough for visitors?"

"She is."

"A visit from me won't alarm her?"

Charlie smiled in relief. "Not at all. I warn you, she'll talk your ear off. She's not well enough to keep up with her contacts, but she's well enough to think. She gets going on these really obscure points we have a hard time following. Her doctors will let her resume her calls next week. Trying to keep up with her thought process is exhausting. We all need a break."

The commandant chuckled and dismissed Charlie.

Two days later the commandant visited the lab. Two armed guards in Marine uniforms ushered him in. Oz greeted him and gave him a tour, showing him the classrooms first.

"I'm teaching all the classes currently." Oz gestured to a whiteboard in the front of the room. "Sara usually teaches theory and programming. I usually teach hardware."

The commandant viewed the board a moment before turning to examine the desks. Each desk held a magnifying glass with an adjustable light clipped to it and small tools set neatly in a holder. "What are they making?"

"Their own wristcomps." Oz flicked his wrist and opened a flatscreen. "I show them each component and they learn how to install it and test its function. In Sara's class they learn how its programming works and how to make their own programs." A tap of his fingers on his virtual keyboard changed the picture. "The midshipmen come up with ideas of their own too. Paul Hayden designed this."

"What is it?" The commandant leaned forward, narrowing his eyes as he examined Oz's screen.

Oz tapped the picture, and the device began moving. He tapped it again and it grew larger, making it easier to see. Another tap stopped the movement. The close-up showed fan blades embedded in cloudy blue glass laced with fine gold wires in an intricate pattern.

"When it's finished, it'll be an engine. Paul designed those blades and helped with the wiring. That first picture was its actual size. It will power a flying security device." Oz opened another picture. "This too is its actual size."

"It's so small. What will it do?"

Oz opened another picture. "We'll make it look like one of these." He tapped the bugs on his screen. "It'll fly or crawl and transmit or record video and audio signals. We're making literal bugs."

"How long is the battery life on something this small that can move around?"

"That wiring was the battery. We don't call it that though because battery implies something that needs to be recharged or replaced— something that runs down. We call it a skein. Those skeins drawn in the energy and feed it to the engine. The skeins you saw there will provide enough power to move the bug continuously indefinitely. If the bug is squashed or stepped on or destroyed it would release the equivalent power of a strong static shock. You'd feel it, but it wouldn't be enough power to actually harm anything."

"You're making these now?" The commandant said in astonishment.

His tone made laughter bubble up Oz's throat, but he managed to keep his voice level when he said, "We have one prototype, yes, and we'll make more soon. We're working on making bigger skeins now to power bigger objects, specifically a car."

"A car that wouldn't need gas?"

"It wouldn't need gas, but right now it would have to run constantly and the energy discharge in a crash would be dangerous. We have to work out those kinks." Oz changed the picture again. "This is one of our security devices your midshipmen work on. We still just call it a buoy. It runs on a similar skein, but underwater. Captain Williams on the

Truman is testing it for us. We add in features he wants, and we send it back. I can show you all its specs, your fully cleared. In general, it sees and hears underwater. It moves relatively slowly, twenty-five knots is about its top speed, but we should be able to significantly increase that once we master our version of a battery, what we call a source. It uses our computers and transmits data through the water to this receiver."

Oz handed him another small black box. "That receiver decodes the information from the buoy and makes it available to anyone with access. We're using our own satellite system now, which of course uses our computers and encryption."

He changed the picture to show a satellite. They were crude devices. He hadn't the time to rework them from scratch and had basically just modified existing technology, which seemed primitive to him. He saw the flaws, but he also saw the potential. It was like that with everything now and very distracting.

He hated to leave his lab because a simple trip for coffee could distract him with ideas for a better cappuccino machine for god's sake.

The commandant clearing his throat brought his attention back to the conversation at hand. He and Brenda had installed the rest of the satellites, and he hoped it wouldn't occur to the man to ask how they'd launched them. They now had three permanent satellites in orbit as well as more ADCs, which as far he knew no one except a few raid members knew about. He'd need to design something capable of launching a satellite though because someone was bound to wonder someday.

He typed a note to his Valory as he said, "Our wristcomps use our satellites as well. We can talk to anyone, anywhere."

Oz showed the commandant every security device they had and were working on.

He finished the tour in Sara's empty classroom. "We're dedicated to security here. Part of security is identifying a threat, that's what I do mostly. The other part is stopping it. That's what Sara does."

Explaining it so simply made him rethink his position on her air shield. She was concerned with stopping threats and perhaps it was better to let her have her way. He'd wanted the shield to reflect damage, but it would be easier to design it to just stop the attack. Besides, he could always do it later.

The mountain of ideas that lurked in the back of his brain grew daily. *What was one more?* he thought in a combination of amusement and annoyance.

Oz showed him the ray-gun test, which distracted his thoughts from the shields. It was a relief to let himself really ponder it as they spoke. This he could spend time on. It was one of their priorities.

He said, "That was our first attempt. We're much better at it now. Our current goal is a shield of impenetrable photons around the vessel and we're very close to success. The ray-gun could be used offensively, but we aren't working on that right now. We're only doing defensive designs. As you can imagine, our designs are highly classified. Sara is working on more than this, but I can't mention any more." Oz paused and gazed at the commandant thoughtfully as he tapped his fingers on her desk a moment. "Sara is a highly trained medical doctor." He gestured for the commandant to leave the room, saying nothing else.

"I can't show you Sara's labs, but you're welcome in mine or my classes any time." Oz led the commandant into his main workspace. Tools and supplies lined the walls. Half-finished projects sat on the tables. Holographic screens flickered to life as they passed the tables and turned off when they reached a new table. A winged woman with white hair, wearing a lab jacket and a navy-blue skirt, flitted from table-to-table, offering sheaves of paper that Oz accepted or flicked away absently as they walked.

Magnifying glasses and microscopes sat on most benches although one bench held a motor taller than the commandant.

The commandant said, "These things you make here are amazing. The engines you make will be world changing. I'd like to attend classes and make my own computer."

"Sure, you're about sixteen hours behind the rest of this semester's class. I'd be happy to catch you up to them or you could take the class next fall or winter."

"When your friends graduate, will you leave, or will the classes continue?"

Oz liked to teach but the classes had the added benefit of pulling him from deep contemplation. He hated becoming mired in thought to the extent that it made normal interactions impossible, and the students helped with that. He wanted the classes to continue but hadn't mentioned his concerns to anyone— not even Sara. She didn't seem to have the same problems that he did shucking off work thoughts and he didn't want to worry her or anyone else.

Besides, he was handling it fine, he assured himself.

"I'm training a few replacement teachers, so I assume they could continue, but I can't say whether Sara and I will be here to teach. Midshipman First class Tillings and Frost as well as Midshipman Second Class Martins are taking extra lessons from both of us. They'll be qualified to teach the basic concepts we do. Whether they'll be assigned here, I have no idea. I've recommended them to teach here. They still need to learn from us, but we'll be available for questions."

The commandant laughed a bit. "These basic concepts of yours are pretty advanced stuff."

"They are. They're brilliant though and a pleasure to teach and work with. I have my eye on Midshipman Third Class Raines as well. I think he grasps the concepts and with more instruction could learn it well enough to teach others."

Oz laughed a bit himself. "I'd love to look through your new applicants and see if any have the math and science skills we need."

"I'll arrange it," the commandant said seriously. "Your criteria may be different from ours. We'll seriously consider anyone you select. All candidates must pass all of our selection process though."

Oz smiled. "We're teaching some civilians as well. If they don't get accepted by you, they might by us. Don't worry, we won't poach them. We have a service clause for our employees. We want to encourage military service, not discourage it." Oz showed the commandant the hiring clause he was referring to. "If an applicant passes us, but not you, he could be hired, but if he passes us both, he couldn't be until he served his full tour."

An idea occurred to him as he examined the list and he typed another note to his Valory, this one marked urgent. His Valory immediately began flicking through the resumes, sorting them by his new criteria. He'd find himself a few apprentices. Intelligent people who could keep him grounded. People he liked and would want to speak with. He liked the cadets, but orders would take them from his lab. He needed a few people that he knew would be around.

The commandant nodded. "Speaking of being hired, Midshipman Hayes said I might visit with Doctor Mitchel and see the game they're all working on."

"I sure she'd like that." Oz led him to the newly installed elevator to the second floor. "She's still in our infirmary, but she's well enough for visitors now. Don't be alarmed at her lack of movement. She can call for help if she needs it. Liz has her hooked to an experimental security device which emits a blue glow. It's the same device your midshipmen are testing. It isn't harmful, it just identifies bioelectric surges. You might see that from her device. If she falls asleep while visiting that's normal as well."

Oz led him to Sara's room and knocked lightly on the door. She welcomed them both with smiles. Oz kissed her cheek and her magic surrounded him briefly. His joined it then it dissipated. They were making no effort to control it. The happier Sara's magic was the happier they all were.

Sara talked enthusiastically about the game, and Oz brought the commandant gear to try it.

Sara donned the glasses and gloves Oz handed her. "You can use my maps and visit the areas briefly to see them all, but without the VR frame you'll have to use virtual legs like me."

She laughed at the commandant's amazement as he strolled through her level. She pointed out he could smell and interact with objects. Oz made notes as the commandant picked flowers, shook small trees, and opened doors and drawers in Sara's small, virtual house. Finally, he took off the glasses.

"That was fun. I'm not much of a gamer, but I'd play that."

"Try Monster Maze; it's my favorite. I'll play with you." Sara started the game. "The goal is to get to the other end of the maze. Monsters hide inside, but we can avoid them by solving puzzles. Or we can run by and they'll chase us. If they catch us, they send us back to the start. This game is super fun and a good work out in the VR gear. It's still fun with a console but lacks the adrenaline rush of really running away. Paul's working on a haunted mansion as well. I have it set for age eighteen, but you could set it for a three-year-old, the monsters would be cute and the puzzles age appropriate."

Sara let the commandant solve every puzzle. She just laughed a lot while they decided what way to go. She fell asleep while he was solving a matching game.

Oz was busily sorting through the applicants for someone to work on the game with him. Someone it would be fun to work with. It was clear to him now that he needed more human interactions. Hawk had been right. They needed more fun. And this fun would make them a fortune. Seeing the commandant play had given him new insights that he intended to take full advantage of. He could barely wait to get started.

The commandant took off his glasses and handed them to Oz. "This game is very fun. I'll be sure to buy it. I have nieces and nephews who'd love to play it."

Oz removed the glasses and gloves from Sara. "You're welcome to check out the entire lineup. I think you'll like the training programs we made for the Scouts— our security teams. We use actual guns for that, modified of course, but with lifelike interactions and responses with a completely simulated environment you can climb and crawl on. Its very fun. The midshipmen here work on that program a lot. We've designed complete virtual ships with every disaster we could think of. We're thinking of opening a chain of them. Not using actual schematics like we do for our training but maybe recreating famous battles or scenes from movies."

"I'd love to see it." The commandant gestured at the gear in his and Oz's hands.

"This all must cost a fortune."

Oz nodded, smiling wryly. "We're going through money like water. Once our game launches, we'll recoup it a hundred-fold though." Oz frowned thoughtfully at Sara. "We need her well. She's vital to Valor Industries. I need her. No one else understands me, not completely like she does. We have so much going on." A finger held to his lips, he gestured the commandant to follow him as Sara stirred in her sleep. They left the room and Marcus entered and sat beside her.

"Sorry. She needs to rest," Oz said. "We're still correlating data from last fall's attack on the president, and she's been working on a theory, tracking leads from her bed in there. It's too stressful, but she's determined to stop Mr. X. That's what we call our unknown mastermind."

Oz waved his hands in the air a moment as he gathered his thoughts. "I'm trying to keep her distracted with nicer thoughts, less stressful things than presidential assassins and people trying to kill Chief or Stasia and Hawk. This visit helps. All normal visitors help. They keep her occupied with nice, normal things. She isn't strong enough to teach yet but I was hoping some of her students could get permission to come here in their spare time and talk to her? She'd love the company, and she could help them with homework or whatever."

He'd make sure that she had some civilian assistants as well. People that couldn't be ordered away and that had families and friends that kept them interested in the outside world.

"I'll see that all of your students get permission to come here as they wish." The commandant said agreeably.

"I'll tell them she can see them all and ask them to visit her. Thank you. Amy and Paul visit when they can, but they only had permission to be here briefly. That will help her a lot." Oz smiled crookedly. "They'll probably come here often and work here as well as see her. They like working on the games and want their own wristcomps."

"How do you afford to give them the wristcomps?"

"We have a grant and it's an ideal learning tool. They learn it and how to use it from the ground up. When they graduate as officers, having and using one will help them tremendously. The Navy likes the Valkyrie operating system and the wristcomps. The cost per unit is down a lot from the original and I expect it to drop even more with next version. We aren't charging the students access fees to our satellite.

"With the newest skeins, the charger will be obsolete in the next model. The worst problem we're having is more people want to take the class then we can accommodate. We choose our students by their GPA. You need a minimum math and science level. Basically, the smarter you are, the better the chances you can get into our class. We can only show sixty people a semester. You're going to have some disgruntled students."

The commandant smiled complacently. "It'll be good for them. Competition is vital for a well-rounded officer. Let me know when it's convenient for you to catch me up to this semester's class."

"I'll email you my schedule and let you pick a time," Oz said.

The students started visiting Sara. Liz monitored her and when she noticed her yawning, she'd shoo them away to let Sara sleep. Sara slowly grew stronger. Eating and drinking no longer made her hands shake. Charlie helped her shower, and someone had to carry her to the bathroom, but once there she could help herself. By the end of the week, she could sit up by herself. She still wasn't walking, but just being able to raise herself into a sitting position lifted her spirits tremendously. Liz got her a wheelchair so she could go where she wanted inside the lab.

She returned to work and spent her days in her office and teaching her students. Her evenings were spent with friends and Charlie. He'd study or do homework while she worked on her own projects or just rested quietly beside him.

He smiled tenderly at her as she dozed. Her magic had stopped pushing her to come to him, it was her own contentment he sensed. Despite the other warriors she was happiest with him and it relieved his soul to know it.

- 8 -

REPORTING

"Thank you for agreeing to meet with me." Liz saluted General Campbell.

"Please, have a seat, Liz. I admit, I'm concerned you've asked for this meeting."

"I have a lot of new information. Let me start by saying Sara is recovering. I think she'll be fully recovered within two months' time although I'm not a hundred percent certain she'll regain the height she lost. I expect her to be walking and doing exercises within a month."

"That's good news."

"It is." Liz smiled in clear relief. "Sara was mostly successful in teaching the magic. All the magic wielders can tell it no now and it listens. I don't know what it will do if it really wants something. They've been keeping it happy." Liz sighed. "One of the reasons I'm here is Sara wants to try to separate them all a bit. I recommend we don't separate any of the couples at first. Sara would like to stop seeing the others slowly. She wants to have it only want Charlie again. I don't think that's possible anymore but she wants to try it. Charlie assures me he won't let her stress the magic. I think we should let her try but keep them in the zone just in case."

"That's fine." Campbell grimaced ruefully. "We've already decided to give them to her. We won't try to order any of them away. It's a waste of training, but their scientific advances are worth more than an entire battalion of highly trained soldiers."

Liz winced. "That brings up my next point— we need that battalion." She told him what Charlie had told her. "Sara has asked it to wait, and it is, but it won't wait indefinitely. We need to be ready for it. If one of them dies or is severely hurt or afraid it could panic again and try to reproduce. We should have our people ready. I wish I'd thought to replace Mike with Harrison to see if the magic would've accepted a replacement for him or if once it chose him it was too late. I recommend we have a full raid ready. If Sara or Brenda do change someone, we can try to substitute our choice."

"Will it stop at the raid?"

"No way to tell." Liz stared down at her fingers twining in her lap and smoothed her hands over her knees. "I recommend we don't change anyone else until we absolutely have to and then add the minimum it will accept. We need information on how long it can go to be able to judge how many we need." She handed the general a file.

"This is an important datum. The new magic wielders, excluding Joy, didn't receive any other buffs; they retain the same strength, agility, and intelligence as they had prior to the change. Mike Wallace received the equivalent of raid buffs, but he isn't as strong as Charlie is. I don't know if it's because he was dispelled and then hit with lightning again or if Sara subconsciously did it. Marcus, Rick, and Mike have all of the spells Charlie does, but Charlie's spells are stronger. He's stronger physically then they are. His endurance is higher; he's a better warrior."

"*Hmm*, yes, I can see how in her eyes, he's better, therefore they were made weaker. Brenda too?"

"Yes, no intelligence buff beyond what she already had. Her damaging spells are stronger than Sara's, but she's a damage class. She can manipulate the magic like Sara can, but she can't communicate as well. Brenda is unable to recharge the bracelets. She lacks the spell to store magic."

"They've both tried to communicate again?"

His eyes as he said it were intent on Liz's. The pressure of them would have made her duck her head if she'd intended to lie but she met them straightly, somewhat amused at her internal thoughts. She bet he could cow the green recruits with the merest glance.

"They did and with moderate success. Sara convinced her magic to let the Scouts touch her, but not naval personnel or Marines. I'm sure it's because she doesn't want them to touch her."

Liz grimaced. "I should say all of the Scouts except Major Nelson. I'll admit that worries me."

"Frankly, I'm amazed Charlie didn't kill him."

Liz winced again. "They speak civilly, but the friendship is gone. Our reputation with them took a serious hit. I know none of them trust him anymore. And when I say none of them, I mean the entire raid. This leads me to my next point. I've written this nowhere and told no one. I'm not one hundred percent sure of my findings. Charlie, and to a lesser extent Sara, can control them all."

"What's that mean exactly?" The general sat back in his chair, furrowing his brow.

"It means, if Charlie says do something, they do it, all of them, even Sara. She can do that as well, but if he contradicts her, they listen to him. It's hard to get accurate results because neither of them order them around, but when they do, they get instant obedience. I think it's more noticeable now because they're together so much. When it was just Team Valor, he rarely asked them to do anything, and almost never asked them to do something they didn't want to do."

Liz made a face. "I can't prove it without talking with them, and I didn't want to bring it to their attention without talking to you and Doctor Gotlieb. I can give you examples of the behavior, but it's just my opinion until it's tested."

"Give me a few examples." The general folded his hands on the desk. His calm reaction eased her fast-beating pulse. She hated to contemplate that Charlie might be controlling her almost as much as she hated to contemplate the general's reaction if he found it to be true.

Liz nodded and opened a flatscreen. "I have a few on video. This is a typical lunch. Charlie isn't looking at Stasia. He wouldn't normally ask anyone for anything while they were eating but he doesn't see that she is. I'm monitoring him closely to be sure his aura isn't affecting his classmates. The reactions are subtle so it's standard practice for me to record him when he's in large groups to better determine if he's affecting them." She waved her hand dismissively. "I digress. There's no noticeable difference but I did notice this. He asked her to get him the report she was doing on cost analysis for the game development, and she gets up and does it. She doesn't say when I'm done eating, which a normal person would do. Before you say maybe it's her, I have recordings of someone else asking her for something while she's eating, and she does say after I'm done. I've seen this multiple times with all of them, they instantly do what he wants."

She turned on a new video. "This one is more subtle. Toric is infatuated with Sara. They all know it. Sara is kind, but distant with him. He visits, and she lets him stay. Charlie orders him to leave and he does. He doesn't even look back. Oz asks him to leave, and he makes an excuse to linger or touch her again before he does. See, it's not conclusive, he could be afraid of Charlie and not Oz, or maybe he's trying to be respectful of Charlie's feelings. The next video is more compelling, but still not proof.

Liz turned on a video of an unhappy looking Hawk. They listened to Charlie tell him to go sit with Sara. Hawk goes. Liz stopped the recording. "What you don't see is him telling Sara to sit with Hawk. She doesn't want to, but she does without complaint. Hawk doesn't want to either, but he does as well."

"Wait, why don't they want to sit together?"

Liz sighed. "I'm telling you this in confidence. It's a bit of a love triangle. Sara doesn't want to hurt Hawk's feelings, so she doesn't want to sit with him and let her magic mingle with his. Hawk doesn't want to upset either of them by airing his feelings. Charlie wants the magic happy, so he makes them sit together at least once a week. It embarrasses both of them. I think this is pretty compelling evidence. A normal seventeen-year-old boy wouldn't go to the object of his affection and be turned away every week. When the magic mingles, you know exactly how someone feels for you. It must be extremely awkward for them."

"This is a big problem! I should've been informed immediately that Hawk is romantically interested in Sara."

"It just became clear when their magic touched, and he isn't in love with her. They do love each other, but he doesn't want to take her from Charlie. He just wants someone like her, a relationship like Charlie has. He does find her attractive and if she weren't Charlie's girl I'm sure he'd make a move, but he never would now. It really isn't a problem. Charlie isn't jealous at all. Hawk is jealous, but not of them, of their situation. He's happy for them. It's just awkward for him and Sara to share that knowledge. It's one thing to know it, it's another to sit by someone and feel it."

"Yes, I see… compelling proof indeed. If their romantic situation changes, I want to know immediately."

"I'm keeping an eye out on all of them and studying psychiatry. I'm planning on leaving the raid once I'm done with these classes. I'll leave sooner if there's a chance of being changed. I do enjoy the buffs, especially the intelligence buff but I don't want to be a host for the magic. I've been taking classes for my doctorate and while I can do it without the buff, the classes are easy with it, so I want to finish first."

Liz handed the general another file. "This is about Joy. She's fully recovered. You know we did a full autopsy on her, removed and weighed every single organ. We dissected her brain and took out her m-nerve and examined it." She traced the picture on her screen of the new set of nerves magic wielders had. "We did every test we could think of on her body. She's perfect now, exactly as she was. She remembers hearing the shots that killed her and then nothing until she woke in the hospital bed. I think we need to reexamine our hypothesis on resurrection. We'd considered it a form of healing, not true resurrection. A sort of advanced CPR that wouldn't work after brain death. Obviously, that isn't the case. There's no doubt Joy was truly dead. Brenda and Rick were resurrected easily. As easily as a healing. In their case I think it *was* basically a heal. In Joy's case, Sara preformed a reset. My theory is she could do it again, and if the body were more intact, specifically the brain, she could do it easier.

"Joy's brain was severely damaged. We'd destroyed much of it during the autopsy. It was much more damaged than Brenda's was when she was murdered. Sara's own brain was severely damaged in the healing. Team Valor was magically depleted for two days afterward. They all injured their m-nerves during that resurrection. I took a biopsy when Sara was sedated and her m-nerves were fried. Her bones had been scorched as if burned and large sections of her brain burned. Without healing it would potentially take years for her to regenerate and it might have been unrecoverable."

"But she has a healing buff."

"Yes, but because her m-nerve was fried, she had no magical conduits. No way to form magic to make the repairs needed. To kill a magic wielder beyond hope of resurrection, the brain needs to be destroyed completely, and in a wielder who possess a healing buff, the m-nerves should be removed too. It horrifies me to think one might be buried and slowly regenerate. All should be cremated when they die. No viable flesh can remain. Sara's current injuries prove that the magic can refashion the body to use it to power the host. It's conceivable and even likely it could injure the host beyond repair if pressed.

"I'll know more as we see how Sara recovers. She's perfectly healthy but she lost two inches in height. It's possible the magic could just use one of them up."

The idea of it gave her the cold shivers.

She cleared her throat and said in a calmer voice, "It's clear memory doesn't just reside in one area of the brain, or perhaps everything a magic wielder has experienced is an indelible part of the magic now.

"It's also clear that removing the m-nerve would only be a temporary solution. It would regrow. I can only hypothesis on the time needed for complete regrowth but I assume it would take at least four days as in a transformation but that's assuming brain function is intact."

Liz tapped her wristcomp and displayed a highly magnified picture. "Our autopsy of Joy taught us the corpus callosum, the fibers that connect the two halves of the cerebellum, are configured differently in a wielder and is where the first spark of magic comes from. These tiny filaments here. Only casters have these. To cast requires reserves of magic that form and are stored in the m-nerve, but it requires these small delicate strands."

Liz changed the picture and the general leaned forward to examine it.

"Those filaments didn't reform until the brain had been completely healed and it took forty minutes or so. I don't think our healing had any effect on that process. Every caster falls unconscious for forty minutes or so when the magic infects them. I think that's those filaments forming.

"When I questioned Sara after Joy's resurrection, she said it felt like her nerves were on fire, and I think they were. It almost killed her to cast that spell. She was forcing too much power through those filaments and burned them out. I know it almost destroyed her ability to use magic. The regeneration of those nerves was extremely painful exactly like a newly infected wielder experiences when they first develop m-nerves. I recommend any dead magic wielder's body be brought to her immediately.

"Brenda has a rez as well, but Sara's is more powerful. A sun priest has the most powerful resurrection spells, excluding druids. We have no druids though because no one wants to be trapped in animal form.

"I have an idea about that too," Liz went on. "If someone were willing to be a druid, Sara, Oz, or Brenda could dispel animal form. I think a druid could learn to do it themselves as well, either using their paws or their mind. I'm still convinced Sara used her mind to cast Call-For-Help, not her fingers. I know testing hasn't been able to reproduce the results, but testing couldn't reproduce the desperation either."

Campbell said, "I agree, especially now that we know the magic communicates through feelings. I read the reports they all made about the meeting and found it fascinating and disturbing. The magic took them all, granted they cooperated— but still."

Liz said, "They were all aware and weren't trying to stop it. They were trying to help it. It would've been unable to speak without their help. Part of the reason Sara is so exhausted is that it was moving her or helping her move when she was trying to show it who could touch whom. She wasn't able to move herself like that, she would've fallen flat on her face. Instead, she was leaning over shuffling hands for a few hours. The magic has no concept of physical limitations or harm. Sara is trying to show it. It doesn't know anything about humans at all. The magic tries to help her but can't because it doesn't know. Like a two-year-old it acts before it knows what it's doing. Like a two-year-old it has no concept of actions and consequences. It doesn't feel bad it hurt her; it just feels bad when she does."

"Can we expect the others to develop the sorts of problems she has with it?"

Liz grimaced ruefully. "Yes. Stasia is working on the same issues now. Her magic wants things she doesn't and it's confusing to separate its wants from her own. It's hard to stop wanting something it does when you want it too. The older ones seem to have less problems with the magic pressing its desires on them but I don't have enough data to be certain it's the level of maturity and not a class effect." Liz shrugged lightly. "Magic enjoys the feel of intimate acts when love is felt. When two magic wielders share magic during sex, it likes it, it wants to feel that again. It doesn't understand inappropriate time and presses its desire on the host. I expect it will get easier for the younger ones as they mature and sex doesn't dominate their minds so much."

Campbell huffed a short laugh.

"It isn't nearly as strong of a desire to mingle for the single ones as it is for the couples. Brenda and Mike don't feel the need as sharply as Stasia and Rick or Sara and Charlie. I'm guessing it's because they aren't in love or not yet anyway. Brenda reports it's getting harder to resist and her magic wants contact more so maybe she's in love now."

She frowned as she considered a new thought. "It's clear the wielders share a connection and I'm wondering if it can be seen by those who can see magic. Charlie has always reported Sara's aura looks as if it's made to mesh with his. I know the fissures he sees and thought were insanity in her aura have almost disappeared. I don't think it was insanity, or maybe it is, but it wasn't a personality defect but the magic imposing its will over hers. When she doesn't fight the magic, the fissures disappear. She's very strong willed. More so than she shows. It could potentially drive a wielder crazy to be deprived of their magical spouse or to ignore the magic's needs. I'll speak to them and have them examine the auras of the entire raid. I'd hate for one to slip into madness unnoticed over a separation."

"We'll make sure the couples aren't separated." The general leaned back in his chair. "I don't know what we'll do about the raid composition. Single unattached people would be best, but then we run the risk of one falling in love outside the raid. Married couples are an option, but what if one falls out of love?"

Liz shrugged. "It's complicated, there's no doubt about that. Add in the fact that both partners need to be happy and it gets extremely complicated. In Sara and Charlie's case we're lucky she doesn't mind going wherever he goes. Stasia and Rick are both happy as active military and being in combat. We have to make sure future raid members have the same life goals. It would make the magic extremely unhappy if one partner wanted to do something that required them to go where the other partner couldn't go or would be unhappy going."

"Yes, we won't separate any ever again. We've learned that lesson. I'll pass this information up the chain. Sara and Oz requested to be sent back to the *Truman* to work on the light shield and some other ideas they have. We'll assign Charlie there as well. I'd really like to keep all magic wielders in the same zone, but is the same ship too close?"

"I'll need some time to determine how far they can be separated. They haven't tried at all since the meeting. I wanted to clear the attempt to do that with you first."

"Do it, but slowly and carefully. Don't stress any of them. Send the unaffected raid members away slowly." He paused a moment in thought. "Keep Drew and Joy together, but let's see how long she can go without seeing him. Don't stress it. Let her see him if she needs to, but we need an idea on how long a magic wielder can go without seeing their non-magic wielding partner."

"We'll need more guards. They don't need to be in the loop, but they do have to be extremely discrete. They're bound to see some unexplainable things. Speaking of personnel, we've been keeping Mike from his team. Now that the patchiness of his skin has cleared up enough to avoid comment, we should let him meet with them and tell them he was recruited to be a Scout. They were told he was on a special assignment."

The general nodded agreement. "Let him meet with them. I'll need some time to find replacement guards. I want to speak with the president and Pierce first. That might be a good opportunity to test potential recruits, set them to guard duty to give them a chance to meet and mingle. I'm not sure though, we need to discuss it. We don't want distracted guards either."

"It has pros and cons," Liz agreed.

"No offense, Liz, but I hope I don't see you again for another year and half at their graduation." Campbell stood to escort her to the door.

She laughed. "Me too. I know we're trying to give them as normal of a school experience as possible, but we're failing miserably. We have full-time guards on both Sara and Oz now. We aren't trying to be discreet. We'll have at least one at their home full-time even when they aren't there. They need a housekeeper and secretaries. I recommend they not only be vetted by Pierce but have defense training as well. Some of our worst threats to them weren't magic related at all. Sara should never have been left alone in that lodge; she should never have had to deal with Philip or gang members robbing liquor stores. They need someone on duty with them at all times."

The general said, "I agree completely. We managed to keep them under the radar magically and dropped the ball for normal dangers. We assumed normal people weren't a threat because of their abilities. I think they're more of a threat because they aren't prepared for them. They aren't suited up and aren't in a team. A simple sedative can kill her."

"She's working on that too with her magic," Liz assured him. "She's trying to teach it what to do if someone on the no touch list gives her one. It's slow going; it's a complicated thing to teach. I'll keep you informed. Right now, sedatives work as normal. She convinced it she was being hurt, not helped when it tried to remove it last time. The good news is once her magic learns they all know."

"That's also the bad news," the general said dryly.

Liz saluted and left to return home.

- 9 -

WORLD DOMINATION

General Campbell met with President Carmichael, Pierce Taylor, and Major Nelson. He told them what Liz had told him and showed them all the files and passed on her requests and recommendations.

"I'm glad they got a handle on this as quickly as they did," Carmichael said as he flipped through the reports.

Pierce placed his copy of the report on his knee. "We learned a lot. It's worth letting them keep the raid near them and not using them for the advances Oz and Sara make.

Carmichael held up a photo of Oz's new engine. "They've made some huge advances. Skeins will revolutionize the power industry.

We're scrambling right now to get ready. Our economy will take a hit, but foreign economy will plummet. We need to assure our allies of our support. His power supply is genius and simple, it's inexpensive to make and safe to use. His technology is patented, but that won't stop other countries from reproducing it. We're looking at the end of the oil age. There's bound to be turmoil. Oz and Sara keep me informed, not only of what they're currently doing, but also of their ideas."

The president used his wristcomp and showed them an email. "Oz wants to launch a probe to the moon. He sent me a two-hundred-page report on what they think they can do on the moon. I'm telling you, they scare me to death. It's exciting and terrifying what they're capable of. My campaign managers assure me that their ideas are brilliant and bound to boost my poll numbers by at least thirteen percent. Sara's website and the few small ads they ran have changed public perception of her completely in less than two months. The ease with which they can manipulate public perception is frightening."

"The only thing holding them back from world domination is their ADD." Pierce chuckled. "They're easily distracted by their next great idea."

"You're joking, but it's true." The president sat back and crossed his legs. "They're perfectly content to design new and better ways to do things. Well, he is anyway. Sara is obsessed with protection. She sends me reports like this one." The president handed them a printout of one of her emails. "Yeah, I don't understand the math either, but look at the summary. She's made a shield. It isn't like hers, but she thinks it'll work and wants to test it. If it passes the tests, she wants to install it on the *Truman*."

The president slid them another printout. "I haven't shown anyone else this. Ignore the math, you'd need ten years of college to understand it. She's working on a smart ray-gun. I call it her death-ray. The ray-gun is based on her smite. She made her smite ignore line of sight and thinks she can do that eventually with the ray gun. In other words, if she's in the zone, she can kill you. Once she targets you there's no escape. Right now, smite will dissipate when it hits walls or other objects— she assures me her ray-gun won't. The ball of light the ray-gun sends will hang outside the door waiting for it to open then smite you. Can you imagine a world where you can just program a ball of light to find and kill someone?"

He waited a moment to let that sink in. "She wants to do that. She says she can make it have a stun effect. She says anything they can do she should eventually be able to reproduce, so Stasia's knockout punch put in a ball of light with Hawk's tracker or Oz's locate." He grinned ruefully at them as he rubbed his temples. "I know, it's terrifying. I'm glad she's so worried about defense instead of offensive. She's designing ways to avoid those scenarios as well."

The printout in his hand shook a moment before he ran it through his shredder. When the last small bit was confetti he turned to Pierce. "Major Harris can now operate on her and they've been doing some experiments. Nothing too invasive, they're waiting for her to fully recover, but what they've already learned..." The president leaned back in his seat and swiveled it side-to-side. "Charlie informs me her goal is to wipe out terrorism.

To make it impossible for terror tactics to work. We had a long talk. Several of them, in fact. He's sure that she'll not only succeed in eventually making her heal available to everyone, but will insist on it being available to everyone, not just Americans. The ramifications of that are staggering. If she can do that— she can make her purify available and a population explosion will follow. Our defenses here better be impregnable, our armament fierce. I'm pretty sure I'll be reelected now. Over the next four years I'll search diligently for a successor that you can all work with. These changes will start soon and happen fast. Oz already started his motor production. The water motor will be available by next year. Who knows how long it'll take Sara to make her heal, but she'll have her shield up in a year. The death-ray will take longer. I'm hoping she leaves development of that for a while at least. I'm going to ask her to concentrate on personal protection. Something safe and affordable for the average person."

He stood and paced behind his desk with his hands behind his back. "No matter what I do— no matter who we share these developments with, the United States will be the world power. No one will be able to compete with us. We need to prepare for that— for the fury of the rest of the world."

"My top analysts have run scenarios." Pierce handed the president a folder. "Imaginary what ifs with our best strategists. Keep in mind none of our strategists are nearly as intelligent as Sara and Oz. I propose we ask them. They can't be unaware of the fallout from their discoveries. We should tell them our concerns and see what their ideas are."

The president resumed his seat at his desk. "I will as soon as Sara is stronger. Liz assures me stress is very bad for her right now. It can wait the two months for her full recovery. We won't use any of them for any situation until we have a better handle on the magic."

"We can use Stasia and Hawk," Campbell disagreed. "I wouldn't use them causally, but in an emergency they could be separated from the rest."

"I wouldn't recommend it." Pierce shook his head, leaning back in his seat and grimacing ruefully at the general. "Yes, they'd agree to help, but the others will be angry. You'd do better using Brenda and Mike or Marcus. Team Valor shouldn't be separated if we want them to keep cooperating. You run the risk of magical backlash if Brenda, Mike, or Marcus is harmed but not the risk of their anger. Talk to them about using the other magic wielders in an emergency. Don't use any of them without telling them first. Don't ever try to use Rick without Stasia. And ask their permission before sending Joy anywhere for any reason."

"I'll speak with them personally," the general said. "We won't use anyone without permission." He sighed. "My dream of a magical army is dying."

"Someday you'll have one. We just need to figure out what the magic wants and how forgiving it will be to changing hosts," Pierce said. "In the game you never die, you can always be rezzed. In real life, everyone eventually dies. Yes, they'll live a long time baring violent death. Liz estimates as much as three hundred years. A heal can't turn the clock back but it can keep you perfectly healthy, which slows the rate of cell decay. In effect, you age between heals. Potentially, if you used a heal daily you could live a thousand years before you grew old. But sooner or later a human dies, it's inevitable and the magic will have to accept that. It's one of the many things the priests need to talk to it about."

Nelson said, "Project Erasure needs to stay current. I'll have to speak to the teams and recheck our plans with these new develops in mind. We should develop a new plan to slow them down."

"Project Speed Bump," Pierce said, and the president winced.

He said, "I'll speak with them personally, but I'm not convinced we need to slow them. What we need is to manage them better. We need to build our reputation back up so that we can guide them and make sure they work in our best interests."

"Are they though?" Nelson asked dryly.

Pierce said, "Time will tell."

- 10 -

HOLOGRAPHIC TECHNOLOGY

The commandant gave Sara permission to use the school cafeteria to throw Stasia a surprise party. She and Amy spent an hour in the morning setting small black boxes and round glass balls that housed holo projectors around the room. A week's worth of programing transformed the space. The entire student body was invited as well as all of Stasia's other friends and family. The Scouts attended as informal guards.

Charlie wasn't certain if he was proud or embarrassed. Speculative glances had followed him all day. The weight of his classmates' stares, the whispers and questions had increased as the day progressed. He supposed he'd need to get used to it. Rumors were rampant on campus about what VI was working on. Few of his classmates took the classes but the entire student body was now aware that the new computers were revolutionary. Once the Valkyrie operating system was officially launched, he was certain it would be more than just his classmates hounding him for the inside scoop.

"Wow!" Dave exclaimed as he and Jeff entered the cafeteria behind Charlie.

"You finished it?" Paul called happily and hurried to Amy.

She turned and grinned, waving them forward. A monster sitting in a broken lounge chair beneath a tattered beach umbrella yawned and used a four-inch golden claw to pick its brilliantly white teeth. The teeth glowed slightly, glints of light shining on the long canines. It shook its head and the purple fur covering it rippled. The hair flowed and waved as it moved, revealing highlights as it stirred and settled, and it continued to stir with realistic movement along its torso and limbs as though the monster breathed and flexed. Its glowing green eyes fastened on Paul as he approached and the monster heaved itself to its feet, crushing the chair, which faded to mist as the monster winked and turned away.

"I'm still working on the noises. I want more creaks and groans, but I got the fur down," Amy said happily as the monster snapped its fingers, making the beach umbrella slid down with a soft clinking sound. The umbrella darkened and elongated, and the monster stepped through the newly formed portal and disappeared. Glowing orange words shimmered across the portal, *Monster Maze! Enter If You Dare!* and glints of eyes and teeth moved in the depths.

"This is your game?' Jeff asked in awe.

"Was that a man in a costume?" Dave asked as Paul nodded.

Amy said, "No, a hologram. Check this one out. Run add for Travel Terrors."

The cadets around Charlie milled and spoke excitedly among themselves as the cave disappeared, replaced by a bathroom door. The metal door was scratched and dirty and the slightest order of disinfected wafted to them.

"It has a really great ominous air, Amy," Paul said enthusiastically. "The vacancy sign is perfect. You were right. It looks just like a plane lavatory and it's scarier than the cockpit I wanted to use in the ad."

"Can we play it?" Dave asked.

"Sure," Amy said and waved him forward.

Charlie laughed as those closest eagerly stepped forward while others hurried to the other three booths.

"You can sit at the table here and play with him using the gloves and glasses," Amy was saying as Charlie turned to scan for Sara. He spotted her beside the buffet she'd set out and chuckled over how proud she was as she spoke to Camila who held a plate of the pasta Sara had made.

His pulse jumped as it always did at first sight of her and her cheeks flushed as her head turned, looking for him.

He didn't have a word for the feeling that bounced between them when their eyes met. It was love, pride, lust, longing, satisfaction, and possessiveness all rolled into one. It was everything. She was everything to him as he was to her. He felt it in his soul and heaved a sigh of contentment that she echoed.

Magic hummed beneath his skin but didn't try to manifest. It knew better by now or maybe it was just content to bathe in that echo.

Amy was explaining how to play as Charlie wove through the crowd that exclaimed excitedly as a stage appeared on the opposite side of the room. Charlie knew there was a wall there, but the projected image looked realistic enough to fool the eye into believing there was an actual stage where the wall had been. People were leaning forward to run their hands over the wall. A door in the back of the stage opened and an eighties girl band strolled onto the stage. Music drowned the excited exclamations, and Charlie reached Sara's side in time to hear her say.

"They seem to like it."

He laughed, and she turned from the woman she'd been speaking with to beam at him as she offered him a plate of pasta. *She was prouder of the food then the programming*, he thought in amusement as he accepted the offered plate.

"Delicious," he said truthfully, nodding with his chin at the stage. "It's really realistic.

You did a great job with perspective. If I didn't know better, I'd swear there was a stage there."

"Doctor Mitchel, Mr. Hayes," the commandant said, "It's fabulous. Have you met our superintendent?"

The commandant introduced Sara to the men who'd followed him while Charlie ate his pasta and watched bemusedly as they questioned her enthusiastically.

Stasia grinned at him from across the room and jerked her head at Oz who was dancing with a girl from Charlie's English class. He snickered as the song ended and a new girl approached.

"Some things never change," he murmured, and Sara followed his glance. He felt her amusement as her gaze lingered on Oz.

"We're being rude," The commandant said, gesturing the man speaking to Sara away. "I'm sure we can talk later, and you have guests to see to. The food looks divine and smells even better."

The men made polite farewells and headed to the buffet, still talking excitedly about the holograms.

"Let's dance before they come back," Charlie whispered and pulled her onto the dance floor.

Life sized holograms of famous singers from the eighties wandered the room.

The room itself had been transformed into an eighties-style dance hall. The tables now appeared to be black rusty metal and the chairs had funky designs. One of the walls was black with a laser light show. The server counters and the entryway were black and white striped. Another wall showed pictures of Stasia and her friends. Amy had designed metallic looking balloons with small wings that randomly floated around the room. They told jokes or made funny noises if you bumped into one, then dissolved into a shower of metallic glitter before reforming elsewhere.

Holographic smoke that slowly changed colors covered the floor. The waitstaff Sara had hired all wore tight leather vests with studs and buckles with their hair spiked and gelled in different colors. Random people were picked out and their clothing holographically changed to eighties style while others were lit with random glows.

A ton of food filled the tables and the holographic band changed with the song that played. All of Stasia's favorite girl bands had been programmed as holograms. Sara, Amy, and a cadre of their new programmers had been working on it for months.

The party was a raging success. Sara only danced with him. He danced with Stasia, Amy, and Joy, which made Sara giggle with happiness.

None of the raid asked Sara to dance and he wondered if she told them not to or if they were afraid to upset him. A few of his classmates asked, likely encouraged by Oz accepting every offer, but she turned them all away. He had to admit he was happy she did, and he knew she felt it. He hoped he wasn't inhibiting her from the raid though.

Between dances she sat in a corner and observed his classmates playing the game and dancing with a smile on her face and in her heart. Charlie sat beside her, and they laughed at Oz who was surrounded by a group of laughing flirting girls between dances.

The party ended at ten and Charlie drove Sara crazy by not telling her Rick planned to propose.

"Come on you have to tell me what's got you so excited." Sara narrowed her eyes at him.

"Sorry can't. You'll find out in a day or two." He kissed her cheek. "Not my secret to tell, sweetheart."

She harrumphed, but she wasn't really angry, she was intrigued and eyed the crowd speculatively, her gaze lingering on Stasia and Rick who danced cheek-to-cheek in the emptying room.

Charlie kissed Sara goodnight, still chuckling to himself, and headed back to his dorm room with Paul.

"I can't believe they let her throw a party here," Paul said as they entered their room.

"The commandant likes Sara." Charlie smiled smugly. "I think he wanted to see how the holograms worked. She told him it was a one-time only request and she wouldn't make a habit of asking to throw parties here."

"It was fun. I'm glad they let her. The holograms looked great, very real."

Jeff said, "They really did. Your games were so cool, Paul. I don't know what game I liked better. When will it be released?"

Before Paul could answer Dave said, "I thought the singers were cool as shit. Did you see Amy had a little Elvis that popped up from her wristcomp to do her bidding?"

"I saw her send a cartoon shark to Paul."

Paul said, "It delivers messages about the games. She uses it so I know the sort of message it is. But it doesn't generally swim through the air. I think she was just playing with the system they set up."

Dave said, "She said we could design our own avatars, anything we want. I'd do my entire house if it didn't cost a fortune. Hell, maybe even if it did. You could have any furniture you liked.

"We might be on to a new business idea here," Charlie said over his shoulder as he changed into sweats. "It only took them a few minutes to remove the hologram equipment. It did take them a week to make the program to cover the furniture, but setup was quick. The program is reusable, and they were teaching Valory to make that program. I see real potential for party designs."

Paul nodded thoughtfully. "A programmer like me could make a killing designing cool themes."

Charlie laughed. Dave and Jeff looked thoughtful.

Saturday afternoon Charlie headed to the boat. Sara was already there and had brought Lucky and Rhea with her. Hawk was training the animals to be safe on board. To Charlie's surprise, Oz and Paul were there as well, taking out the boat's engine and replacing it with one Oz had made. Sara greeted him with a hug and a kiss.

The touch of her lips on his made his bones feel light. She pulled him down for a deeper kiss when the first one ended. Warmth spread from his center, filling his hollowed bones. He pulled away before his eyes could flare blue, smiling ruefully at her, lust echoing between them.

"We have company."

"I'm going to go take a nap to be well rested for tonight when our company leaves." She trailed her hand across his chest, kissed him again, and made a contended sound that he felt more than heard before heading to their cabin.

Grinning, he went to help Oz and Paul move the old engine.

Hawk joined them a while later. “I put sensors around the hull earlier,” Hawk said as he handed tools to Oz. “If Lucky or Rhea fall off, you’ll be notified immediately. They both have the new chips in them. Even without me or Oz, you should be able to find them anywhere. I tested it on Lucky.” He leaned closer and lowered his voice. “I dropped her off at the other end of the pier. She stayed off the roads just like she was trained to do, and the satellite found her in seconds. Your cat should be fine even if she does get off the ship. I was thinking we should chip Sara and Stasia.”

Oz sat back on his heels, grimacing at Charlie over his shoulder. “I’ll make enough to do all of us. Liz is going to Texas to do our parents. There’s no point in taking chances with any of us.”

Rick picked up Stasia from her mother's apartment later the night. "Is she okay with you spending the night with me?" He glanced back at the apartment as they walked to his car. Anticipation was keeping his stomach in a knot.

"She isn't thrilled, but yes." Stasia leaned into his side and pulled him down for a kiss. "I miss you so much. Since you got magic, it's much harder to be apart. I have to hold my magic back constantly. It wants you desperately too."

"I love you," Rick murmured as he kissed her brow.

His magic pushed for release, but he held it back with little effort.

"We're getting better at this." He opened the car door for her and kissed her again once she was seated. Her breath on his lips sent a delicious thrill through his entire body. He couldn't resist running his fingers through the soft thickness of her hair.

Her soft exhalation made his fingers tighten and he reluctantly moved away before his magic could begin to press harder for release.

He drove them to the mountain where they'd had the meeting. They had to hike into the camping spot where he had a tent already set up with a picnic laid out nearby. "I wanted to be alone with you. Somewhere our magic could do as it wished as well."

When she smiled, he sighed in relief. While the area was perfectly private it did have some unpleasant memories associated with it. His pulse fluttered and his palms sweat when he took both of her hands in his.

"Anastasia Morales, I love you with all of my heart and soul. I want to be your husband, to have children with you, to be together forever. Will you marry me?"

Stasia started to cry and threw her arms around his neck while her magic swirled wildly around them both. She nodded, too overcome to speak.

"Is that a yes?" He knew it was because her happy excitement enfolded him like a warm blanket, but he wanted to hear her say it.

"Yes! Oh, Rick, yes. I love you so much!" She pulled away and held his face in her hands, her brown eyes shining with tears. "I love you!" she continued to speak but her words were just sound lost in the thumping of his pulse, but he didn't need words. He laughed as he whirled her around and the magic sparked as it flowed about them. It was as happy and excited as they were.

The head of the registrar's office came to the commandant a week later.

"We have a slight problem. Ninety percent of the student body wants to take Doctor Simmons' and Doctor Mitchel's classes. Even if we asked them to teach every single day all day, we couldn't accommodate them all. There was already a waiting list, now it's just ridiculous."

The commandant smiled in satisfaction. "Competition is vital for a well-rounded officer. Use the same system we have been to fill the class. Inform the applicants of the requirements. I've requested Midshipmen First Class Tillings and Frost to be assigned here next fall and Midshipman Martins the following year. We might be able to offer a few more classes. But keep that confidential for now. Let them compete."

The registrar laughed. "You planned that?"

"Planned— no. Took advantage of— yes. Most of the student body had only hearsay to judge those classes on until the party. They all wanted one of the wristcomps, but they hadn't seen or understood what the programming was capable of. They see it now and want to be a part of it. There are so many applications for the holograms alone it overwhelms. Doctor Mitchel and Midshipman Second Class Vlase have made a holographic program to hide ships at sea from sight visually." He paused a moment to let that sink in.

The registrar's eyes widened. "If they can do that, they can hide tanks. Good lord, they could probably hide aircraft. Holy mother of God, the United States won't be the only ones with this technology, other countries will reverse engineer it."

"Doctor Simmons assures me they can and it will take them approximately one year to make hardware once they acquire some to copy. He thinks it will be a bit longer until they can program effectively. Doctor Simmons and Mitchel are already working on a hologram detector. They're working on so many things my mind boggles. The point of this discussion is we need highly trained, competent programmers of our own as soon as we can. We need our cadets to want this, to strive for it."

"You've succeeded brilliantly. Your entire student body is clamoring for the chance to learn it."

The commandant smiled complacently.

- 11 -

PROGRESS

The president received a phone call from Sara asking for a private meeting with her and Oz. He granted it immediately. She'd never called before, preferring to email him. If she wasn't comfortable sending the information in an email, it had to be big.

Their security escorted them to the White House. His security escorted them to him.

"We wanted to talk about our findings personally," Sara said when they were alone. "We're ninety-two percent certain we're correct in all of our surmises. I have the math to prove it, but I think you'll just have to take our word for it." The report she handed him contained over fifty pages of equations and graphs.

Oz tweaked Sara's ponytail and grinned at her when she made a face at him. "What Sara is trying to say is we found Mr. X. We won't be able to prove it in court though."

"He means we found Mr. X, Y, and Z." Sara opened a flatscreen. "These are the men people mean when they say 'They' - meaning the mysterious men who really run things. There are other behind the scenes mover and shakers, but these three are the ones trying to get you out of office. They'll do whatever it takes to do it and they have the manpower and connections to do so.

"First, we have Mr. X. The owner of Liniar Corp headed by Joseph Liniar, billionaire, philanthropist, maker of everything from children's toys to car parts. He has interests and investments spanning the globe and just bought massive amounts of land in Alaska two years ago. A huge investment."

Oz leaned forward and adjusted her screen, highlighting portions of text. "Well, he didn't buy them. He leased them. Long term leases from the government. He did buy some outright, but he leased the majority."

"Then we have Mr. Y." Sara put up another picture. "Tro Industries is based in China and headed by Mr. Tachimori. Again, he has interests everywhere with a sixty percent overlap with Liniar Corp. Then we have Mr. Z. Mr. Nguyen who's based in Vietnam. The head of Sinder business conglomerate. They have a seventy percent overlap. That means all of their businesses depend on each other. They're aware of the dependency although maybe not as aware as we are."

Oz took up the explanation. "You know we've been correlating data from every source, from Ingra Arnault, the gang, your secretary, Senator Bishop, and every single one of the other men and women we even thought might be involved. Libya was an information windfall— our first solid connection. Joy has been searching for us, illegally I might add, totally non-admissible."

Sara changed the picture on her screen. "I have copies here in my report of her findings. Questions are bound to be asked on how you got the information. I wouldn't recommend showing those reports to anyone except Pierce. We can prove legally they've all met numerous times, but that proves nothing. We have illegal recordings that are very damning, but we'll get to that."

Oz laid a hand on Sara's arm, interrupting her. He said, "I'll skip ahead here; we can go over our evidence later on how we received each piece. What you need to know is they aren't done. I don't think they'll ever be done. They have too much to lose. They need to control the White House to control the power industry. All their big money is in power, either producing it or manufacturing parts for it."

Oz showed a diagram to the president. "Your secretary sent them the transcript of your conversation about the skeins. They were already trying to replace you to put their choice in office and aware of us as a threat to the election. That made them aware of us as a threat to their investments. They still hoped a simple regime change would be enough to keep us in check."

Sara interrupted. "They're unaware we have working models. They think it's all in development still. We have recordings that confirm that. Their information pipeline is closed at the moment. I'm sure they're scrambling to open it again. Right now, they're proceeding along the original plan; replace you and put in anyone else they can control. Their frantic now though because they see how much they'll be hurt. Skeins will crush their plans. This is no longer about greed and power for them but in staying afloat with their assets intact. They need time to dump their industries that will take a hit. Oz did the math. They need twelve years minimum. They can't just dump everything. People would notice and their stock would plummet. If they want to recoup a fraction of their investments, they must go slowly and stick together. Their finances are too deeply meshed to allow otherwise. They'll try again to replace you, they have to."

Oz said, "Their businesses are profitable, but these are greedy power-hungry men who were willing to murder to rig an election. Now that they realize their infrastructure is at serious risk, who knows what they'll be willing to do? They could cause enormous amounts of trouble legally, and I don't mean by speaking against you but by manipulating the market by letting their own businesses fail. Millions of people work for them. They have their hands in banking both here and abroad. Liniar is setting himself up to rule the world behind the scenes and he's close to success."

Sara frowned and shook her head. "We disagree on what they'll do. I think Liniar's ego won't let him allow his business to fail even if it would help his end game. Sure, he'd write off a few, but to destabilize our economy he'd have to intentionally ruin himself." She shook her head again and changed the picture on her screen. "No, his next move will be an attack. If he can put his man in office, and the man himself is irrelevant— he just needs someone he can control. If he gets his man in, he can manipulate the market and foreign affairs to position himself as the world power. Oz has worked up the most likely physical attacks. I've produced public opinion and economic attacks scenarios. I really think it's their next hit."

Oz showed the president another graph. "Billions and billions of dollars are at stake here. Joy found their plan to hit our existing pipeline in Alaska. They're in the process of ruining Exon, specifically their ability to ship oil. They need the price to rise to sell their own investments. They're doing everything they can to insure it does and it's working.

"Unfortunately, a lot of what they're doing is perfectly legal. Set guards immediately on the pipeline. They can't afford to be caught. We have a list here of at-risk installations sorted by probability of attack.

"We also have a plan that will make whatever they do irrelevant as far as price gouging goes. As to them attacking you physically, you have a few options. The one that would work best you'll like least. Meet and work with them to preserve their assets as best you can." Sara held up a hand. "I know it's distasteful. Let them know you know the entire score. Our economy will take a hit as the United States changes power sources, it's inevitable. People will lose jobs as the new technology replaces the old. There's no reason we can't go slowly enough to let as many as can convert gradually enough to hold those employees. Mr. X Y and Z will still take a hit, but they could recoup some of their investments.

"You could release Liniar from his lease. It might be enough that he drops the other two to fend for themselves. If he drops the other two, they'd flounder and sink within five years. Oz has graphs to show the probable repercussions worldwide of that."

Oz flipped the screen to show his report. "On the other hand, you could make him keep those leases until he's bankrupt, which by my calculation would be in fifteen years if you do nothing to help him. If you try, you could ruin him in six years." Oz gave the president a tight smile. "We could always assassinate them. That's my favorite plan. Their inheritors will fight over the companies and probably not even notice they're going broke until it's too late.

The president frowned. "No."

"Yeah, I knew you'd say that." Oz heaved a heavy sigh, looking disappointed. "Sara has been working on the best way to move to the new technology, not just for us, but worldwide. Whatever you decide to do, we recommend meeting with all current power suppliers to give them time to prepare. We've been running simulations and can guarantee an extremely bad outcome if they aren't told privately with assurances for help."

Sara said, "Even with help we can't guarantee a smooth transition. Some of our existing power infrastructure can be repurposed, but most will be obsolete. I've put suggestions in there on how to retrain the employees to work with modern tech and the sorts of jobs that might be available in the future. My report has my recommend approach to the change with math backing it up. You should have Pierce's people look at it. I'm not a trained psychologist and have very limited experience with people. My plan needs to be vetted by people with experience."

Oz handed the president a folder. "We also think you need to order our full security package. Having our security just inside the White House won't be enough. You're at risk everywhere you go, and we can minimize that risk. We would absorb the cost ourselves, but you need everything to do with us to be clean as a whistle.

"Our recommendations, costs, and timeline are in here." He tapped the blue folder. "Sara included a graph showing the improvement in your life expectancy with our security in place. We put in the minimum amount you could do with the maximum protection. If congress won't allow it, you could afford the minimum yourself. We really recommend you do it for the first lady's sake."

"Consider it done," the president said. "Get me the minimum installed as soon as you can. Bill me personally. My wife's safety is your top priority."

"We'll start tomorrow." Oz touched Sara's hand, letting the magic feel the relief as well. A blue glow surrounded their hands and was gone in seconds. "Read that report so you know what we're going to do."

"I hope you take all of our reports seriously." Sara leaned forward. "Our math is sound. Our proof solid. You must decide very soon on a course of action. I wish you could wait until after the election, but that isn't an option. Keep the report somewhere secure. I've put in a scenario if our secret is leaked. The information we have from your secretary makes it unlikely, but not impossible."

"Thank you both." The president stood, shook their hands, and lead them to the door. "I'll read it carefully. Just knowing who my enemies are is a weight off my mind. I'll personally hand the report to Pierce."

The president read the reports and called Pierce in for a meeting. "They've already run their own scenarios and want your teams to look them over. I want your recommendations as soon as possible. I won't be dealing with my enemies. They get the same consideration as anyone else." The president laughed shortly. "Sara's recommendations for that are her most complete and in-depth ones. She knows me well."

"Personally, I like Oz's recommendation," Pierce said as he glanced through the summaries.

"This office will be above reproach while I'm in charge," the president said firmly. "I could order the death of someone, but not for personal gain."

Pierce cleared his throat and rattled the paper he held. "These are very bad, corrupt men. This isn't the first time they've funded terrorists. Their greed has cost thousands of lives. Killing them would be a public service." He stood to leave and shook the president's hand. "As always, it's been an honor."

- 12 -

NORMALCY

"So, have you made any plans yet?" Sara grinned at Stasia as they worked on a new configuration of her shield emitters on her model of the *Truman*.

Stasia laid her screwdriver on the desk and smiled dreamily. "As soon as I graduate we'll have a private ceremony. Just us two, and we'll take our first vow. We're debating on which magic wielder to ask to officiate. They'll need to get a license to do it."

Sara frowned down at her desk and began neatening the files scattered across it.

Stasia nudged a pile of notebooks aside and muttered, "You guys with your books."

She shook her head laughing when Sara snorted and picked up her screwdriver.

Sara said, "So we like physical books..." She took the notebook from Stasia and placed it lovingly with its fellows. Floor to ceiling shelves to the right of her desk held identical notebooks. "It helps me think when I can see the work," she said defensively when Stasia snickered.

Stasia said, "You need more help and to slow down. You have crap everywhere."

She took a stack of spell bracelets that needed to be refilled from Sara's desk and put them into one of the storage cabinets that lined the wall by the door.

"I leave them out until I get around to filling them."

Stasia rolled her eyes and said, "Valory, put a sign on that cabinet door saying recharge needed and remind Sara to fill a bracelet every two hours." She returned to the desk and began neatening the tools. "It isn't like you need to do them all at once. You need a system. We need to give Valory hands so she can bring you things. Think how much more we could do if Valory could do physical work too."

Sara resumed work on the model. "Don't change the subject. What about the wedding? Aren't we invited?"

Stasia said, "We'll hold a reception, but we want our vow to be private."

"A captain of a ship could do it legally." Sara absently tapped the tool she held on her desk as she spoke. "We have a captain in the know. Is all he'd need is a ship, and we have one of those too. Captain Sanders could stand on one end with you two on the other."

"Sara, you're a genius!" Stasia hugged her. "You won't mind if we use your boat? We don't know what our magic will do when we take a vow."

"No, we'd love for you to marry there." Sara hugged her again as their magic mingled. "You'll be Mrs. Hayes before me. I'm jealous of that."

"Speaking of Mrs. Hayes, are you two okay?" Stasia picked up the screwdriver and returned to work, glancing at Sara from the corner of her eye.

Sara sighed. "Yes and no. She loves me and I love her. I know she must resent the harm I do to her sons. Just because I don't mean to do it doesn't make it less painful for them."

"I'm sorry I ever said a mean thing to you. I didn't understand how hard it is to stop the magic when it wants something. It's hard to even know when it's manipulating your feelings."

Stasia let her magic loose so Sara could feel her remorse. "Rick and I've talked about children, and we'll include that in our vows. You've helped us so much. I'm so grateful. Every painful lesson you learned we can avoid."

Sara smiled ruefully. "I wish I could be as confident as you are that the magic will understand. My biggest lesson is, don't ever go far from him."

"We'll be careful," Stasia promised. "Joy and Drew have no problem being separated, magically, I mean. They miss each other, but the magic is fine with him being away. Brenda and Mike can also separate. She needs warrior magic more than he needs hers. I think it's because she loves him and he doesn't love her."

Sara nodded sadly. "She knows. It breaks my heart. He knows she loves him too. That must be so awkward for them. Is she having a hard time with him dating others?"

"He isn't as far as I know. He does like her. He could fall in love. Not everyone does instantly."

Sara shrugged. "Maybe. I'm sure Liz is watching the situation. Mike could be in for a shock. Brenda goes to Marcus a lot and he's a great guy. She could learn to prefer him."

"What a mess."

Sara snorted. "It is. I'm staying out of it. As long as she leaves my warrior alone, I don't care which one she picks."

"Well, she can't have Rick either, he's mine." Stasia grinned, a fierce blue light in her eyes.

Sara laughed. "No one would dare. Everyone knows rogues own priests."

Stasia laughed. "I haven't thought of the Harpies in ages."

Charlie and I ran into two of them in town at a dance club once." Sara snickered. "They haven't changed. Hannah calls Paul whenever she's in town here. He's stopped seeing her though. I'm sure that drives her crazy. I could live my entire life and never see any of them again and be happy about it."

Stasia laughed again. “I hear that.” They returned to placing the sensors and running the simulation.

That Saturday Stasia and Sara went to the storage facility where Sara stored her mother’s clothing. “Any one you want except this one.” Sara held out an elaborately beaded wedding dress. “I’m saving this for our wedding. Isn’t it beautiful?” She held it in front of her and swirled around. The dress glinted and sparkled in the light.

“It must weigh forty pounds,” Stasia said as she ran her fingertips over the beaded bodice.

“At least.” Sara closed her eyes and smiled. “I’ll wear this dress and feel my mother’s presence at my wedding. If my mother where here, she’d want me to have someone to love as much as she loved my father. Even though he was a horrid parent, you can’t deny he loved her.” She opened her eyes and blushed slightly. “I want to legally be Charlie’s wife, to call him my husband in public and belong with him in all ways. This wait is so hard.”

Stasia stopped sorting the dresses and turned to Sara with a serious expression. “I’ll never liked your father. He gives me the creeps. He always has. I'm sorry your mother won't be here for you but mine will be. She loves you." She started going through the dresses again. "Christmas will come again before you know it."

Sara shivered. "I sometimes wonder if Christmas is a bad omen for us. We hardly ever have a peaceful one."

"Your wedding will be perfect. The dress is magnificent, and you'll be beautiful in it."

Sara nodded and handed Stasia a dress. "This would look amazing on you. There's enough fabric to let the bodice out and the hem could be shortened easily."

Stasia held it up, using her wristcomp to see her reflection. Sara held out a different one. They sorted through the large collection, pausing over their favorites. "Take all three," Sara said when Stasia couldn't decide which one she liked best. "We'll have more dances to attend. Get them all fitted to you."

"I couldn't. One is more than enough. I know how much they mean to you."

"I have so many I could never wear them all. I'd love to see you in them. Your mother is so important to me; I wish I had that for you too."

The girls picked up their choices. Sara took the shoes that matched hers, but they wouldn't fit Stasia. "I have jewelry to match them in my safe-deposit box and you can borrow whatever you like. Don't worry, it's all insured. Besides, Oz can find it all."

Charlie waved goodbye to his roommates as he headed to the gate closest to their home. He'd gotten leave for the weekend and planned to spend it on the boat.

Sara, Oz, Stasia, Rick, Hawk, and Camilla were in the living room watching the news, which was unusual enough to make him join them.

The president was holding a press conference and showed a simulation of the skeins powering one of the new motors and made a speech about progress. He warned that progress would bring change both good and bad. He finished his speech by saying, "Progress can't be stopped and change is hard. This nation has been blessed with more than material wealth. The wealth of her people's industry and inventiveness will lead the world to a new age of prosperity. Clean, cheap, renewable energy will open our horizons. We've progressed from horsepower to gas power in the past and progress in all aspects of our lives followed. We'll progress from here with unlimited potential to better the lives of man everywhere."

"Wow!" Hawk said when the speech ended.

"Wow indeed!" Sara grinned and hugged Oz. "I'm so proud to be your friend. You're a great man."

Oz blushed lightly and hugged her back. Rick brought out champagne and they toasted Oz and his invention.

Sara texted the commandant as Charlie drove them to the boat. *'The new engines are Oz's design. It was classified until now. I'm sure he'd be happy to speak with you, Sara.'*

Charlie laughed at her. "I don't think he'll care."

"I'm sure he'll want to know what's happening on his campus. I promised to inform him right away when possible."

Charlie shrugged. He didn't want to think about school or the secrets he was keeping from his commander.

"Let's say we take the boat out instead of staying in dock?"

"Sure." Sara picked up her small clothing bag and a much bigger hard-sided case from the trunk. Charlie grabbed his own bag and a cooler with food in it.

"Leave it. I'll come back for it," he said when he saw Sara struggling to carry it.

"I got it." Sara set it down on its wheels and rolled it along. She did let him lift it onto the boat for her.

"What's in here, rocks?" The case thumped to the deck, rocking the boat.

"New buoys I want to test."

He picked Sara up and swung her aboard. Sam came up and took her heavy case. Tony saluted from a nearby motorboat. Sam brought Sara's case below deck for her and tweaked her ponytail when she thanked him.

Charlie waited for him to rejoin Tony before taking the sailboat from its slip.

Sara glanced over her shoulder at the trailing motorboat. "I miss our privacy."

"They face out, not in. Just ignore them. It isn't rude, that's why they're there. I'm taking no more chances with you."

"I wish we could sail away just the two of us," Sara said when they were headed back in on Sunday.

"We will during spring break, just us." Charlie ran a hand over her arm, enjoying the feel of her warm skin.

"You won't be bored?" Sara asked anxiously.

"*Uh-huh,*" Charlie said as he nuzzled her neck.

She giggled and made a soft sound of contentment that he felt in his soul.

The next Friday was the formal dance. The girls got ready at the lab. "Who's Hawk bringing?" Sara asked as she put her makeup on. She and Stasia had just gotten back from the beauty parlor where they'd had their hair and nails done.

"Paul's younger sister, Abby. Paul is going with Amy. Amy and Abby are staying with my mother."

"God, I'll be glad to get our house back," Sara said as she put on her high heels. "I'm tired of the trailer. I sleep here most nights."

"Speaking of the trailer, could Rick and I, *um*, borrow it over break?"

"Sure, we'll be on the boat." She cleared her throat and blushed a bit. "It's not exactly private. Oz is right next door and the entire thing creaks and moves."

"Oz has kindly agreed to stay in the lab." Stasia grinned. "He offered his trailer but I'd rather use yours."

"Make yourselves at home." Sara went to her desk and rummaged through the drawers. Stasia pulled out a notebook and flipped through the pages. Sara took the notebook from her and handed her a black case.

"Impressive," Stasia said, waving at the notebook and Sara laughed.

Stasia's breath caught as she opened the case. "I meant that diagram of our m-nerves. This… I can't borrow this."

Sara removed the diamond necklace and fastened it around Stasia's neck despite her protests.

"It looks beautiful on you." Sara handed her the earrings and put the bracelet on her. "You look beautiful." Sara stood back and admired her.

Stasia removed her wristcomp and put it in her small purse.

"I'll be fine. Everyone will be there," she said when Sara frowned.

"I know. I'm tempted to take mine off too, but my gloves cover it." Sara added a wide crystal bracelet over her light-blue silk gloves to cover her wristcomp.

Arm-in-arm they went downstairs to meet the boys. Charlie's eyes lit with appreciation as she approached. She frowned at him. "How am I supposed to not kiss you all night when you look this good?"

"You can kiss me now," Charlie said huskily as he pulled her closer. Her lips were soft and the touch light, but it heated his entire body. He wondered for the millionth time if all men felt this way, as if their wives' kisses were light and heat, or if the heat of her was because she was a sun priest. He kissed her thoroughly, basking in the heat before stepping back to admire her. Her face was flushed and her lipstick slightly smeared. He'd never seen a more beautiful girl.

She smiled at him and twirled around, showing off the sky-blue dress. It floated gracefully around her. Charlie admired it; she always wore the exactly right thing, looking beautiful without looking overdone. Her clothes were never too tight or too revealing and always managed to look incredibly sexy.

He took Sara's arm and gave Stasia a quick kiss on the cheek, taking a moment to admire her too. Stasia didn't make his heart beat faster, but he could appreciate how beautiful she was.

He drew Sara away from Rick and Stasia and the magic swirling around them. *Apparently she made Rick's heart beat faster,* Charlie thought with an inward laugh. He waited by the door with Sara for his brother to control his magic.

Sara kissed him again, running her hands over his chest and down his back. He forgot he was waiting for his brother until Rick cleared his throat. He stepped back from Sara and lightly rubbed the lipstick that was smeared on her face. She reapplied it hurriedly and they walked together to the car.

“Sit in the back with me, please,” Stasia said to Sara. “I need some space from him for a minute.”

Sara laughed and got in back. Charlie turned to wink at her. Her kiss lingered on his lips and he knew she was still thinking of him.

They met Hawk at the dance. Paul’s sister Abby was sweet and shy and clearly intimidated by them. Sara greeted her warmly and kissed Hawk’s cheek. The girls had met before in Vermont. Charlie shook her hand then wandered off with friends. Sara stood with Abby, introducing her friends and pointing out different people.

Abby had applied to the academy for the next term; she was seventeen, a year younger than Hawk. Tall and thin like her brother with the same dark hair and eyes. Freckles were scattered across her face and long elaborately curled, brown hair softened her classic features. Her dress was simple and elegant, half-black, half-white.

“Your hair is so beautiful,” Stasia said wistfully.

"I'm enjoying it now." Abby ran a hand over her hair. "I'll have to cut it soon enough if I get in."

"It's a crying shame," Charlie said as he came up. "Hair this beautiful shouldn't be cut."

Abby blushed a bit and looked away.

"Her hair will be beautiful short as well." Sara pursed her lips and examined Abby critically. "I bet I could make a program to show different styles on you. Could you come back after break for a day or two? I could do a really good one if I could program how your hair is now."

They started talking about what Sara would need to do, and Charlie wandered over to the boys again. The last thing he heard her saying to Abby was just a little trim.

Amy had joined the girls talking about the program, leaving all the boys together.

Charlie stood back and viewed the room. His classmates all wore dress uniforms with their dates on their arms or talking like the girls were. He glanced back at the girls and smiled. "We're the luckiest men alive."

Paul laughed. "We are indeed." He turned to Hawk and frowned. "She's my little sister, show respect."

Hawk laughed. "She's staying with my mother; respect is all she'll see. Thank you for introducing us and talking her into coming."

Paul smiled at his sister. "She's my favorite sibling; we were very close growing up. I don't think she really wants a military career though; it's just a tradition with us. We've all gone here, and it will break her heart if she doesn't get in."

Charlie said, "She's in. Sara told me. They looked over all of the applicants." Charlie didn't mention she and Oz had requested her for Paul's sake, ensuring her acceptance. She'd met all the criteria on her own and would likely have been accepted without them. Abby was mathematically gifted like Paul. "Tell her to keep it quiet though."

Paul punched his shoulder and went to whisper in his sister's ear. Abby squealed and jumped, then clapped a hand over her mouth and glanced around guiltily. She gave Sara a quick hug and turned shining eyes to Charlie, mouthing, '*thank you.*'

Charlie nodded and smiled, happy Sara would have another girlfriend.

He had a great time at the dance. More than he was expecting. Sara accepted dance invitations from his roommates, Hawk, and Rick while Charlie watched happily. He danced with Stasia, Amy, and Abby, saving the slow dances for Sara, cutting in whenever the music changed. He found it hard to resist kissing her when she lifted her face to his, her eyes shining. Small tendrils of blond hair had escaped her braided bun and framed her flushed face. The heat of her skin called to him. He wanted to run his hands over her. Anticipation echoed between them, growing as the evening progressed.

Rick and Stasia disappeared halfway through the dance, unable to hold back the magic.

Charlie and Sara made plans to pick up Hawk, Abby, Paul, and Amy on the boat the next Friday. Everyone would stay on board until Sunday. The girls planned to work on the new program.

"Bring warm clothes and a bathing suit." Sara said to Abby as they parted for the night. "It gets cold at night."

She gave Abby her email address and a quick hug.

Hawk winked at Charlie before taking Abby's arm to escort her to his car.

Hawk's obvious happiness made Charlie chuckle with delight. He hoped Hawk would find true love like he had.

"What?" Sara asked, sensing his sudden unease.

"I was just thinking how difficult it will be for Hawk— and Oz too, to find someone who can accept all of this." He gestured vaguely, knowing she'd understand what he meant.

"What wouldn't you do for love," she asked dryly and not altogether happily.

"Touché" he said as he bent to kiss her lips.

"Thank you for coming with me, I had a great time," Hawk said as he glanced at Abby. She sat beside him as he drove her and Amy to his mother's house. Paul and Amy were talking quietly in the back of the car. Amy had stayed often in the past with Stasia and would sleep in Stasia's room with Abby.

"I was wondering if you'd let me bring you home." Hawk asked her hesitantly. "I'd love a chance to get to know you better."

"It's a long drive," Abby said doubtfully.

"It's a short flight. I could fly you back. I wouldn't mind the drive though." Hawk cleared his throat and licked his lips, hoping he didn't look as nervous as he felt.

"You're a pilot?" Abby sounded surprised.

"Yes. If your uncomfortable going with me... I mean, I know we just met. We have time to become friends. There's no rush." He winced as he felt himself flush.

"I'd love a ride home," Abby said. "Before I fly with you, I should get my parents' permission though and I'm sure they'll want to meet you first." She giggled, covering her mouth with her hand. "Maybe you'd better bring your pilot license and have Paul vouch for you. You're awful young to have one."

He grinned at her, his heart expanding as if it was his very first breath. "I'll get you home safe and sound."

She smiled back, making his heart pound. When they arrived at the apartment complex, Hawk and Abby exited the car, leaving Paul and Amy to say goodnight. They emerged a few minutes later. Paul gave his sister a kiss on the cheek and Hawk a measuring glance when she said Hawk was bringing her home. He shook Hawk's hand, kissed Amy quickly and left in his own car. Hawk escorted the girls inside.

He threw on sweatpants and a T-shirt before heading to the kitchen to fix a snack. Abby joined him after she'd changed. She sat at the small, kitchen island and fed Tank bits of cheese. Tank rested his head in her lap, wagging his tail. His blue eyes closed in bliss when she scratched behind his ears.

Hawk ruffled Tank's ears. "He'll be your devoted slave for cheese. I warn you though, he weighs a ton and he's a bed hog."

She giggled, kissing Tank's head. "Will you bring him Friday?"

"Yes, he likes the boat, and Rhea will be there."

"Rhea?" Abby glanced at him then away, her eyes mysterious dark pools, leaning over Tank to rub his belly.

"Sara's dog, his mate." The smile on Hawk's face grew when Abby glanced back and returned his smile, a pink flush on her freckled cheeks.

They sat together talking until she yawned and glanced at the kitchen clock. He laughed and offered her a hand to rise. “We can leave whenever you like. I’ll rent a car and fly back,” he said as they paused before the bedroom doors.

“Do you have to be back at a particular time for anything, or, *um*, anyone?” she asked.

He took a step closer. “I don’t have to report until Sunday evening formation. I have no girlfriend.”

Her smile widened. “We can take our time then. I’ll buy you lunch.”

A blue glow flickered across Hawk’s hands. “Sorry, security device— it’s nothing to worry about.”

“I’ve seen Paul’s.” She gestured to his wristcomp. “What causes it to go off?”

Unease and embarrassment made his voice tight. “My pulse,” he mumbled.

A half smile on her lips, she leaned forward and kissed him quickly on the mouth. “I don’t have a boyfriend either,” she said over her shoulder as she headed to Stasia’s room.

He grinned after her.

Charlie pulled into the dock on Friday. Hawk, Paul, and Amy had flown to pick up Abby and should be back soon.

“This is good,” Sara said softly as she hugged Charlie from behind. “This life we have now, our home here, our work. I like our life. I like it better when we can spend our nights together, but this is good, Charlie.

He turned and kissed her. “I like that better too, and soon we can spend every night together. On the *Truman,* I’ll be with you whenever I don’t have night duty, then just a few months more of school.”

“Is this the life you want?”

“This is perfect,” Charlie said and kissed her again.

- 13 -

TOMAS RETURNS

A week later Joy and Stasia stood at the window of Stasia's office and watched Sara's father leave the lab.

"It's a bit too convenient for me," Stasia said sourly as she watched him go. "He doesn't speak with her in years, and then when she's a big name in business he wants to be close? This is the fourth visit in two weeks." Stasia rose an eyebrow and pursed her lips. "Let's visit him, shall we?"

She and Joy snuck into Tomas's home and office and found hidden safes with passports and money with his picture and different names but left them. Shredded papers filled the garbage can in his home office. The files yielded nothing about either Valor Industries or Sara.

"Maybe he really is sorry?" Joy asked doubtfully.

Stasia snorted. "I believe he's sorry, but not of the way he treated her. He's sorry he has no hold on her now."

Charlie was aware of Tomas's visits and concerned too.

Not wanting to upset Sara, he questioned Oz about her father's visits.

Oz leaned back in his chair and put both booted feet up on his desk. "He tried to talk both of us into giving him a wristcomp with the security programs or selling them to the public." Oz dropped his feet and rummaged in a bottom desk drawer a moment and handed Charlie a thick file. "He had an entire report done showing the profit we could make. It horrified him that we weren't interested in profit." Oz lightly slapped Charlie's back. "Don't worry, man. Sara isn't being taken in. She likes to hear about her mother, but she's aware he's more interested in business. Tomas brings her pictures of her mother on every visit and lets her copy them. The man's doling them out like rewards for good behavior or something. Sara isn't stupid, she knows he's using her mother to find out what we're up to here and get in her good graces. Although he is trying to get to know her outside of the lab too. Every time he comes, he takes her to lunch."

Charlie crossed his arms. "Damn, I want to tell him not to come around before he messes with her head. But how's that fair? He's her father."

"Tomas always invites me along. I'll start going and keep an eye on her. If I think he's doing more harm than good, I'll scare him off." A blue glitter lit Oz's eyes. "The man can't have her. She's *our* sun priest."

Tomas took her to her mother's favorite play in Washington and dinner afterward. Sara's security followed discreetly. Two days later they went to a cinema showing one of her mother's movies. Both had tears in their eyes at the end.

Tomas took Sara's gloved hand. "I know I'm rushing getting reacquainted, but I don't have long to stay in this area. Business will call me away soon. Come to lunch with me tomorrow. "Bring your friend, and I'll show you both where your mother and I got engaged. We can take my jet to Newport and be back by supper time."

Sara removed her hand from his grasp and put her hands in her coat pocket. "My security needs to come as well."

"I hope you're not relying only on them for security." Her father glanced back at Manny and Todd who trailed them.

"No, we have these." Sara held out her wrist. "My guards can locate me anywhere with theirs, even if I don't have mine."

"Glad to hear it." Her father smiled. "They're welcome to come with us or follow."

They spoke of the movie they'd just seen until the car arrived back at the Valor building.

Tomas said, "I brought you the photo album of pictures we took on our honeymoon. If you'd like to copy it, that's fine, but I don't want to leave them here."

"I can copy them in my office," Sara said eagerly as she accepted the large album.

Each picture was covered with tissue paper inside its own envelope.

"Please be careful with it. It's my prized possession," Tomas said as he peered over Sara's shoulder.

"I have tools in my lab I can use if you don't mind waiting in my office for me?"

"No, take your time. I'll play with your game system, and maybe we can talk later about an idea I have for that?"

"Sure," Sara said happily and hurried from the room, clutching the album to her chest.

Tomas stare after her, grinning.

Sam went with Sara and Oz the next day to Newport. Rick followed in his own car and waited outside the park. He was shocked when his wristcomp dinged, warning of a sudden change in status. He slapped his white bracelet down as he opened the raid channel.

"I'm summoning. Both have lost consciousness," Rick said as he casted the spell. Nothing happened. He hit his bracelet down harder and panic made his voice rough as he reported it wasn't working. He fumbled for the door handle as he took his spell-bracelet off and reapplied it to no effect.

"Rick!" Charlie shouted.

"I'm going to them," Rick said as he pulled his gun and rushed into the park that they'd entered minutes before.

A woman screamed and ran, dropping her bag in her haste. Two men who'd been talking approached but both ran before getting close, Rick's aura forcing them to flee. He ignored the commotion he was causing.

Charlie overrode Sara's wristcomp, but it wasn't on her wrist anymore. He activated the tracking device. It claimed to be with her wristcomp, and he swore furiously.

Rick found Oz and Sara's wristcomps beside an unconscious Sam and Tomas. The microchips Oz had installed lay in a puddle of blood. Someone had known where they were and cut them out. The park was large and tree shaded with branching paths that wound through the greenery. It was impossible to see very far at all.

He picked the closest path and ran. A police officer shouted for him to stop but he ignored him. Trees and buildings blocked his view and the path split in three directions. He hesitated and then ran to the right, emerging on a road with busy foot traffic but seeing nothing at all suspicious.

Swearing savagely, he turned and ran back the way he'd come.

The same officer was waiting, speaking into a radio clipped to his shoulder.

He again ordered Rick to freeze, and Rick ignored him again, running past him and down the left-hand path.

Charlie was yelling directions to the Scouts in his earpiece and a map formed above his right arm, showing the roads leading from the park.

Yellow highlighted a road leading to the closest airport and he swore again as he spun back to take the center path to reach that yellow road.

Sirens screamed in the distance and the original officer had been joined by another one. Both screamed for him to freeze.

"Private security," he shouted, and the younger man shot.

The bullet lodged in his shoulder but didn't slow him.

Major Nelson shouted, “Rick, get on the ground and put your hands behind your back. You won’t be able to catch a car on foot and you’re going to cause us a serious problem. That’s an order, Marine!”

Rick glanced back at the police chasing him. He’d have to run right past them to get to his car, although he could steal one…”

Nelson said, “We’ve alerted security at the airport. There’s nothing you can do. Give yourself up, Rick.”

Stasia said, “Please, I need you… They’ll lock you up.”

Charlie snapped, “Stasia!”

Nelson said, “Do you want them to kill your damned brother too?”

Rick stopped running. They wouldn’t be able to kill him, but Nelson was right. He couldn’t catch up either and trying could expose them. He knelt and then lay face down, wincing as another bullet impacted his back. He felt it like a sharp tap, and he hoped his aura hadn’t scared them enough to ale them keep shooting because his lack of injuries would be impossible to explain.

The Scouts scrambled to get to Newport. No one had seen or heard a thing. Hawk began searching.

Charlie strode into Tomas's hospital room followed by Joy and Major Nelson, leaving nurses and orderlies rushing away in his wake. A gray-haired man sitting beside Tomas's bed jumped to his feet and skittered backward, holding a hand up to his face.

"Have you found her," Tomas asked in a quavering voice and reached for the water glass.

Charlie's magic hated this man and urged him to kill. It took effort to hold himself back and he stopped in the doorway to get himself under control.

"Who are you?" Joy asked, and the cowering man lowered his hands.

"Henry Richmond, my vice president," Tomas said.

Charlie eyed Tomas thoughtfully. Apparently, he'd been medicated. He spoke woozily, and his tone had changed completely from the worried inquiry if they'd found her to dismissive unconcern as he mentioned Henry. Joy waved Charlie back as she crossed the room.

"She's got this," Nelson murmured.

Charlie shrugged off the major's hand but hesitated.

"Have a seat. There's nothing to be afraid of," Joy said to Henry.

"No. I've stayed too long already." Henry darted a nervous glance at Charlie. "Feel better, old chap. We can talk more at the office."

He sidled past Joy, and Charlie stepped away from the door to let him pass. A glance down the hall showed the nurses he'd passed were huddled in a tight clump. Security would be arriving momentarily.

Tomas pursed his lips, eyeing Charlie dismissively. "My Meredith was the same. She had a thing for brawn too until she met me. A beautiful woman. Not as brilliant as Sara—but my genes, you know. And Sara found herself a brilliant man too."

Henry fled the room, his shoes echoing along the tiled hospital corridor as he ran from Charlie's aura. Tomas didn't seem to feel it and continued speaking as if he hadn't noticed Henry's abrupt departure.

Charlie didn't know if Tomas was speaking to Joy or him or himself. "It must hurt. God, I was so angry…" he shook his head and his gaze drifted to Joy.

"What were you angry about?" she asked as she casted Sweet-Talk and sat on the bed beside him.

"I thought she was having an affair, but I should've known better. Such a waste. We might've had more children. Imagine how amazing my son will be. My grandchildren." He giggled, then burped and looked surprised and embarrassed as he sipped his water. "Excuse me, miss," he said to Joy as if just noticing her there.

Joy said, "Tell me about your grandchildren."

"I have none yet. But soon, I hope. And they'll be brilliant and so beautiful. Meredith was gorgeous. The most beautiful woman I'd ever seen, and she left her oaf the minute we met and married me. She recognized my brilliance. It wasn't the money. She adored me. I saw her letters." He laughed a moment, then began to cry. "But I was wrong and she's dead. She's dead and it's all my fault."

"Who's dead?" Joy asked softly, casting Sweet-Talk again.

Nelson gripped Charlie's arm tightly, but he needn't have. Charlie was riveted with both fear and horror. He clenched his shaking hands and let his breath out sharply when Tomas answered.

"My beautiful Meredith." He glared at Joy and leaned forward, stabbing a finger in her face. "But I have a second chance. Sara. My beautiful Sara. I should never have let her go live with him, but I didn't see it then."

"Where is Sara?"

"I don't know." Tomas leaned back and closed his eyes, his expression dreamy and relaxed. "Somewhere on the ocean with her brilliant scientist. She found one just like her mother. She's gone but I can have her back."

"Do you mean Oz?"

"Oz?"

Tomas opened his eyes and peered at Joy doubtfully and then glared at Charlie. "You thought you could take her from me." He cackled and rubbed his hands together, his expression becoming smug. "But my beautiful Sara wants a brilliant man. She doesn't care about the money either. But it doesn't matter if she wouldn't sell her plans. She'll give me beautiful children, as beautiful as her and as brilliant as him— as me." His expression became thoughtful and a bit angry. "Think of what we could make. Her designs were brilliant. How did I not see it earlier?"

"What didn't you see?" Joy asked.

Tomas's smile returned. "She's as smart as I am. She has vision."

Charlie said, "Ask him where she is again."

"I told you where," Tomas snapped. "She's on the ocean with him, making me beautiful grandchildren. I should've got her to tell me about her work first though. That was stupid."

"You think she and Oz ran away together?" Charlie asked doubtfully.

Tomas laughed so hard tears trickled from his eyes. "You think she'd stick with you when she could have a brilliant man? A man worthy of her? Don't be ridiculous! She's just like Meredith," he said dreamily and closed his eyes again. His eyes opened, and he glared at Charlie. Your threats mean nothing! You mean nothing. I'll never let you have her again!"

Joy frowned and waved Charlie away.

Nelson pulled him from the room.

"Tell me about your last lunch with Sara," Joy was saying as the door closed behind him.

Nelson said, "He doesn't know anything. I almost feel sorry for him."

"Well, don't! He's an ass. She'd never leave me for Oz."

"I know that, but you can see how he hopes it's true, and Meredith did leave that football player— what's his name— and run away with Tomas. They were gone for a month and returned married, and everyone was shocked.

"I know, but there's no way!"

"But you can see why he thinks there might be. Or did you think he was lying?"

"No." Charlie rubbed his face and slid down the wall to sit weakly on the floor.

"She's so afraid. I'd hoped he was involved. I don't know what to do. I never should've let her leave the zone with only two guards."

"It should've been more than enough. If you'd been with her, they'd have you too."

Charlie glowered and stabbed the icon connecting him to Hawk. "Find anything?"

"No. Not yet. I won't give up."

"Nothing?"

"Too many people and planes have been through. Sara and Oz left no prints. I can see the tracks from the passengers and luggage racks, but the people went in different directions and the luggage racks stopped at four different vehicles before returning to the main terminal where they were handled by over twenty people. I have no way of knowing if they were moved that way or carried off or if this plane made another stop somewhere first. I don't even know what leads to pursue. The tracks won't last much longer."

Charlie glanced at the time display in the upper corner of his HUD. "Four more hours. Follow the cars and if one led to a plane follow that."

"Is she…"

"Awake and afraid, angry and confused. I wish to god I could tell more."

"We'll find them."

Charlie disconnected and tapped the icon to connect with Rick. “Stasia?”

“She’s still searching Tomas’s office. I’m so sorry. I have no idea why the bracelet was empty. I took it right from the shelf in her office.”

“Guthrie has security on it to see who entered.”

“Her father?”

“Is convinced she ran away with Oz,” Nelson said.

“Really?”

“If he’s lying, it’s an Oscar winning performance,” Charlie admitted. “I think he was telling the truth. Damn it!” he jumped to his feet and ran for the exit. “I wanted him to be involved! He was our only lead!”

“Excuse us,” Nelson said to the shrieking nurses as he chased Charlie.

Small shrieks and clatters followed Charlie out the door.

“That was stupid,” the major said as they got into the car.

“It wouldn’t have matter if I’d walked. It was better to get out quick.”

I guess... You can’t be involved in the search like this.” Nelson grasped his shoulder hard. "Hear me out. Your aura is causing a major scene wherever you go. Let the rogues do the questioning. Hawk has reported his findings to Agent Lewis, and he has men on it. We'll have the footage from the airport soon, and I'm sure we'll get some new leads."

"And every hour they get further away!"

"And we're spreading out in a grid and summoning."

"We're too damned slow!"

"We're going as fast as humanly possible. We have a squad up in the jets. Get back to the school where your aura won't affect anyone and oversee them from there."

"Sara could fool me if I didn't have this connection with her," Charlie said thoughtfully and reached for the door handle.

"Don't be ridiculous. What will killing her father get you other than jail time? He was drugged to the gills and not fighting Joy's magic." Nelson slapped Charlie's hand from the handle. "I'll have her find out what he's on, and we can go talk to him again after she reports if you think it's necessary. But I mean it, Charlie, I'm not covering up a murder for you! That man had nothing to do with it!"

"Then why isn't he dead?"

"Why isn't Sam dead? Who the hell knows why? Maybe they just didn't have time. They drugged them and removed their microchips in seconds."

"Three minutes and forty-six seconds," Charlie said as he gripped the steering wheel to stop himself from running back inside.

"Exactly. Rick found Tomas, Sam, and the wristcomps and trackers within minutes. This was an orchestrated attack, planned to the tiniest detail."

Charlie closed his eyes and rested his forehead on the steering wheel. Sara's fear beat at him and his magic was furious that he was doing nothing. The fire beneath his skin was distracting, and he hoped she didn't feel his pain and fear and think he was captured too.

"Let's go see what Guthrie has to say," he said, and Nelson relaxed. Charlie glanced back as he drove away, he'd wanted Tomas to be involved but the man had really thought he'd have grandchildren.

- 14 -

WE KNOW NOTHING

Joy positioned her screen so Charlie could see it. “He’s dying, Chief. He’s got a year, tops. Henry Richmond is running his company. He’s been in charge for two years now. But he was the one running it before Tomas was sick. The man should really be a partner. Tomas did design the S-30s and still works in the lab but it’s Henry who keeps development going. Tomas spent all his time wheeling and dealing. He owns stock in so many companies it will take months to sort it out.”

Guthrie said, “If he’d been involved with Liniar and company Sara would’ve told us.”

Joy shook her head. "I asked him about that, and he says the skeins and new engines won't really affect his bottom line, then he raved for ten minutes about how smart Oz was and how clever Sara was to hook up with him. He's one hundred percent convinced that she's with him and going to give him a grandchild. So much so that he calls this mythical child his son. He gets Meredith and Sara confused in his mind, but I spoke with his doctor and he said confusion is to be expected and will grow worse as his symptoms progress."

"What's he dying of?" Guthrie asked.

"Syphilis."

"Jesus," Charlie gasped.

"I know. He has massive brain lesions already, but he's convinced he can beat it. So convinced, I questioned him extensively to see if Sara had mentioned she could heal but he said her medical degree was ridiculous and laughed as if it were the funniest thing he's ever heard. He thinks she designs weapons like him and was working on bioweapons. I honestly think he's a bit conflicted about Sara. He's proud of her accomplishments but in a sort of it must be

Oz thinking of them way and then it's like he remembers she's his daughter and it's okay for her to be smart as Oz as if he literally can't envision a woman being his better intellectually. I have no idea why he started coming to see her. He rambled about Tara and the game deck and wristcomps and money and how he thought he could talk Sara into selling but every avenue of questioning led back to grandchildren.

"He must know he's dying," Liz said. "A man like him would find that an impossible truth. I've never met a more self-absorbed person in my life. A grandchild, especially a boy grandchild, might be his version of immortality."

Joy said, "He has no real affection for her. I'm sure of that."

"We always knew that," Charlie said bitterly, and flicked Joy's report closed. He'd read it so often he'd memorized it. This was the third doctor she'd spoken with and they all confirmed the first reports. Tomas was dying and since as far as Charlie could figure Tomas only loved money, there was no reason for him to kidnap Sara. She was worth more to him working in her lab. He loved the idea that she was a brilliant scientist. Both Tara and Tomas were milking her disappearance for all the publicity it was worth.

"She's alive," Liz said consolingly.

"It's been a goddamned week!" He jumped to his feet and began to pace. "We have no leads. We—" Sara's fear buffeted him, and he cried out. He could practically hear her screaming for help. "Oh god, Sara, how?" How!"

"What?" Liz asked breathlessly as Nelson exclaimed. Charlie realized he'd fallen but Sara's fear was so strong he could hear her shouting for him in her mind. She wanted his help with a need past desperate.

"Charlie?"

Liz took his arm and he screamed with rage and fear.

"She wants me so badly, Liz. She's so afraid. She's terrified."

"I feel it," Liz said, and Charlie hugged her. Liz was afraid too. He realized the others had left the room and he was glad. His magic was frantic as it swirled around him, and he knew it would infect anyone it touched with its fear as it had Liz.

Nausea roiled his stomach and he vomited. Small skeins of lightning began to careen around the room, impacting the walls and desk with sharp crashes, breaking into scintillating sparks and reforming to do it again. Charlie barely felt the sharp shocks but Liz's pain as they impacted her made him cringe.

"Go!" he said and roughly pushed her away.

"I—"

"Go!"

Liz left him huddled on the floor.

"Please, Sara, please! Where are you?"

Thunder rumbled, and the window blew out. Lightning scorched the desk and Charlie leaped to land in it. "Where are you!" he bellowed, but the lightning held no answers he could understand. He felt its urgency but no pull and he wished with all his soul that he'd rolled a paladin and could find evil.

"Take me to her," he screamed, envisioning himself by Sara's side, pleading mentally for it to summon him to her but the lighting flowed around him unchanged. The heat beneath his skin was matched by heat from the lighting. It sought as desperately as he to form a connection. And Sara's fear built until she blacked out. He felt her go as a grateful fading to black. The table caught fire and the alarm shrieked. He fell to his knees, barely feeling the flames that washed over him. The physical pain felt good, giving his rage an outlet as his magic healed his wounds. Water cascaded from the sprinklers in the ceiling, quenching the flame but not the lightning. It faded to a thin line, and he jumped from the table to peer from the shattered window. But his relief was short-lived. She became aware again within minutes so terrified that he screamed too. His magic raced around the room, a whirling vortex of blue. He screamed with frustration and jumped out the window.

"Where!" he bellowed and ran west to the lightning that flickered overhead. His magic followed, mixing with the smoke drifting from the broken window. Distantly, a siren wailed. Sudden pain made him scream. Her pain grew and her terror with it.

"Where are you!" he shrieked until the pain overwhelmed him and darkness pressed upon him. He awoke moments later and felt nothing at all. The lightning had faded, and he lay in the parking lot. She'd gone eagerly into the dark again or maybe he had. He was just grateful her pain had stopped. Sirens blared, police, fire, and ambulance, but it felt distant and disconnected. He felt nothing at all from Sara. No magic surrounded him, no lightning lit the sky and he felt weak as if he'd fought for hours, not the mere minutes that he'd felt her. A glance at his wristcomp confirmed it had been just twenty minutes since her first spike of terror.

"Charlie," Liz called hesitantly, and he realized he could hear murmuring voices, but it was too much effort to lift his head to see who spoke.

A minute later Liz crouched beside him and took his hand. "Can you get up?"

He closed his eyes and sobbed.

She said hesitantly, "Is it— over?"

"It will never be over until I kill them all."

"Is she…" Liz sobbed and stopped speaking.

"I don't know. I feel nothing now. It can transport me anywhere. Why didn't it take me to her?"

"I don't know."

"This is my fault. I should've never let her leave the zone without me."

"You can't blame yourself."

"Why not? We both know this would've never happened if I hadn't wanted this." He lifted a hand and waved vaguely at the school. The voices in the distance grew louder and took on clarity, and he knew he should rise and pretend to be fine or the emergency personnel would want to see him, but he couldn't muster the energy.

Manny ran up and handed Liz a blanket that she draped over him. "Get a stretcher and we'll get him into my lab," Liz said.

Charlie heaved a sigh and forced himself to sit. "I can walk."

Liz tucked the blanket around him again, and Charlie impatiently threw it from him.

"Chief, your uniform is burned. Keep covered," Manny said as he handed him the blanket again.

Charlie glanced down and grimaced at the remains of his clothes.

"Let us help you," Liz murmured as she tried to tug him up.

"No one can help," he said but he pushed himself up and let Manny support him.

Scouts and their hired security bustled about the parking lot, and Liz released him to say loudly, "Just a concussion! No broken bones. I'll see to him."

She continued to talk as Manny dragged him away, half carrying him.

"Take him right downstairs," Joy said. "I've got them distracted."

Her voice made his magic stir, a weak ripple of sadness, and he suddenly wanted to cry, not for his pain but for hers. The walk to Liz's lab passed in a daze.

"He's in shock," Liz said, and he opened his eyes to see her leaning over him. He glanced at his HUD. *Four minutes.* He'd lost four minutes. "Of course, he's scared," Liz continued angrily, and Charlie glanced around to see who she spoke with.

Nelson frowned at Joy and snapped. "Control your damned magic. Give him some privacy!"

"You aren't helping," Liz said angrily and put an arm around Joy.

"I *am* scared," he said, wondering if that's why he felt so weak. He was so scared he had no room left for anger. "Please wake up," he murmured and closed his eyes, trying to force a connection to Sara.

"Leave them alone," Liz said as Joy laid her head on Charlie's chest and began to cry.

He smoothed her hair as he concentrated. Stasia, Hawk, and Rick entered, and he felt their pain. Their magic swooped about the room for a moment before sinking to the floor in fear and confusion.

They spoke and cried, and he heard nothing but white noise as he concentrated. It got easier when the magic dissipated and Joy fell asleep. Her pain made it hard to concentrate. But asleep in his arms he could feel her heartbeat and was able to commune with his magic.

It wanted Sara and hummed beneath his skin, but the gap was too large, and he couldn't make it understand or it couldn't make him understand. Static began to flicker but it petered out before manifesting into lightning.

"I don't think it knows what to do either," Liz whispered.

Charlie opened his eyes and tightened his grip on Joy.

"Leave her here."

"We will. But if she wants to go— She loves Drew."

"It isn't like that. Sara isn't replaceable, and I haven't given up. She could just be sedated. They've done it before." Anger returned with a force like a blow.

"What happened?" Liz asked hesitantly.

"I don't know. Something that scared her almost to death. I think it made her pass out. And then she was in pain. So much pain and so afraid..." he began to cry, waking Joy who began to cry again too.

"The magic could transport me. Zones are so arbitrary. Why can't it cross them? She wanted me so badly." The anger felt good, refreshing, and he let himself become furious. "What good are you!" he screamed as he jumped from the bed and ripped an oxygen tank from the wall. He smashed the metal tank to pieces, then attacked the bed. Joy joined him in his destructive frenzy, and Liz ran from the room.

He and Joy destroyed the room, ripping chunks from the ceilings and walls with their bare hands, shredding everything to pieces until all that remained were scraps of cloth and chunks of dented metal.

"We need a mage," Joy said through panting breaths. She glanced at her wristcomp, keying it on with a blink. "Drew, we need you or Lee. We need a mage."

Lee ran into the room a minute later and Charlie rose his arms. The lightning came but try as hard as he could, he couldn't get it to leap to Lee. He wasn't sure if it didn't want to or didn't understand or was trying and couldn't.

"Brenda, will you try?" Charlie asked on the open raid channel.

"Enough," Liz said and knelt beside Charlie. "It isn't going to work. Let them rest and we can try again tomorrow on our mountain."

He lay on the floor panting. Brenda was hurt and scared and magically depleted. His magic regenerated much faster than hers and wound slowly about the room, bringing him her despair as if she shouted Sara is dead and gone forever. Joy knelt beside Drew, handing him a water bottle that he waved away.

"I'm sorry," Charlie said to Lee.

"It isn't your fault. We want to help. I wish I could be the mage you need."

He pulled her up and hugged her, smoothing the burnt wisps of hair back from her face.

"Thank you for trying so hard. I do want to try again on the mountain, but we won't try to force it."

I'm willing…"

"I know. But I'm not willing to hurt you like that again." He turned to Drew. "I'm sorry, man. I had no right. I should never have—"

Drew cut him off with a curt gesture. "We'll try again tomorrow."

Charlie grimaced but nodded, hating he'd hurt his friends so badly but what choice did he have?

Liz helped them up and to the door, waving Charlie back.

"You owe them your protection too," she said as she hugged him.

"I have to try."

"We all do but you have to control yourself too. Don't let fear or pain make you a tyrant."

He stumbled from the room and to his office where he fell onto his couch exhausted. Sara's silent screams for help rang in his head and he saw her terrified face behind his closed eyes.

He rose to go through all the reports one more time.

"It's been a week; I haven't felt her in a week." His head in his hands, Charlie sat at Liz's desk trying to convince himself Sara was just unconscious, that their broken connection didn't mean she'd died. "If Oz were here, we could find her. He could figure it out even without Locate."

He glared at the screen behind her desk. The sound was muted but the news anchor was clearly talking about the abductions.

Liz said, "We'll find them, have patience. Go back to school. Stasia and Joy are searching. Brenda is traveling and calling."

"School," Charlie said bitterly.

"Yes, when we find her, she'd hate to be the cause of your expulsion. There's nothing you can do, Charlie. When we get a lead, we'll all go."

"Without Oz none of this—"

The words clogged in Charlie's throat. They all knew Oz was dead. Nothing could hold a mage. He'd have portaled away if he couldn't fight free.

Charlie had barely contemplated the loss of Oz, too caught up in the loss of Sara, but without Oz's amazing intellect Valor would be reduced to brute force.

On the television, conspiracy theorists were having a field day claiming the government was behind the abductions. Experts gleefully debated the loss of the new power source on the economy. He turned away from the screen as two new men joined into the debate.

What good was magic without a mind to guide it? Without their mage, they'd never develop the tech they needed to ease the world's distress when the magic became common knowledge. There would be no heal to share with the world just anger and unending fighting. Whoever had taken them had taken the world's hope with them.

- 15 -

A MAJOR DISAGREEMENT

“What are you doing?” Liz asked as she entered the lab.

Major Nelson glanced up from the boxes on the counter but continued to tape them closed.

“This is the only magic we’ll ever have and they’re wasting it.”

“It’s hardly a waste.”

Nelson rested a hip on the table and gestured at the empty shelves behind him. “How many times do you suppose they’ve cast Call-for-Help? They’re dead. The Scouts can cast a million more times—”

“We don’t know that!”

"Charlie hasn't felt a glimmer from her in a month. Not one glimmer. She's dead. I'm sorry, Liz. I really am but he felt her die. You saw him…"

"He felt pain and fear."

"Followed by nothing."

"If her m-nerve was removed…" Contemplating that made Liz nauseous and she had to stop speaking, afraid she'd vomit.

Nelson shook his head. "Even if they were alive, which I highly doubt because no one has even tried for the other three, but let's assume they are. There are thousands of zones. We don't have enough magic to keep calling randomly. Not in the spell-bracelets anyway. Brenda can continue her search. The bracelets need to be reserved for healing, for emergencies that we can actually do something about."

"Charlie will be furious."

Nelson snorted softly. "He's already furious, and besides, he won't know. He has no idea how much magic she had stored. I'm not planning to take the bracelets they have on them. When they run out, there won't be more, that's all. It'll just happen sooner than they thought."

"Did the general order this?"

Nelson sighed deeply and turned away to gather the last rods of stored magic.

"Did the general order this!" she repeated, angrily.

"No. But I could ask for the orders if you try to go over my head."

"I outrank you."

He rolled his eyes. "You're a nurse." He cleared his throat and offered her an apologetic smile. "Excuse me, ma'am, but this is my sphere, combat."

"I have to disagree. This is my lab and you're confiscating my supplies."

"Fine. I'll submit a request. And I know exactly how many are in here, Major Harris."

Liz said nothing as he stalked from the room but as soon as the door closed she called General Campbell.

"Major Nelson was just in my lab, trying to remove the remaining magic Sara had stored," she said without preamble. "I agree it needs to be rationed but removing it is a horrible idea. Charlie needs it. I've been weaning him off but it's going to take time and patience and his cooperation. If he comes here and I have none of her magic to offer him, I can't predict his response, but I can guarantee it'll be hostile if he knows Major Nelson has her magic and won't give it to him."

"I agree," Campbell said. He tapped his wristcomp. "I just sent you a copy of the letter John received this morning. The commandant is concerned and asking John to get Charlie to withdraw."

"I'm not certain it's Charlie causing the problem. It might be the lack of Hawk's aura, I'm sure the commandant won't expel Charlie with a month to go. He has no grounds."

"He could make a case for depression and not accept him back next year. I'll set up an appointment and we'll speak to him. I think it's even more imperative now that the bonds are tight with us." He glanced at his wristcomp, tapping the face, grimacing ruefully. "Major Nelson. I'll get back to him. How much magic remains for the spell-bracelets?"

"Not enough to keep on as we are. The major was correct about that. But I don't think they're dead. When Joy died, the magic wanted more instantly. Wouldn't it hit Brenda and demand she make more if they were dead? Charlie has been trying to make a mage, but the magic doesn't want one. It wants Sara. Why would it want her if she were dead?"

"They all report no compulsion to transform anyone?"

"So far," Liz agreed. "They report the magic feels confused when with Charlie but behaves normally when away from him. Charlie riles all of them. Rick handles it best, but Marcus and Mike need the target dummies after being near him, speaking of which, I need more. I sent a new design idea to Oz's father. It seems to help when the dummies break and I'm not sure if it's the breaking or if they're rage is just spent. I'd like to test that."

"Of course."

He seemed surprised she'd asked for permission and she frowned as she considered. "Normally, I'd send requests of this nature to Mary. She ensures the magical research funding is hidden but the company is a bit disorganized at the moment. John's been in meetings trying to salvage our schedules but without Sara and Oz we'll never meet our deadlines. Our programmers just don't have the speed. The board meeting this month was canceled and I spoke to John and asked him to give me one more month before calling for another. I'm afraid of Charlie's reaction."

That was such a massive understatement she winced.

"The company… I hadn't really considered."

Liz shrugged. "Valor Industries will survive, but on a much smaller scale. John can continue producing the components they already manufacture but won't have new ones to offer."

"The light shield?"

"Nowhere near ready. I don't know that it will ever be ready without Sara or Oz to finish the design. Sam has been working on it. He'd been helping them, but he just doesn't have their vision. Maybe, given enough time, he could get it working. I really couldn't say. Team Valor might be able to pick up where Oz and Sara left off, but I hate to ask them. Asking would be tantamount to giving up and we can't afford to give up or our reputation will plummet."

"We need to find them."

"I'm open to suggestions."

Campbell winced. "Lewis and Taylor are doing everything they can."

"And we don't have one lead."

"Someone out there planned very well. We need to remain vigilant and catch them when they try for the others."

"You still think it's magic related and not about the new motors?"

"Honestly, I have no idea. I don't understand why they'd kill Sara if it was about magic but maybe they know of her link to Charlie and thought he could find her using it."

"It gives me hope and nightmares." Liz wiped her suddenly teary eyes.

"They'd have to remove the m-nerve."

Liz closed her eyes. "And keep her in the dark."

"It makes me sick to think about it."

"Oz— they'll have killed him. He's too dangerous to let live. They all know it. If he'd woken, he'd have portaled away if he knew he couldn't fight free."

"Or he's in the dark with Sara."

"I don't think her healing buff would be enough. He'd need medical care after a double amputation, although, I suppose they could keep him alive if they tried hard. Her buff would eventually heal him. But I don't think he'd stay alive long if he had a way to end his life."

"No, I don't suppose they would."

"Sara will hold out as long as she can for Charlie's sake."

"It makes me sick to think of what they'll do to get her to talk."

"She'd do anything for him, and he knows it. His rage feels like a scorching summer day from twenty feet away."

"I almost hope they're dead."

"Sometimes…." Liz shook her head. "It doesn't matter what we wish. We can't change it by wishing. If it could be done, Charlie would've done it by now he's been thinking so hard at the magic."

Campbell glanced at his wristcomp in annoyance. "I better take this. He's marked it urgent."

"Tell Major Nelson I'm taking his advice and removing the magic from my lab but in the future, I'd appreciate a polite request before he enters it."

Campbell saluted her and disconnected before she could respond.

Liz finished packing the boxes and debated a minute before tapping an icon on her wristcomp. "Camila, could you meet me in my lab? I have a favor to ask.

The commandant met with Liz. To the commandant's shock, President Carmichael showed up at the meeting.

The president said, "Major Harris informs me Midshipman Hayes is disrupting the student body."

The commandant's lips tightened. "Not exactly disrupting. In fact, the average GPA has risen. But school spirit is at an all-time low. Athletics are at an all-time low. The entire school is depressed and unhappy. I'm not saying its Cadet Hayes's fault. The midshipmen feel the loss of the doctors keenly and blame themselves—"

The president held up a hand. "Mr. Hayes has done nothing to merit expulsion. For reasons I'm not at liberty to say it's imperative he attend this school, that he considers this school his home. I'm sorry this situation is disrupting the school but for one more year you'll have them here. During that time, do everything in your power to bond them to this institution."

The commandant leaned back in his chair and folded his hands on his chest. "You don't believe the doctors will be found?"

Liz winced and glanced away as tears filled her eyes.

"*Ahh.*" The commandant cleared his throat. "You believe they've been killed."

The president rested a hand on Liz's shoulder as she stifled a sob. "Irrelevant. We *will* keep searching. Found dead or alive, we'll bring the perpetrators to justice. Taking them was an act so foul— the loss for the world is so great— the possible consequences so grim…" The president trailed off.

A moment later he cleared his throat and resumed. "Because we can't know what their captors learned from them, we must prepare for the worst. Our only hope to survive as a nation resides in the three we have left. Anastasia, Sebastian, and Charles. This incident could push them from us, make them hostile to the United States. And we can't afford that. If we're attacked by weapons that Sara and Oz designed, we'll need them to counter the effects. Those three are the only ones who could hope to understand whatever Sara and Oz's genius has thought up."

"I see." The commandant gazed at Liz with his lips pursed. "My intention was to ask him to withdraw for the good of the school. To ask all three to withdraw and have the Valor building reassigned before the start of next term. This situation puzzles me. I mean the depth of the student body's feelings over this matter. Cadets have died before, both heroically and tragically and it's never produced this sort of all-encompassing funk. A year of that might be enough to permanently harm the school."

The president nodded. "And yet, without them the United States is doomed."

"The weapons Doctor Simmons and Mitchel developed are that strong then?"

The president sighed and spread his hands on his knees. He spoke without looking up. "Doctors Simmons and Mitchel are world changing."

"Then I'll do my best to make the midshipmen happy here."

"Loyal, we want them loyal. Think team building. Nothing you do will make them happy, but you can work on *esprit de corps*."

- 16 -

STUCK ON BASE

Charlie's fellow students left him alone. Moody and irate, he swung from rage to bleak acceptance to desperate hope, calm only when forcing himself to study, sublimating his fear and anger by concentrating intensely on schoolwork.

He cursed softly as he crumbled his orders. He'd been assigned to the *Truman* again for the summer.

His anger surged hard enough to cause his magic to manifest as he packed up Sara's supplies and schematics. *What was the point?* Why order him to bring her things as if she were going to appear and be able to install them? A month with not even a flicker of contact. His wife was dead.

The anger faded replaced by sorrow so intense he thought he might smother on it. Time hung heavy on his hands. Stasia and Joy spied. Brenda traveled, casting her Call-for-Help everywhere she went. Hawk and Agent Lewis searched. He did nothing except reign in his magic.

Without his conscious control his magic burst from him and swirled away in eddies in every direction as if it sought her but didn't know where to go. He'd tried following it, but it circled endlessly. He went to the mountaintop every few days to beg it for help. Thunder always sounded and lightning crashed but he'd never gotten a response he could understand.

Hawk was waiting in his office.

His magic left him a rush that left him breathless. Hope swelled and crashed, leaving him feeling sick.

"Liz asked me to come." Hawk set Lucky on her feet and gave Charlie a hard hug.

"You should be out searching." Charlie winced and pulled him back for another hug. "Sorry. I didn't mean it like that. I'm glad to see you."

I'll never stop looking," Hawk said.

Charlie didn't need the magic to feel his sincerity. It shone from his eyes.

"I know. They'll know too." His voice caught on a sob and he turned away to rub his face.

Rhea whuffled softly, her hopefully gaze darting between him and Hawk as if she expected them to take her to Sara.

"The damned dog is killing me," Charlie said, consumed with fury over the dog's pain as its head drooped and it flopped to the floor.

Lucky meowed plaintively and brushed against his legs.

Hawk stooped to pick up the cat. "They miss her."

Lucky began to purr, and Charlie strode to the window, consumed with fresh rage. Just seconds ago he'd been angry his pets were unhappy and now he was furious to hear his cat purr.

"I'm going crazy. I hate that damned purring! What the fuck is wrong with me?"

"I'll take them with me."

Charlie spun to see the animals meekly leave the room, guided by Hawk's magic.

"You—"

"Abby will watch them. Don't worry about them." Hawk hesitated them grasped his shoulder. "You need to get control of it though." His eyes narrowed and his grip tightened. "It won't work."

Charlie huffed a short angry laugh. "Her magic takes her to me."

Hawk shook his head and released him to perch on the edge of the desk. "It takes her. But she knew both times right where you were. Letting yourself grow this angry won't make it more powerful."

"We don't know that, and it doesn't matter anyway. I am this angry."

Hawk batted at the blue wisps that still swirled around him. "It's already desperate. If it could take you to her, it would."

"And it makes me so goddamned mad! Why won't it!"

Hawk's lips compressed and he said nothing, but Charlie felt his despair.

"They can't be dead, Hawk. They just can't be."

School ended for the year and Charlie went to the *Rheal Lucky* for the first time since her disappearance. He stared at his ship, her home, tempted to leave and never come back— or sink it— but she'd loved it.

Lucky cried from the cat carrier in his hand. He glanced down at the cat, then at Rhea who followed him. In a week, they'd go back to Abby and he'd report to his ship. He didn't want them around really, but Abby had brought them, trying to comfort him. When he returned them, he'd give them to her. They offered no comfort, only reminders. Charlie straightened his shoulders and marched onto his boat.

Sara had left drawings for the game on the chart table with notes in the margins. One-by-one he picked them up and examined them. The notes in the margin made him smile despite himself. *'Charlie loves this NPC. Amy thinks this one needs bigger claws. This looks too much like Paul's. My father thinks this looks like Anchorage.*' Charlie paused. He hadn't been aware her father had been there. He'd examined her father's records obsessively and couldn't recall that as a stop. He called Stasia. "Can you find out when Sara's father was in Alaska?"

"April first," she said instantly. "Why do you ask?"

"Why do you know the date so quickly?" he countered.

"It was an odd stop; he was there three days, and it was right before he came here and on none of his calendars."

"What was he doing there?"

"Business, what else? I'll text you the company he was hunting."

She texted him the name. More for something to do then he thought he'd find anything, he opened Sara's wristcomp, entered the name and hit search. It was owned by another company. He searched again; in an hour he was five companies in when he hit a dead-end, owner unknown. Once again, he wished Oz where there, he could track this easily. He spent two days of his vacation tracking down company owners trying to keep himself busy so the crushing misery of her absence wouldn't destroy him. He frowned at the final owner— Liniar Corp. He was going to Alaska.

Most of the raid accompanied him on the company jet. They landed in Anchorage. *Sara's father was right; it did look like the drawings,* he thought as he gazed around at the stunted trees. He was walking across the tarmac to the car when Stasia screamed. He turned to her and felt himself sway as a roiling cloud of magic engulfed him. He fell to his knees and screamed as her magic engulfed him. Unable to deny the truth to himself any longer misery overcame him. Sara was dead, they both were. They'd been killed here. The magic was in pain, afraid and lonely. He screamed in fury. The magic recoiled from his pain and loss.

"It needs someone," Rick said in a heartbroken voice as he knelt beside his brother.

Charlie was beyond caring. He could feel Sara in the magic and he wanted it for himself.

Joy laid a gentle hand on his arm. Her face was as bleak as he felt.

"She's dead."

"I know. I'm sorry."

"I should've felt it— why didn't I feel it?"

"I don't know," Joy said softly and turned to Brenda. "Can you place it in one of them?"

Charlie tightened his grip on Joy's arm.

"I can try." Brenda bit her lip, turning her white face to the raid. "I'll need two volunteers."

They all stepped forward. "Lee, Todd, the rest of you, step back," Brenda said.

Charlie knew why she'd picked them. Lee was a mage, Todd a ranger. They'd find who did this. He placed his hand in Brenda's. He'd find them and kill them. They had a lead now. Her father had been involved. It was too much of a coincidence that he'd been here days before her death.

Together they called the lightning and this time it worked.

Charlie staggered to his feet, grinning in triumph as the lightning lingered on Lee and Todd. He was so furious that he shook. His anger felt thick like tar that would trap him, not the smoothness of honey.

Sirens sounded in the distance and men spoke heatedly behind him. The lightning had been harder to control than he'd imagined. It came so easily to Sara. It had taken all of them chanting give us a mage before it had shifted from him to Brenda. It still lingered on Lee and Todd.

"Two more minutes," Liz said from his HUD.

"I got this," Manny said and slapped his shoulder as he strode past him to the approaching siren.

Charlie squatted beside Stasia who knelt on the tarmac crying. He had no room for tears. Anger filled him with purpose. "When we first spoke, you said this stop wasn't on his books. How did you know about it?"

She sniffled and wiped her eyes on her sleeve. "From the pilot."

"I came here to search the office," Joy said.

"When?"

"As soon as we heard. Forty-three hours after they were taken. It seemed suspicions. But there was nothing. Just a stupid parts manufacturer."

"It's too much of a coincidence. Did you cast Call-for-Help?"

“We’d already tried twice here.” Joy looked stricken. “I should have. God, maybe—”

Charlie cut her off, slashing his hand through the air as he stood.

“It isn’t your fault. I believed that lying sack of shit too. Joy, you come with me. Stasia, Hawk, you guys search here.”

The lightning flickered and faded, and Marcus began CPR on Lee as Harrison felt for Todd’s pulse.

“He’s breathing,” Harrison said.

“Where are you going?” Nelson asked in the raid channel.

Charlie glanced at his HUD, checking vitals. “Home to beat some truth from him.” He flicked the icon to end the call and turned to Mike. “Get them to Liz. You and Brenda stay with them until they’re completely recovered. Brenda will be fine,” he said in a softer voice and crouched beside Mike to take Brenda’s hand. “The lightning hurts, but she’ll recover and be on her feet again in an hour.”

He glanced over his shoulder as the voices behind him escalated. Manny was arguing with a man in a golf cart and two security guards. "Get them back on the plane. Joy, talk them into leaving and smooth things over here." He crouched beside Stasia again. "You need to pull it together. We can cry after we find their bodies."

"It won't work," she said sadly.

"We don't know that!" He took a deep breath to calm his wildly beating heart. "We don't know that," he said again in a calmer tone. "We don't know what happened or when. Maybe they kept her sedated and she died hours ago. If we can find them, we might be able resurrect them! If she was dead all this time, why didn't the lightning come when we called at home?"

"Charlie—"

Charlie glared at his brother. "We don't know, Rick, and I won't give up!"

Stasia pushed away from Rick and stood. "You're right. We'll search."

Charlie glanced around for Hawk then checked his HUD. Hawk was already a mile away and moving fast. He hadn't even seen him leave. He hesitated, his hand hovering over his spell-bracelet, then tapped the icon to connect them.

"Hawk?"

"The magic came from this direction. If we have enemies, I'll see them."

"I don't like you running off alone."

"I'm not alone, Tank is with me, and no one will see me. This is a wilderness. I have an army at my beck and call."

"Call me if you find anything."

"And me," Stasia said.

Charlie was happy to see the hard glitter of magic had replaced her tears.

"Let's get them on the plane and get them home to Liz."

"I'll oversee this," Glenn said.

Charlie turned to examine the police and ambulance who'd arrived. They faced away from them, speaking with Joy. Drew and Manny were being ignored. *A good sign*, Charlie thought and dismissed them from his mind. He picked Todd up and headed back to the plane.

"We need faster transport. It's going to take hours to get home."

"He doesn't know we're coming," Toric said.

"Can you fly the plane?"

"Yes…"

"Good. Let's get going."

Toric glanced back, "Shouldn't we wait for Joy?"

"She'll catch up."

Toric said nothing else. He hurried ahead and opened the door for Charlie, leaving it open as he ran to the cockpit and the engines sprang on before Mike boarded with Brenda. Charlie waited impatiently for Marcus to bring Lee.

"Everyone's on board," Charlie said as he yanked the door closed. Marcus glanced at him but turned back to Lee.

The plane began to roll as he knelt beside Marcus to feel Lee's pulse for himself. He had a mage now, but Sara was dead. He'd traded one for another, he thought bitterly as he helped Marcus make Lee as comfortable as they could in a reclined airline seat.

"The world is a big place," Mike said without glancing up from Brenda.

"I'll make him talk.

"If you kill him, you kill our chances."

"I can handle it." *And that was true*," Charlie thought bitterly. His magic had stopped pressing him, either tired of fighting him or having nothing to fight for. He released his control and let it go. It oozed from his skin and slide along the floor as if drawn to Lee despite itself.

"It's afraid," Marcus said.

"Me too," Charlie said tiredly and closed his eyes.

- 17 -

CONFRONTING TOMAS

"You can't go in there," a secretary said as she ran for the elevator.

Charlie smiled. Security had already tried to stop him and his aura had made them run from him.

"Stop this right now!" Nelson snarled and grabbed his arm.

Charlie shook him off.

The major had been waiting when he'd arrived.

"The police are going to come and you're going to cause a riot!"

Charlie ignored him and burst into Tomas's office. His magic rushed Tomas and hated with a passion that lit Charlie's eyes.

"Where is she?"

"I'm ordering you to return to base!" Nelson said angrily.

Tomas rose to his feet, glaring at Charlie.

"I have no idea…" His expression became pinched, and he opened and closed his mouth as if he'd changed his mind on what to say. Charlie stalked forward and braced his hands on the desk to loom over him. To his shock, Tomas appeared unaffected by his aura. His gaze stayed on the magic as it darted about him and he almost appeared smug.

Goosebumps rose on Charlie's arms.

Tomas said, "I can make allowances. I know you're upset over her death, but I had nothing to do with it. For god's sake, she's my daughter!" he said it indignantly, but Charlie knew better. Tomas had never cared about Sara.

He grabbed Tomas, and Nelson shot him. He threw Tomas from him and reached for the major but fell to the floor before he could grab him.

"If he comes here again, I'll have him arrested." Tomas's words faded to blackness as Charlie struggled to open his eyes. He knew Tomas knew where she was, and when he woke, he'd beat it out of him, even if he had to kill the major to do it.

He woke manacled to the stasis chamber and snarled at the major as he yanked on the chain.

"Cut it out. I sent Stasia to question him, but you saw him. He's either disconnected from reality— crazy as a loon— or your magic knows he's not involved, or it's confused and thinks he's her or something. But it doesn't matter. Stasia will get better results—"

Charlie's wristcomp chimed and Stasia overrode his controls when he didn't answer immediately, appearing before him in a three-dimensional image. She looked furious and the room she stood in was ransacked.

"He isn't fucking here! We're too late. I sent a team to his house and his plane and no one knows where he went!"

Charlie yanked at the chain and glared at the major who back-peddled away, holding out his hands.

"Did you search—"

Stasia interrupted the major. "Of course, I did! I found nothing!"

"He has other homes. Search them. This is a solid lead—"

"One you let get away!" Charlie yelled, so angry he was hyperventilating. He yanked again, and the chain ripped from the stasis unit, knocking it to the floor.

"I know and I'm sorry. But I really did think Stasia would get better results.

Charlie absently rubbed his wrist as he considered. He knew Nelson was telling the truth. His magic was darting around him. His momentary hope had energized it and it flitted wildly about the room.

Nelson grimaced but didn't try to run or go for the gun on his belt.

Charlie said, "If you ever shoot me again, for any damned reason, I'll kill you."

Nelson sighed and shook his head. "Look, it isn't personal. I'm trying to help. How would it help Sara if you're in jail? Or did you intend to break out? Jesus, Charlie, think about this logically. If Tomas killed her, we'll find her body, but beating him to death isn't the answer. It won't bring her back."

"Maybe it will. Maybe we could resurrect her."

Nelson shook his head, and Charlie turned away. He knew it was a slim hope, but it was all he had. If they could find their bodies before they decayed too badly, maybe with all of them casting resurrection it would be enough.

"We have to find them."

"We're trying," Nelson said as he slapped his shoulder.

"I'm going to talk to Liniar myself," Stasia said.

Charlie glanced at his HUD. All the Scouts had joined the channel while he and the major were arguing.

Nelson said, "Joy should go. She can keep a cool head."

"I'm going," Charlie said flatly.

"No, you're not. I'm not kidding. That's an order, Charlie, and if you won't follow it, I'll have you dismissed from the service. There's no point in your going. What can you do except intimidate him? Your anger is a liability here. This isn't a fight; its surveillance."

"I'm going," Hawk said. "The major is right. Lee, Joy, and I will go. And not just to him. We'll recheck Tachimori and Nguyen too. If Tomas has contacts here, let them think you've given up and maybe they'll grow careless. If he did force them to tell our secret, he'll be prepared for rogues, but he can't be prepared for me and my Hidden Nature. I can spy using the animals. The mice and the birds will be my eyes and ears, and the minute we have a lead, Joy and I will question him, forcefully if we have too."

"Look, Chief, Stasia and I will go," Joy said firmly. "We'll find out everything there is to know. You stay here.

"I'll be with them," Nelson said cajolingly. "We'll call when we find anything. It'll be easier for Hawk and Joy to sneak into Vietnam and China than the group of you. Go do your duty. That's an order. Stasia, you stay here to oversee the search. Talk to all of his acquaintances and find out if Tomas made any other undocumented trips." He turned to Charlie as he said, "Now that we know Tomas was involved, we'll question everyone again. I'd really believed he was innocent. His own daughter…." He trailed off, looking grim, and Charlie sagged.

He found it hard to believe too and he'd known Tomas had no love for Sara. He'd believed the man when he first questioned him and might even have been persuaded to believe him now despite the huge coincidence of his visit and her death if he hadn't run. He wanted to rip Tomas apart with his bare hands, but the major was right— violence would get them nothing.

"Find them, Hawk," he said as commandingly as he could.

Hawk saluted, his eyes shining so brightly they cast shadows on his face.

Lee started searching for their dead bodies as soon as she recovered. She traveled the world looking while the rangers and rogues searched.

Charlie reported to the *Truman* and did his duty efficiently and quietly. He oversaw the placement of the light-shield emitters and holographic projectors, knowing they wouldn't be used. Without Sara and Oz it would take years to write the programing and iron out the kinks.

"It's been a month," Captain Williams said as he examined the schematics Charlie handed him. "When will they go online?"

"When Sara and Oz are retrieved, they can come do the tests." Rage boiled up and he tamped it down with ruthless efficiency. "This is an untested system, and I'm not qualified to test it." Charlie's hands shook with fury, knowing that would never happen. He pushed the rage back with practiced ease now. The magic remained beneath his skin, a burning sensation he'd become all too familiar with. *Soon. Soon they would find who'd done this and all those involved would pay. He'd kill them all himself, then join her.* He lived now for revenge and the slim hope that her body would be found, and she could be resurrected.

"Right." Captain Williams cleared his throat. "Dismissed," he said softly.

The more time that passed the more desperate Charlie's hope became. Joy had only been dead for days and it had almost killed Sara to resurrect her, but he refused to give up the hope, it was all he had. He returned to his bunk to reread the reports for the hundredth time.

Stasia had joined Joy and the two rogues traveled from Vietnam to China, from China to Florida, from Florida to Vietnam again.

Gina's call was a welcome distraction and his damn heart leaped with hope.

"Yes?"

"I'm worried. Hawk is losing too much weight. He's using too much energy."

"Get him energy bars," Charlie said impatiently.

She glared at him so hotly he could practically feel heat emanating from her holographic image.

"Don't be stupid. Of course, I'm giving him energy bars."

"Shut up!" Hawk barked, and Charlie winced at his scratchy voice.

"Take a break, Hawk."

"No."

Hawk sat in the dirt beneath a towering pine with his eyes closed, flicking his fingers as he directed a horde of lesser animals.

Charlie bit his lip. "I love you too, Hawk. Take a break."

"Send them back to China. Wait, there's a man here, a doctor…" Hawk leaned forward, cocking his head and scrunching his face, his head swaying slightly as if he read although his eyes remained closed.

"Back up," he murmured and twitched his fingers again. Gina knelt beside him, her anxious gaze flicking from her wristcomp to Hawk.

"Get him into the sun," Charlie said.

"Sam is searching for a safe sunny spot for him. There aren't many spots close enough. Mr. Nguyen hardly ever leaves his offices—"

She snapped her mouth closed when Hawk gestured impatiently.

Hawk said, "He's involved with her father. They want the skeins." Hawk frowned as he flicked his fingers.

Charlie recognized the spells, but they made no sense. Hawk was sending an animal back and forth and left and right so fast it was hard to make out the patterns and he wondered if Hawk were just stretching his fingers.

"Liniar and he are bargaining with Tomas."

A mouse crept into the clearing and dropped a scrap of paper at Gina's feet. She reached for it as three more crept in. Within seconds the small clearing was teeming, each rodent bringing a scrap of shredded paper.

"Holy crap," Charlie whispered, stunned over the amount of animals Hawk was bending to his will at once.

Gina gathered the papers, and Hawk slumped as the mice scampered away, opening his eyes and rubbing his shoulders. She immediately offered him a water bottle and granola bar. He waved both away.

"I've sent One and Two into the filing cabinet. It'll take them a little while to chew through. Six and Ten are dead, and I released four, five, and eight. I need a bird or two and a racoon. Wake me in an hour." He shook Gina's shoulder hard. "An hour, Gina. He'll be done eating by then and this is our first solid hit. We can't afford to miss anything he says.

Gina nodded. Hawk released her and spoke to Charlie. "The man I sent Stasia to saw them. He was there in Anchorage. We'll find them, Chief."

"How are you controlling so many?"

"I'm not. I'm switching quickly. I can only control ten lesser animals at once."

There had to be fifty mice there..."

Yeah, it's a pain in the ass to make them go back and pick up the pieces, which is why I need a racoon."

Can't you use some ferrets or something?"

"I am. Look, we can talk about this later. I'm exhausted and I can sleep while they work. Every second counts."

Hawk's eyes were bleak, and Charlie knew his hope for a successful resurrection was waning.

"Sorry. Sure. It's just I'm worried about you too."

"Well don't be. I'm fine. I'll have all the information from the files within a few hours and then Mr. Nguyen and me are going to speak face-to-face."

"I wish I was with you."

It's good you're not. I can concentrate better without you looming over me, and Nguyen told Liniar that Tomas was a fool for running when you were powerless to hurt him. They're discussing his return. Let that bastard think you believe him or are cowed by his wealth. The second he shows himself, we'll get him."

"Let it be soon," Charlie said prayerfully and disconnected the call.

Stasia called him four hours later in hysterics. Joy and Nelson yelled at her to hang up in the background. "Tell Lee to search for them, not their bodies," she said through gasping sobs.

The background grew quiet. "Major Nelson didn't want me to call. He says it's false hope, but, Charlie, they could be alive."

"Stasia..." Charlie's voice trembled.

"They ripped out the m-nerves in their hands. Charlie, if they did that and then moved them again, the magic would be free wouldn't it?"

"God, I don't know? How do you know what they did?"

"We have one of the doctors who did it. He doesn't know what he removed. I mean, he doesn't realize it was magic. He thought it was a bioweapon. Her father was definitely involved, oh god." She started to cry again and sobbed incoherently for a minute, gasping and trying to talk.

The major got on the line. "We have more leads to follow up here. As you can see, the girls are very upset. I've sent for Rick and Drew. The rogues collected quite a lot of paperwork that I still need to go through while they return to the search."

Joy yelled, "Don't tell him," in the background as Stasia cried.

"Don't tell me what?" Charlie's hands were shaking and his palms sweating.

"The details, there's no need. Charlie stay there. That's an order!"

Nelson hung up. Charlie couldn't catch his breath. Hope burned like a flame fed with his rage. He called Lee. "Search for them, not their bodies— them! Go to Vietnam and China and do all provinces. If you find them, call immediately. Take three Scouts and keep a warrior in the zone."

He hung up and called Hawk. "Nguyen can't know we're onto him. If they're still alive—"

"Alive?" Hawk gasped and his eyes brightened.

"Stasia found a lead. That doctor removed their m-nerves. And maybe she's right and it was enough to keep their magic from regenerating. God, Hawk… I need it to be true!"

Hawk said, "And if they are and we tip our hand…" He trailed off and nodded grimly. "Did Stasia kill him?"

"I didn't think to ask. I sent Lee to you. She's been searching for their corpses." Anger at himself for not having more hope, for not insisting she search for them, washed over him in a hot wave, making his voice tremble. "She'll be searching for both now. Whether they're alive or dead, if they're in China, she'll find them."

"If they removed their m-nerves—"

"Yes. They must know." His throat felt tight. "They'd keep her in the dark so she doesn't regenerate."

"It's been weeks." Hawk snapped his mouth closed and his grim expression deepened.

"I don't know if she's alive or dead. How can I not know? Wouldn't I know it? How could she be gone so completely and yet I still have hope?"

"Her fucking father," Hawk muttered. "Liniar is practically stealing his businesses. Tomas will have to show soon or he'll lose everything. And I don't get it. His businesses won't be hit that hard by the new engines. Why would he subject his own daughter to that?"

"Tomas's business is weapons and he must see how powerful she is and want it for himself. Why else hire a doctor? He must be trying to figure out the magic. He needs a heal." Charlie laughed bitterly. "God, it must be killing him to know she could heal him if she loved him." His thoughts raced and hot and cold waves traveled him. "Tomas isn't trained in medicine. There must be more doctors."

"And I'll find them. I need to talk to my sister."

"She's pretty upset. The major sent for Rick and Drew. God, it's killing me. I want to go to her and you."

"No. Stay there. I'll talk to Amy and get her to write another program, but it's going to take her a few days at least."

Has Toric spotted anyone?"

"No but he reports the holograms are completely believable. If anyone is watching, they'll believe Stasia is at your parents with Rick."

"If he went to her…"

Hawk shrugged. It won't be as realistic without a real person manipulating the environment, but your parents can interact with the projections, and I'm sure Amy could make a quick one so Rick appears to be inside, but no one is going to worry about the warriors just the rogues. And Amy has them covered. She's a brilliant programmer with an artist's eye for detail. I thought myself the images of Joy yelling at Captain Sanders were real."

"And you?'

"I'm in the woods sulking. Tank is there and making me look real. He's sensed no one except one lone hiker, and Glenn has set a team on him, but I think he really was a hiker. He hasn't been back. No one cares where I am."

"I care. And not just because we couldn't find them without you."

"It'll take me a day to be sure One and Two are sure of their tasks. I'll set them to watch Nguyen and they'll call me if he mentions either of their names."

"Call you? You'll be out of the zone.

"It's not that hard to teach a mouse to hit a button."

Hawk disconnected.

- 18 -

HORRIFIED

Joy held Stasia while she cried in a shabby hotel room in Vietnam. Major Nelson paced around the room, his face tight. "Take a sedative— that's an order. I'll go through the papers while you sleep, or at least rest."

Nelson was sitting at the small desk staring thoughtfully into space when they returned in the morning. "Rick and Drew are on the way here." He indicated a pile of papers. "I have work to do. You two take a break. I think we go to China next, but I want to think about this first."

Later that night Rick came into the room followed by Drew. Tear streaked and pale, Joy and Stasia greeted them with hugs.

Their magic collided with enough force to make the windows rattle. Rick glanced uneasily at Drew as Stasia grabbed him and began sobbing.

"Jesus, what happened?"

Unable to answer through her sobs, Stasia shook in his arms. Rick pulled Joy away from Drew and surrounded her in his magic. "Their horrified, literally sick with horror. The magic is terrified," Rick said, sounding sick himself. "What happened?" Dread laced Rick's voice.

Joy shook her head. "It's better if you don't know."

"We'll share this burden. What happened?"

"We found a doctor and he had video and pictures," Joy said slowly.

Stasia pushed away to run to the bathroom and vomit.

Drew took Joy from Rick and smoothed her hair as he pulled her close. Joy winced and licked her lips. "I can't, I'm sorry I want to forget." She turned her face into Drew's shoulder and cried quietly.

"Where is it?" Rick asked.

When she didn't answer, he searched the room. Joy hugged Stasia and both cried. Rick slammed from the room and pounded on the major's door.

"What's going on!" he snapped.

Nelson glanced at his television and Rick pushed past him.

"Excuse us, sir," Drew murmured.

Nelson snorted but didn't try to stop them.

The picture on the screen showed Sara in a brightly lit room with a glass window that looked into an adjoining room. A man grabbed her by her manacled hands and tugged her closer to the glass. When she tried to turn away, he slapped her and yanked her hard by the metal collar she wore.

The glass was tinted, obviously one-way glass. Oz lay unconscious on a table in a much smaller darker room in front of her, wearing the same bulky manacles on his neck and ankle. A Vietnamese man was in the room with him cutting open his hands while Sara yelled for them to stop. Blue clouds of magic gusted about her. The man in the room with her handed her a paper.

"We know you tried to give him a weapon built into his hand, and you've been experimenting on yourself as well. We want you to remove the weapon or we will." He spoke heavily accented but understandable English.

Sara said, "I can't remove it. It's part of his DNA now and will grow back. It doesn't work well. He isn't a danger. It isn't a weapon, it's a cure." Tears streamed down her face.

"*Ah*," the man said as if enlightened. He left the room and the screen flickered. A new man entered, and Rick realized it was a different day. Sara rose from the corner where she'd been crouched and backed as far as she could go.

"We want you to show us this heal."

"You've seen it." She rubbed her face, and the man grabbed her chin, tipping her head but he released her in moments and wiped his hands on his pants.

"There's no denying it works," the first man said, giggling as he stroked Sara's hair.

Sara cringed but let him touch her. She said, "Sometimes, but it doesn't work that well either. The passive regeneration effect works better. I really can't remove it. Please, don't hurt them," Sara begged. "If you remove it, it will release this gas." She gestured at the magic that fluttered around her. "It's dangerous and uncontainable and bonded to the new nerves. The gas will stay with them. Please, I'm telling you everything I know. I discovered it by accident and I'm not sure what it is. You know I'm telling the truth! I'll help you. I can try to give you the heal too, just please stop."

The magic surrounding her disappeared.

"Does your boyfriend have any modifications? He doesn't appear to have this heal."

"No, he doesn't even know I do." Sara started to cry. "Please, I'm begging you. I'll do whatever you want."

The man tapped the paper. "We want this!" The second man grabbed the first's arm and they argued heatedly in Vietnamese.

"What are they saying?" Rick asked.

"Arguing on whether to fulfil their contract or not."

Which is?"

Nelson said nothing

On the screen Sara said, "There's no guarantee that my child would be as smart as

I am." She wiped the tears from her cheeks and turned pleading blue eyes on her captor.

"That's why we have him. You cooperate, or he suffers."

Sara nodded. "Let me go to him, please." She glanced at the paper again, and her hands clenched. "My father gave you this?"

"No, he sold us that. We're renting you. When we're done, he gets you back."

"He gets all of us?"

The man smiled at her. "When we get what we want. First, we want you to try to heal what we did to his hands."

Sara nodded. The man pulled her into the other room. She reached a trembling hand to Oz, acted like she was trying very hard, and then casted her weakest heal.

The man leaned over Oz, staring at the blood oozing from Oz's lacerated arm. His eyes widened as the blood slowed to a trickle. "That will do. How often can you do it?"

"A few times a day." Sara fell over Oz as if she couldn't stand. "It's tiring and hard to do. Sometimes it doesn't work at all. We really aren't a threat.

"He knows more than me. He could probably tell you more if you let him wake. You can't keep him under like this or he'll get brain damage."

The first man giggled, making Rick's skin crawl.

The man pulled her off Oz and patted her cheek. He shoved her into another room and Rick gasped, his heart thudding hard even though he knew Stasia was safe in the other room.

A girl with hair her exact shade and style lay on a stretcher in a dimly lit room. Her face was to the wall and a blanket covered her chest, ending at her knees. She wore the same sort of manacles Oz had.

"Stasia," Sara moaned, and the doctor laughed that high-pitched giggle that rose the small hairs on Rick's arms.

The doctor said, "I don't think you're telling us everything. We've fixed the connector now. If you mess with your bonds again, well…" He turned to the door and said something in Vietnamese to someone off camera. A moment later a new man entered the room with the girl.

"Your friends haven't been too cooperative. We've killed this one's brother already but maybe you can save her."

The man in the room used a long pole to tap on the latch on the manacle on the girl's neck. Rick jerked back and closed his eyes from the explosion that followed. When he opened them, the doctor had turned a smiling face to Sara. Blood and bits of bone were sprinkled about the room like gruesome confetti.

Sara crouched sobbing at the doctor's feet, grasping the manacle on her neck as the doctor said something in Vietnamese.

"Stop, please! I'm—"

The doctor slapped her cheek, clearly angry that she couldn't or wouldn't heal the injury. "You're nothing." He reached into his pocket, pulled out a needle and injected her in the arm.

Nelson hit pause. "I have no idea if she knew that wasn't Stasia or not. You don't need to see the rest. Sara was clever, and they believed her. They thought removing the m-nerve removed the danger from them. They removed them and ensured their cooperation. Those men have no idea it's magic. They think it's tech she dreamed up and her genetics make her smart."

Rick pushed play.

Nelson turned away.

Grainy footage played of Sara unmoving and obviously unaware of her surroundings. She wasn't tied just placed on a metal table in a small, dank room. She still wore the thick metal manacle on her neck and leg and a simple hospital gown although it was stained now.

Water marks marred the walls. Dented metal tables held medical implements on trays and Rick wondered when the footage was taken. It was clearly a different day. The doctor wore different clothing as did Oz. Oz was tied to a similar table and dressed the same as Sara.

The doctor cut Oz's hands and arms opened again and removed pieces. Rick turned white when the man started to saw on his head. He groaned when Oz woke and the man kept sawing. Oz started screaming as the man cut into his brain and Rick closed his eyes. Sara woke as he was screaming and began screaming too. Deep gasping sobs swayed her body as she vomited. She huddled on the floor with her head buried in her arms as the man continued his gruesome work while Oz screamed and begged her for help and her magic swirled in a frenzy.

The other man entered and tried to capture a sample and swore as the magic began sparking. Sara fainted and her magic returned to her body as if she'd vacuumed it up, which made the men talk excitedly amongst themselves a moment. The man finished with Oz and picked her up.

The doctor ran his hands over her arms, his smile growing before he held a vial under her nose, and she woke coughing. The doctor laughed as he chattered, his words undecipherable to Rick. He brought her to the doorway and dropped her. They argued for a moment, then Sara casted a heal-over-time on Oz. The man patted her head and wheeled Oz from the room. "Why isn't she fighting?" Rick moaned.

The major stopped the video. "The doctor said he had Charlie and if she didn't cooperate they wouldn't let her try to heal him. If she cooperated, they'd let her heal Oz when they were done. They can kill her remotely in a second with that bomb strapped to her neck. There's nothing she can do, and she knows it. He timed it perfectly so Oz would wake and scare her to death."

Rick hit play and the major turned it off again.

"That's enough."

Rick turned his blue-eyed glare on the major and hit play again. The major threw his hands up and stalked away. On the screen, the doctor entered and strapped Sara tightly to the table. He cut her hands open while she screamed and begged. When he was done, he stood back. She tried but couldn't heal herself. He removed the manacles and watched a while, checking her vitals and hooking her to monitors.

"I think he's making sure she's healing before he continues," Nelson said softly.

The man wrapped her hands in bandages and put an IV in her arm as the other man carried the covered tray containing the ripped-out nerves away. He held it at arm's length, swaying away from the magic darting between him and Sara.

"How can he even touch her?" Rick asked.

"He's a masochist, he loves her. He touches her all the time and smiles. He's disappointed that it stops hurting him after he removes her m-nerve. See him run his hands over her and frown?" Nelson pointed to the screen where the doctor was running his hands across Sara's face and over her neck. Sara's eyes were closed as she struggled weakly against her bonds.

The doctor frowned and ran his hands up her bare legs before stepping away and turning to the tray of medical implements.

"Never let Charlie see this." Rick turned it off as the man started to cut her head open while she screamed and begged. Sweat trickled across his brow and he raced to the bathroom to vomit. Pale and shaken he returned to Stasia and Joy. Drew followed. The four of them huddled together in the magic, which sank to the floor at their feet unmoving.

- 19 -

MISDIRECTION

Two days later they traveled to China. Major Nelson sent them with a list of businesses and homes to search. They traveled the country for a month and Charlie was frantic. Hawk and Todd had found leads but they never panned out.

Stasia and Joy brought mountains of papers and recordings back to the major.

Hawk called him. "Liniar has disappeared as have Nguyen and Tachimori but I have a solid lead. I know Tachimori has taken his boat and I want Stasia to go and find out what she can, but the major won't send her. He says it's a waste of time, that they weren't involved but I think we need to check this.

They're still talking about a deal with Tomas. They must be in contact with him!"

Charlie immediately called Major Nelson. "Send Stasia—"

"Chief, I'm handling this. The leads here are better."

"What leads?"

"Nothing you need to worry about, and I don't have time to coddle you."

Nelson hung up on him, and he called Stasia, too shocked to be angry. "I'm sending Brenda to you. I want her to see the papers. Major Nelson won't answer my questions. He's being very evasive."

Stasia knew why the major wouldn't answer, they hadn't told Charlie about the recordings they'd recovered, but she agreed to sneak Brenda in.

"I hate doing this," Brenda said as Stasia snuck her into the major's room.

Stasia squeezed her shoulder. "It'll put Charlie's mind at ease, and who knows, maybe the major missed something. Some of the papers are in Chinese."

Brenda read all the papers while Stasia watched the door for the major's return. It took Brenda a day to read through them all.

Brenda said, “That was gruesome reading, I’m so glad they don’t remember it.”

“What?” Stasia rose an eyebrow as she turned to her.

“They don’t remember it. There’s an entire file about their recovery.” Brenda rummaged through the files.

Stasia took the paper Brenda handed her with shaking hands. “He didn’t tell us. Why wouldn’t he tell us that?”

“I don’t know. Maybe he thought you knew?”

“God, I’ve been sick, literally sick over this! He should’ve told us! It would’ve been a huge relief to know that. I’ve been picturing them tied and helpless, waiting for that man to come back.”

“No, they don’t know. They don’t remember anything at all. It was all in that report.” Brenda tapped the file in Stasia’s hand.

“Read it to me!”

“You could read it yourself— it’s in English.” Brenda opened the folder and held out a paper.

Stasia paced. “Brenda, he had to know.”

“Yes.”

"What does it mean?"

"I don't know," Brenda said worriedly.

"I don't remember giving him this file. If Joy gave it to him, she would've told me. Brenda— he must have another source we don't know about." The two women stared at each other in mounting horror.

Stasia quit the raid and followed the major. Rick held her wristcomp in his hand. Copies of the report were spread across the bed in their hotel room. Glints of blue shone in his eyes as he put her wristcomp on his wrist to hide her whereabouts.

For four days Stasia followed Nelson while pretending to be elsewhere. She'd almost given up when a Chinese man approached him in a coffee shop, handed him an envelope and walked away. Stasia followed the man to a small flower shop where he entered the back and made a call. The man spoke Chinese, so she recorded it. Stasia shadowed the man as he made deliveries before returning to a nearby apartment. She made a note of the address before returning to Nelson.

She followed him from a local restaurant to the hotel they were staying in. He'd brought them dinner as usual. She released her invisible and joined them.

"Any leads today?" she asked as she took a few of the takeout containers from him.

"Nothing."

Nelson told them about going to the library and the courthouse pursuing leads but made no mention of the man with the envelope.

Stasia pickpocketed the major and excused herself. In the room she shared with Rick, she opened the envelope. It contained a picture of Oz with a bandage around his head cuddled with Sara under a blanket in front of a big fire. Oz was kissing her. Sara's deeply scared hand rested on his face. A picture window behind them showed the sun either setting or rising. A small bird sat on the windowsill. The furniture in the room appeared expensive.

She flipped the picture over. *'They still believe they're happily married.'* The picture cupped in her hand, she called Rick from a disposable phone.

By the time Rick arrived moments later magic swirled around the room in agitated gusts and eddies. Rick scanned the picture and sent it through Oz's locate program. The magic began to send off sharp shocks of static.

Stasia glanced at the screen floating beside Rick, and her eyes flared brighter. "It's a tropical place. That's a Bonin petrel and it only lives in the southern hemisphere."

Rick sat on the bed with his head in his hands. "He knew. The major knows right now where they are. Oh dear god, what will we tell Charlie?"

"The truth and right away before the major figures out we know and tells them, and they move them." Stasia grabbed the picture back and put it in the envelope. "I'm going to go put this back, and then you're going to invite me to the raid. Call Lee and send her south. Joy and I will watch Major Nelson and do what he tells us too. We'll copy every piece of paper we gave him, and Charlie will go through them all. We shouldn't have trusted him again."

She tapped her wristcomp and Hawk answered. He paled as Stasia spoke.

"I can't believe this," he said when she'd finished.

"He might not be working on his own."

"I'm on my way to Iraq."

"Be careful. Liniar and Tomas don't appear to know about the magic, but the general does."

"*Ha.* No one will ever see me. And it won't be mice I send in if I find he's involved."

"Make sure first," Rick said.

"Be safe," Hawk said and ended the call.

Stasia hugged Rick. "I feel your rage. Stay here. We have to hide it until we find them, and then they can feel ours."

A moment later Stasia left the room and slipped the picture back into Nelson's pocket. She sat and picked at her food.

"Where'd Rick go?" The major glanced up from his meal.

"Our room." Stasia continued to pretend to eat. She'd never eat another thing he brought her. "I need a break from this." She pushed back from the table and left the room.

Rick greeted her with swirling magic and a hard hug. "I've called Lee and sworn her to secrecy. She's headed south. Todd is wearing her wristcomp, it's the best I could do. Major Nelson shouldn't notice unless he taps for info."

"What do we do now?" Stasia's voice was muffled in Rick's shirt. "I can't tell Charlie this."

"I call my father, and we get Charlie home."

"The major will know it's a ruse."

"Let him. We can tell him Charlie needs Dad. It wouldn't be a lie."

"Call him."

Rick called his father. "I need you to trust me and do something for me," he said without preamble. "I need Charlie to go to you in Texas right away, and he can't ask the major for permission to go. You or Mom need to pretend to be dying, a car accident or heart attack or something. Call his ship and get him sent home. Do it right now. Tell him its Project Blackout. I love you guys, and I'll be home soon to explain."

Stasia quit the raid again and snuck into the major's room that night. She snuck out his files and copied everything she took.

"If Oz were here he could probably download the contents of his wristcomp for us to see," she said bitterly to Rick.

“If Oz where here we wouldn’t have to do any of this.” Rick kissed Stasia hard on the mouth. “I love you. Be careful; he’s a snake.”

At three a.m., Stasia snuck into Joy’s room and woke her and Drew. Joy stared at the picture in her hand as her eyes filled with tears. Drew leaped from the bed and paced furiously around the room.

“Don’t let on you know. Lee needs time to find them.” Stasia pulled Drew back to the bed and pushed him down by Joy who stared blankly at the picture crumpled in her fist. “Act normally. Joy and I will follow him. Rick will meet Charlie.

“We should beat the truth out of him.” Low and angry, Drew’s voice shook. “First Rinto, now the major. I can’t believe this.” Drew took Stasia’s hand in his. “I swear to god, I had no idea.”

Stasia nodded and kissed his cheek. The magic darting between them made his sincerity clear. “Act normal. Don’t let him suspect we know. Brenda needs to be told.” She left them dumbfounded, sitting in bed holding hands.

The next day Stasia and Joy took turns following the major. Rick flew to Texas with copies of everything.

"Where's Rick," Nelson asked as he accepted the stack of papers Stasia had grabbed at random from an office workers desk.

"Sleeping. My nightmares keep him up."

She ducked her head to hide her glare. The major said nothing.

Charlie received notice that his mother was dying and she wanted him to finish her Project Blackout for her. He rose both hands to cover his eyes, which had flared blue. *Brenda had found something.* Major Nelson had been lying to him. The magic within him pushed hard, and he locked it down ruthlessly. When he dropped his hands, his eyes were their normal brown color.

Captain Williams turned from the security screen as Charlie boarded a jet. "He had everything last year, now... I feel sorry for him."

Charlie took a cab directly to the hospital where his mother winked at him. Relief made him lightheaded. He'd been sure it was a ruse, but what if it were based in truth? His father greeted him with a hug and a worried expression.

Rick called from their parent's house. "Come home. Leave Mom there. She doesn't need to know this."

Charlie and his father arrived home. Rick paced the floor beside the entryway, his boots echoing against the hardwood. He grabbed Charlie's shoulder when he entered and shook him lightly, then gave him a hug before pushing him away and resuming his short, sharp movements. "Let me start by saying I have proof they're alive and relatively uninjured at the moment."

Hope surged hard, tightening Charlie's throat enough that he wouldn't be able to speak even if he could have found the words. He nodded mutely for his brother to continue. The slight movement was slow and ungainly as if the rage he'd carried inside himself had condensed to tar, making all of his movements difficult.

Rick glanced at the file he'd placed on the small table beside the door. Charlie followed his glance and reached for the file, his eyes narrowing as Rick put his hand down on the folder and shook his head.

Charlie's magic burst form him to swirl around his brother and he knew Rick was nervous and scared beneath a raging anger.

Rick licked his lips. "Lee is looking right now. We've narrowed the area down considerably. Major Nelson knew for at least one month. I don't think he was involved in taking them, but... I've been wrong about him before. Stasia and Joy are following him around. Drew is tracking the man who contacted him. Tony and Sam are on the way there now. Toric and Gina are still looking for Sara's father."

"Hawk?"

"Is in Iraq."

John inhaled sharply.

"Mike is joining him."

John's expression grew grimmer.

Rick hugged Charlie, surprising him. "I never wanted you to know what we found, but you need to be told to understand when I show you the proof that they're alive. I don't want you to ever see the pictures. You'll take my word for this."

Tears came to Rick's eyes as he glanced at their father and he held his hands out helplessly. "I'm so sorry." Rick took a deep breath and grabbed Charlie by the shoulders. "They cut up their brains when they removed their m-nerves," he said quickly as if pulling off a bandage, hoping speed would lessen the hurt.

Charlie staggered unable to keep his balance in the suddenly spinning room.

"They don't remember anything. Not who they are, or what happened— nothing. For two weeks they were vegetative. They're regaining function with increasing speed but they don't know who they were. At this point they can walk and talk again and believe whatever they're told. The scars are healing. They're regenerating."

The room continued to whirl around Charlie. His father looked sick.

"Their brains?" Charlie said haltingly, the words felt foreign. He glanced at his father questioningly, wanting him to say he'd misunderstood, and John winced.

Rick put an arm around his shoulder and his magic surrounded them. "Charlie, they don't remember it. It's a blessing, believe me." Tears leaked down Rick's face as he glanced helplessly at John.

"Will they regain memory as they regenerate?" his father asked as he rubbed Charlie's back.

"I sincerely hope not." Rick stopped talking and shrugged. He opened his mouth, then closed it without speaking.

Like a child seeking reassurance Rick took his father's hand in his. The three men stood in the hallway unmoving a moment. Rick released his father and brother and opened a flatscreen where he displayed the photo Stasia had copied.

Charlie leaned forward and made the screen bigger. One finger traced the red lines on her hand and face without touching the picture hanging in the air. Knowledge burned like acid on his soul. He'd wanted to know what had happened for so long, but the truth was unbearable. *His beautiful Sara…*

Rick flipped the picture, showing the writing for a moment before turning off the screen. “They don’t know, Charlie. No memory remains. Not of who they were, or magic, or us, but they do have each other.”

“Their brains,” Charlie said in a soft voice full of horror. Rick hugged him. A fine tremble shook Charlie’s entire body. *Oz’s beautiful mind…* Vomit burned the back of Charlie’s throat.

“Don’t think about it. Think about getting them back.”

Charlie pushed away from his brother and the table and stumbled away in a daze. Her terror, she’d known. He ran to the bathroom and was sick.

- 20 -

PROJECT BLACKOUT

John turned horror filled eyes on Rick.

Rick closed his eyes, pressing them with the heels of his hands. "Don't ask me. I told him the truth, but not the full horror of what they did. He can never know. God help us if they ever remember.

John paled and cleared his throat. He started to speak and had to clear his throat again. "You'll find them soon?"

"Oh yes, if I have to beat it out of Major Nelson one scream at a time, we'll find them very soon." He slid the file to his father. "Don't open the sealed ones. Lock them somewhere he won't find them. Go through the rest of them."

John took the sealed pages by a corner as if they were poisonous and carried them from the room at arms-length. Minutes later he returned and started to go through the files with Rick.

Every few minutes Rick wiped his eyes. John took his hand. Rick turned to him and cried on his shoulder for a moment. "I'm sorry," Rick said gruffly as he pulled away.

John squeezed his shoulder, and they returned to searching the files.

Charlie returned to the table and sat but couldn't concentrate. Memory of her terror kept intruding.

He tapped the icon that connected him to Stasia. "Take him and force him to talk."

"We can't," Rick said.

Charlie growled, so angry words deserted him.

"I'm not protecting him. We don't know who he's working with but he's obviously in touch with the men who have them. We can't afford to tip our hands. Stasia already called Amy and she's working on a program that will show Nelson in the hotel, but she needs one day. We can give her one day."

Charlie screamed in rage. He was thwarted at every turn, always too late and too trusting— but Rick was right.

"One day," he bit out and called Hawk.

"Hawk, if you find the general's involved, do nothing. I'm handling him."

"Charles," his father said, laying a hand on his.

"If they're involved, if they did this after we trusted them, I'll kill them all. They know it too. I've never hidden my nature from them. Her father, her stepmother, they hide what they really are. If the president is lying too, he deserves what he gets!" He stomped from the room and went to his target dummy in the basement and beat it until it was small pieces crushed into the cement of the wall.

That night the major disappeared.

Stasia ransacked his room in a towering fury. Her voice shook with rage when she called Captain Sanders. "Where is he?" she screamed.

"Who, Stasia? What's happened?"

"Don't play with me, Captain. Tell me right now where Major Nelson is!"

"I thought he was with you."

"If you're lying to me, you'll be very, very sorry!"

Stasia called the general next and got the same response. Wild now, she called the president on his wristcomp. "Where is Major Nelson?"

"Stasia, Captain Sanders called and said you were looking for him and very angry. I don't know where he is—"

"Fine! No one knows! I'm coming. I won't be alone, and I won't be friendly!" Panting hard she raced from the room to ransack the home of the man who'd given Nelson the pictures while Joy searched for Nelson himself. They'd known he had spell bracelets and she cursed herself for not stealing them when she'd had the chance. He could evade her for a very long time by spell stealing Invisible.

Brenda called Stasia.

"He hired a plane. Joy's chasing."

"Use deadly force. Don't hesitate. He knows we're onto him."

The man's home, who'd given Nelson the picture, was small and Stasia searched it in moments, linking pictures of all the documents to Brenda.

"I'm on my way. We'll make him talk," Brenda said grimly.

Stasia grabbed the man as he came in the door, hitting him hard and following him down to kneel on his chest. She waved a copy of the picture in his face.

"Where did you get this?" she snarled.

He babbled a spate of indecipherable words.

"I got it," Brenda said. "I'm marking your HUD. Sam, cut the damned links already!" she said in an aside. Tie him but don't kill him. If it doesn't pan out, we can go back."

Stasia tied the man to his own bed and raced out the door.

The address he'd given was a stinking hovel, squalid and filthy. Two men half passed out in the corner yelled something to Brenda and an armed man stepped onto the stairs. Stasia laughed as he reached for his gun and appeared behind him, slitting his throat in one clean move, and letting the body tumble down the stairs. She killed the next guard just as quickly and let herself into a locked room at the top of the stairs.

Brenda followed her in and began rifling the papers as Stasia grasped the man at the desk and shook him hard before hitting him once. Knock-Out Punch left him unconscious on the floor and she threw a glance at a naked woman in the bed in the adjoining room but she slept on.

"Anything?"

Brenda clamped her lips tight. Charlie had just sent a raid wide message asking the Scouts to gather and observe Project Blackout.

"Another address. Let's go." She grabbed Stasia's hand and yanked her from the room. "Leave him. We don't have time to move him, and they'll just untie him. But maybe he'll be dumb enough to stay here if we need to question him again."

"More pictures," Stasia said triumphantly and scanned them into the locate program as Brenda flipped through the files. She withdrew a folded letter and slapped it into Stasia's hand.

"Head to Hawaii. Limited time remains to find them before they do that again."

Stasia handed it back and wiped her hands on her pants. Brenda waved the letter in the air, her face grim. "This says, *'No child yet. Keep trying for four months, then repeat procedure.'* We have less than two months remaining. If she has a baby, God knows what they'd do to it. Two months," Brenda repeated angrily. Let's do it in one. Lee is in serious danger. The major will have to kill her to stop her from finding him and them."

Voice a repressed snarl, Stasia said, "We're all in danger. Get Marcus, Todd, and Mike and tell them to come to Hawaii without the others knowing where they are."

She scanned the pictures and entered them into the locate program.

Stasia called Lee. "Go to Hawaii. Call me, not Charlie, when you find them."

Lee said, "You think the Scouts are involved?"

"I know our commander was. Until we have them back and are somewhere safe, it would be foolish to trust he wasn't acting under orders. We've been trusting fools. Stupid ones at that. Not once did we consider it would be in the United States best interest to take them when it should've been obvious. This is a modified Project Erasure. And we fell for it."

While she spoke, Stasia was texting and sending copies of everything to Rick.

Rick called the raid. "Get to California and we'll meet there. Keep a low profile. The team is on the way." Shoulders tight and scowling furiously, Rick turned to his father. "Major Nelson is in hiding."

"Our jet is in Florida. I'll get you the next flight out." His father said as he called the airline.

"Not a flight. A plane. Rent us the fastest jet you can. I hate how slow we are!" Charlie said savagely.

Rick paced the room fuming while John made tea with a generous helping of whisky in each glass and handed it to his sons.

Charlie was so angry he felt sick. Without thinking he threw his glass of tea across the room. His father said nothing. He gave him a shot of whiskey without the tea.

"Sorry." Charlie shook his head but his brain felt muddled from the clash of hope and anger. "Get the *Rheal Lucky* there and all of the magic she had stored." Charlie knocked back the glass of whiskey without tasting it.

Rick called Liz. "Hang the cost and get the *Rheal Lucky* shipped to Hawaii in one day. We need the magic it contains. The boat can't be taken apart. By land, by sea, by air, by rail, I don't care— get it there!"

"I'll do my best."

She hesitated for a moment when she hung up, then called General Campbell.

"Major," the general said angrily.

Liz winced. She'd been ignoring all phone calls not from Valor. "General, Charlie has ordered no contact. None of the raid will disobey him."

"What's going on?" the general sounded gruff and tired now.

"Major Nelson was involved with kidnapping—"

"What!" the general bellowed. "Sorry— carry on."

"The proof is inconvertible. The depth of his duplicity unknown. Valor is panicked and taking the raid with them."

"Jesus Christ, they think we ordered it?"

"I'm afraid so, sir."

"But you don't?"

"No, I believe this was Nelson's idea. If the president wanted them stopped there were easier ways available. Give them time to calm down, and they'll see that."

"Meanwhile, how do we keep the president alive? Stasia informed him she's coming for him."

Liz winced again. "Stasia is busy now. Until they retrieve Oz and Sara, everyone will be busy. You have until then to convince Charlie that the president wasn't involved.

"Right. And how do we do that?"

"Sorry, sir, I don't know. This puts me in an untenable position. If I call and report movements, I'll be perceived as a traitor. If I don't, I'll *be* a traitor."

"No." The general took a deep breath and exhaled loudly. "Call me if and when you can but stay with them and help smooth the situation. I'll cut the orders. In fact, I'll cut orders for all of them leaving them under your command. Do your best, Liz."

Yes, sir. I will, sir." Liz hung up and began making calls to get the *Rheal Lucky* moved.

Charlie gave up trying to sleep and paced for hours, circling his father's dining room table while his Valory scanned the internet for information on Hawaii. His father had hired a jet, but it wouldn't be ready for five more hours and he cursed his aura that wouldn't let him travel on a regular plane.

Anger tightened his shoulder muscles when he considered he didn't dare ask for the president's help. A military jet could get him there in hours but putting himself in their hands was foolish when he wasn't certain they weren't behind her disappearance.

His magic pressed him to attack, and he hurriedly turned his attention to the search, flicking through the mountains of data his Valory had gathered.

Most of it was useless junk but he had his Valory compile the information into maps.

A hologram formed and gained detail as his Valory built a 3D map of the islands.

Charlie said, "Run every name in the Hawaiian tax registry through Locate program. Mark every building in red that could be associated with Liniar Corp, Sinder Business Conglomerate, Tro Industries or anything owned by Tomas Mitchel or any of his known associates."

"Complying," his Valory said as red began to speckle the map.

"Mark buildings in purple that are owned personally by Tro, Liniar, Sinder or Mitchel. Remove all buildings that can't match photograph 1."

His father and brother joined him as he was examining the map. Red and purple speckled it. He needed more information to weed out the false positives.

He tapped to connect to Stasia and got an away message. He was tempted to hit the emergency override but if she was screening calls from him, she was busy.

He left a message instead. "Check his room again and search for hidden. We need more pictures."

Rick said, "She just sent me more."

Rick gave Charlie the pictures Stasia had just sent. Charlie's pulse pounded when he read the memo about repeating the procedure.

"Regeneration must be slow if they can wait two more months before they need to redo it."

Charlie barely heard him. He traced the curve of Sara's brow with a fingertip. "Thank god they have each other."

His father looked dismayed. Rick relieved.

"I have a gun and money, take both." John rose to get it.

"I won't need a gun," Charlie whispered. Unable to hold it back, he screamed his attack cry. Rick echoed him.

Rick's magic twined around Charlie, then disappeared, leaving thin wisps of his magic. He'd never felt it so agitated. It was as confused as he was, and its conflicting desires dizzied him. Charlie sat at the table with his head in his hands, not knowing what to think or do.

His father returned with the money. "I can get more and put it in your account."

"I have enough money." Charlie jumped to his feet. "Let's go wait at the airport until our damned jet is ready. Maybe we can steal one!"

His brother didn't argue. As he rose to his feet, his phone rang with a video call. Blue surged into Rick's gaze as he answered it.

"I found out they were alive and didn't remember a thing." Nelson said quickly before Rick had a chance to speak. "Rick... They were better off there, happy and safe. The world isn't ready for them yet."

"Happy— safe? Would they be happy when the procedure is repeated? When I find you, I'll find out how happy you are," Rick said in a strangled voice.

The major's eyes widened. "Repeated? No, why would they? They don't remember a thing. There'd be no need."

"They're regenerating," Rick snarled. "Does it matter why? You decided to leave them there where anything could happen to them— without us— their family. How could you do that?"

"The world isn't ready for them, Rick. I read the reports. You have them. You see what will happen!"

"When I find you, you'll see what will happen!" Rick's eyes blazed brightly.

"They're not safe! You delude yourself to salve your conscious. You're afraid of them, of her."

"You should be afraid of me." Charlie said as he stepped beside his brother to glare at Nelson. "I'll find you no matter where you hide. We'll find them too eventually."

"I'll help you find them. I should've told you, but I thought you'd be happier not knowing. They could live a life together untroubled by magic, safe and comfortable. You'd be sad, but how much sadder would you be when she comes home in love with him? I swear to you, Chief, I meant to help everyone!"

"Not one more word!" Charlie said through his clenched teeth. "I'd never put myself above her. You disgust me. I'd gladly watch them together happy every day and know she was safe and well, then not know and have her in the hands of psychopaths."

"I'm sorry—"

"You will be." Charlie ended the call. "He'll tell them we know— if he hasn't already. We have to move fast before they move them."

"He might not, he might've been sincere." Rick laid a hand on his brother's arm.

Charlie panted with rage, angry with Rick now. His magic burst from him and swirled about Rick and his father.

"I don't care if he thought he was saving the world! He left Sara in the hands of psychopaths because he was afraid of her! We act on her behalf, on Oz's behalf! Major Nelson is untrustworthy! We treat him as the enemy!"

"I'm not disagreeing; I'm just saying there's hope he won't tell them we know."

Charlie took a deep breath. "I'm sorry. Let's go, please."

Rick glanced over his shoulder at his father's drawn face, then straightened and followed Charlie.

- 21 -

RESCUE

"We're in the zone!" An exultant grin formed on Lee's face. "They're that way!" She pointed east.

Drew landed the copter and Joy jumped out as she engaged her white bracelet and casted Call-for-Help.

She clasped Drew's arm hard as she waited out the timer. "Fucking perception! We need to physically find them; they aren't in the raid anymore."

"Let's go," Drew said as he jumped back into the helicopter.

He followed Lee's pointing finger.

"Below us," Lee said in excitement.

The helicopter passed over a large house that sat on a steep cliff overlooking the ocean.

Joy called Stasia who called Rick and Hawk. "We found them," she said.

"What!" Charlie said sharply when Rick growled. "I swear to god, if you don't answer me—"

"They found them."

Charlie screamed his attack cry. His vision darkened and resumed but with odd halos and angles on familiar objects. He shook his head and gritted his teeth. His magic wanted her right now and careened wildly around the cockpit.

"No! Pain!" Charlie said emphatically, concentrating as hard as he could. The magic returned and his vision cleared, and he screamed again, this time in triumph. His soul was chanting *we'll kill them all* and the magic believed him. It burned with impatience beneath his skin, but it would wait.

"Can you summon—"

Joy cut him off with a sharp, "No! We tried. They don't remember us. The perception—"

"God fucking damn it!" Charlie took a deep breath and exhaled slowly. "Fine. We know how that works." Internally he raged at himself. It had never occurred to him that she wouldn't be able to accept a summons. They'd wasted so much time assuming their magic would work, that all they'd need to do was enter a zone and summon them. But, without memory they'd been effectively logged out. Pierce hadn't sent operatives to search locally, assuming that a summons would find them whether or not they were unconscious, and whoever had taken her had done so knowing what they were and would keep them moving overseas where the zones were smaller and blurred. But all of his assumptions were shit.

Charlie growled in annoyance.

Stasia said, "I'll beat you there. We stole a jet."

"You what?" Rick said, sounding more incredulous than angry.

"This Falcon is a sweet ride," Brenda said enthusiastically. We should get a few. Too bad we'll have to ditch her in the sea."

"Dear Lord," Rick mumbled.

"Perfect," Charlie said. "We'll ditch this too."

Hawk said, "Mike, Gina and I land in thirty-five minutes. Major Nelson has been in contact with the general but General Campbell is furious. I don't think he's involved but he knows enough to be playing me. Liz called me. She claims the general isn't involved, and I believe she believes it, but they wouldn't tell her if they were involved. I sent Mom into hiding."

Charlie's heart thumped hard. It hadn't occurred to him, and he felt like a fool. "Hold on a second." He put the call on hold while he called his father. "I need you and Mom to get somewhere safe. Trust no one except us."

Charles—"

"Just do it, Dad! I can't worry about you guys too. I need you safe!"

"Okay. We could use a vacation."

"You can't use your credit cards."

"I'm not a fool. I've planned for this. No one will find us, not even a mage. Are the wristcomps secure?"

"Yes. Only Oz or maybe Sara could hack them. If anyone else tries, we'll know it."

"Good. Then we can stay in touch. Your takeoff made the news. Before we go, I'll call and see what I can do about that."

Charlie had barely noticed the people who'd run at his approach at the airport and hadn't given it a thought.

"Who cares? Just go. I'll worry about it later."

"You're burning your bridges, son."

Major Nelson already burned them. What they did to her…" Just thinking of it sent his magic roiling about the plane and knotted his gut.

"He might've acted alone. I can't believe President Carmichael would do such a heinous thing."

"We'll find out when we get them back."

"You've found them?"

"Joy is with them now." His gaze was glued to the video Joy was sending.

"Sara," he breathed, overcome with relief as Joy crept into a bedroom. He widened his screen and leaned closer.

Sara led Oz to the bed and lifted his legs to make him comfortable. Her smile was sweet and slightly crooked as she covered him with a light blanket.

"She's partially paralyzed," Joy whispered. His speech is much more slurred than hers and he doesn't move well. I'd get closer but my magic..."

"No! Take no chances. Wait for backup if you can. Guards?"

"Two outside the patio door and four in the hallway."

"Did you check for explosives?" Stasia asked.

"No traps or explosives. Lots of hits on find hidden but nothing in this room. It'll take two of us to get them out though. I can't carry both.

"How many summons do we have?"

"My spell bracelet is full," Lee said. "Liz gave me a full rod and I still have most of it. I can do about thirty channeled spells but that's just an estimate."

"I have about four spells," Drew said.

"I have about four too," Marcus said.

Charlie said, "Lee has enough to summon us. Joy, stay with them. Don't leave them for a second. Keep your line open."

"They're getting ready to go out," she whispered. "Some kind of dress event."

"Out?"

Charlie examined Oz's attire and frowned. He'd been so caught up watching Sara brush her hair that he hadn't notice Oz wore a tuxedo. Sara applied makeup. The harsh lighting of her dressing room table wasn't kind to the scars on her hands and face, but they didn't seem to bother her. She spent no time trying to cover them. *Or maybe they do bother her*, he thought as she rubbed her arms and wiggled her fingers as though they hurt. She rose and limped to the closet. Her left side was slower than her right, her foot, hand, and the left corner of her mouth weren't responding as quickly, making her awkward as she dressed. She donned a blue silk dress that left her shoulders bare and revealed more cleavage than she would normally show. She tugged at the bodice but finally gave up and pulled a sweater from a drawer before returning to sit beside Oz.

Sunlight streamed through the open window beside the bed, slanting across her face and she closed her eyes, turning her face into the sun.

"Their bags are packed," Joy whispered, and another screen flickered to life in front of Charlie. "The house is busy beneath me. I think they're leaving soon."

"Stay with them," he repeated. "Lee, try to summon Stasia every six minutes. Brenda, as soon as you arrive, try to summon Hawk."

"I think we need a good thirty minutes," Rick said.

"I know."

"Marcus and I could get in the house to get them out," Lee said.

"I'm tempted. Let me call Liz and see what sedatives she recommends."

"It's going to scare them no matter what we do," Joy said sadly.

"I'm more worried about the m-nerves regenerating. It's clear they have no magic. If they did it would be swooping around Joy whether they wished it to or not. So it's going to hurt like a bitch when we heal them. We need to be ready. Marcus, hang back. Lee, can you recharge his bracelet with the rod?"

"Yes."

"Great, give it to Drew and he can get close enough to summon both you and Marcus. I don't want either of you to let your magic loose," he said as commandingly as he could. “Wait for me if you can but don’t let them get away.

Charlie disconnected and flicked the icon that put him raid wide. “Most of you have heard about Major Nelson’s betrayal. If you were involved, you’re only hope for mercy is to come forward right now. If we find out later, I won’t be merciful or quick.”

“Charlie,” Rick said softly.

Charlie ignored him.

“I know none of you signed on for this. If you feel you owe a duty—”

“Fuck that,” Manny said harshly. “If they’ve turned on Sara and Oz, they’ve turned on all of us.”

Mutters of angry agreement clogged the line a moment.

“If the major was ordered to act as he has, I plan to declare war on the United States.”

Liz gasped. “Charlie, you can’t! Don’t even think it. Your rep—”

“I can, and I will. But I’ll wait for proof. Honestly, Liz, I don’t care about them. I care about Sara and Oz and it scares to me death to think we might be hours too late.”

He debated saying he’d found them, but the risk was too great. It was better if the

Scouts didn't know. "I know we can find them if given time, but the major knows that too. He'll warn them to burn the bodies to ash."

Saying it made him shudder. He was so close, but he'd been close before and had let her slip through his fingers.

"Liz, what I need from you is information. I need to sedate them, keep them under while their m-nerves regenerate. When we find them, our magic will want them and it will hurt."

"Jesus," Hawk whispered as Stasia made a soft sound of distress.

"Keep your magic contained," Charlie barked, using his Voice of Command spell.

Liz said, "I have sedatives on me configured for their chemistry."

Charlie glanced at his HUD. Liz was in California, even on a jet it would take her hours to reach them.

"What can Joy get a pharmacy?"

"I'll text her the best choices." Hope filled Liz's voice, and Charlie knew she thought he was closer than he was saying. He hesitated then in sudden decision cut the feed to everyone except her.

"We found them, Liz."

"Oh, thank god. How bad—"

"Bad. They need extensive healing. I need all the rods we have. Get a jet and come to us in Hawaii as fast as you can."

Liz was already examining a display hanging in the air before her. "I can get the *Rheal Lucky* to Maalaea harbor in three hours, rerouting from Pearl Harbor. That's as close as I can get. "I already have every canister of magic from the lab with me."

She lifted troubled eyes to Charlie. "Captain Sanders arranged the transport to Hawaii. He's truly horrified about Major Nelson's actions."

"We're done with them!" Low and full of hate, Charlie spit the words. "Don't tell anyone we're so close!"

"You have my word," Liz said.

"Bring the Scouts to Hawaii but keep an eye on them."

Charlie tapped the icon connecting him to Joy's channel.

"Lee?"

"Three minutes and I'll try to summon Stasia again."

"Stasia, if you can't control the magic, don't go near them, that's an order! Marcus, head back to town and find us a pharmacy or hospital that has what we need. As soon as Stasia is on the island summon her to you and steal what we need. Hawk, how close are you?"

"Forty minutes out."

We're too damned slow!"

"We're going as fast as we can," Rick said, and Charlie growled.

Every fiber in his body wanted to be with her with a need so fierce it hurt but his magic stayed beneath his skin. Rick's magic gusted about the cockpit in agitation, stinging when it touched Charlie and making the humming beneath his skin louder.

"Sorry," Rick mumbled.

"Don't be. I love your anger. Be angry."

"Chief," Joy said worriedly. "A man in the hall is talking about going."

Charlie tore his gaze from the screen displaying Sara sleeping in the chair and focused on Joy's screen. She was facing the opposite way, peering through the bedroom door at two men. Both wore black suits and headsets and carried assault rifles. Charlie's trained eye picked out the holstered guns and knives, automatically categorizing each threat while his soul rejoiced to have a face for the Enemy.

"— idiotic but we get paid." The bigger of the two men said.

"You couldn't pay me to fuck the shamblers. They give me the willies," Shorty said.

"Just get them to the boat. Mitchel's guests will be arriving, and he wants her on display."

"We've done some shit but this guy—"

"Right? I could understand wanting a grandchild. I mean, she *was* a fucking genus, but selling her like a prized mare? We never should've taken this gig. A man who'd do that ain't going to pay his damned bills."

"When do we leave?"

"Not until tomorrow, or hell, they might need a night to recover. They've got some choice blow, enough they won't miss some." Shorty glanced down the hall at the guard facing away from them and leaned closer. "Perkins is on guard duty at the dock. We could score a real haul if we're quick."

"Let them get going real good first and they won't even notice it missing." Tall man slapped Shorty on the shoulder and sauntered down the hall where he stopped to speak to the guard at the head of the stairs.

Joy whispered, "Should I let them move her?"

"How many are in the house?"

Drew said, "I've counted fourteen servants and seven children. They're having some kind of children's party on the back lawn. None of our main targets are in attendance. It looks like the hired help. Chief, these are innocent bystanders. The kitchen is worried about her picking at her food. They like her and she likes them."

"How—"

"I stole Joy's invisible. They won't see me. But those women have no idea who she really is. Look."

A screen popped up in front of Charlie and he frowned at the woman slicing the fresh fruit.

"— he prefers the melon, Nan. That doctor of theirs has no bedside manner but he sure is getting results. Zach seems better every day. See that Ioki packs those beach towels. I never saw such a pair for sunbathing."

"Shall I bring the cake out?" the girl the woman spoke to asked.

"Yes and refill the punch bowl."

Charlie flicked the screen and it dwindled to a black speck.

"Let them move them to the ship."

"I'll get us a boat of our own," Marcus said.

Charlie tapped the display to see where Marcus was. He was running down a dirt road and once again Charlie lamented their lack of fast transport.

"Can you get a car?"

"None have passed me yet but there's a house up ahead."

"Don't kill them," Drew said.

Marcus made a dismissive sound.

"Don't kill them!" Charlie ordered, using his Voice of Command, which was the best he could do. He didn't think Marcus would kill people who weren't involved but he wasn't certain how the magic would influence him. He should probably order him to wait at the copter. It was a risk to let an angry Warrior run around the countryside where he might run into someone who the magic perceived as getting in the way of the mission, but they needed those drugs.

"Kill no one," he said again as forcefully as he could.

"Yes, sir." Marcus saluted but didn't stop running.

Charlie wished he could run too. He wished he could do anything. Waiting was intolerable but it was all he had.

"Joy, stay with them—"

"I've got it," Stasia said, and Lee whooped.

"Ditching the jet," Brenda said and despite himself Charlie grinned at her disappointed tone.

"Marcus, summon Brenda too. She can help Stasia while you get the boat. Get one big enough for all of us, legally if you can but do what you have too. I want us ready to go in one hour."

One hour, his soul rejoiced. *Soon, very soon,* he promised the magic.

"Drew, see if you can get on board their ship and place the sensors, but be careful. Don't give us away!"

"Yes, sir."

Charlie muted his end and stretched, shaking out his hands before rising to grab his duffle bag. It only contained two swords and a shield. It was all he needed.

- 22 -

MY SARA

Charlie crept along the top rail of a four-story yacht and observed the crowd below him.

Only one guard manned this topmost level, and he was paying no attention. He sat in a lounge chair on the opposite side of the ship, smoking and admiring the stars.

“Target one in sight,” he said, and his pulse leaped. His magic rushed from him so fast it hurt and made his ears pop, but he recalled it quickly, holding it back in an iron grip. Men and women spoke and danced on the lower deck below him, and all eyed his wife with avarice. The enemy his soul screamed but he couldn't tear his gaze from Sara to memorize their faces.

Just the sight of her was enough to fill the hollow places inside himself with light. It was enough to begin breaking up the tar-like feel encasing his limbs. His magic hummed against his skin and he imagined it too was working to free him from the sensation of being mired. Thoughts of the coming fight made his breath come fast. *Passion*, he supposed. His hatred heated him the same way. He passionately wanted to kill those responsible. Muscles in his arms flexed, the feeling smooth and freeing. The sight of her had given him back his soul, freed him to be what he was— a warrior— and he hadn't even spoken to her yet.

His pulse jumped as he imagined the feel of her warm skin under his hand. He hadn't let himself think of it, not even when he knew she was alive, and he didn't really want to think of it now, but he couldn't stop himself from staring, memorizing the curves of her. The brightness of her hair, the blue of her eyes, all called to him. But it shifted the heat that was filling him, redirecting his passion.

He closed his eyes and forced himself to count to ten. The magic was as conflicted as he was. It wanted to touch her as much as it wanted to kill their enemies too.

Soon, he thought and the hum beneath his skin increased.

Anticipation. He burned with it. The familiar feel of honey coated him. He was ready.

He opened his eyes as a man approached her and handed her a glass of wine. She smiled but seemed uncomfortable, peering over her shoulder with an anxious expression. A real smile crossed her face when she spotted Oz. She left the man and hurried as fast as her limp allowed to Oz, linking her arm in his. Oz kissed her, placing his hand over hers.

Charlie's pulse leaped again. "Target two spotted."

Oz and Sara danced slowly, smiling into each other's eyes. The music was low. Charlie could hardly hear it. He glanced at his HUD.

Five minutes remained on the countdown.

Arm-and-arm Sara and Oz walked slowly to the bow of the ship away from the rest of the guests. Charlie followed on the top deck, keeping them in sight. They talked for a moment before Oz left her side, limping heavily, leaving her alone on the bow. "Target two retreating" he said softly and jumped down to the lower deck.

Sara started in surprise when he cleared his throat.

"Oh, good evening. You startled me." Her voice was heavily slurred but understandable. Her scarred hand clutched her throat where her pulse jumped. She eyed him uneasily, and he didn't blame her. It was odd to be wearing sunglasses at night, and he wasn't dressed at all like the other guards. He'd left his sword and shield in the boat but wore his combat clothes except for his facemask.

Charlie gritted his teeth and forced the magic back, forcing his gaze from the red scars on her face and hands, forcing himself not to touch her. She had no idea who he was.

"Did you see my husband?" Sara peered over Charlie's shoulder, biting her lower lip. "I thought you were him returning."

Charlie stepped forward and her eyes widened and she took a step back.

"I did," he murmured huskily. "I'm sorry, we haven't been introduced, Charles Hayes." He stared at her intently, but she showed no sign of recognition.

"Beth Blake," Sara said. "You must be a friend of my husband's or maybe my father's?"

"Yes," Charlie agreed without specifying which he was friends with.

"Zach should be back soon." Sara backed further away, opening the small purse she clutched under one arm and taking out a bottle that she fumbled and dropped.

Charlie picked it up, reading the label. She was taking pain medication and it made his pulse pound again. He dropped a pill into her hand without touching her.

"Thank you," she said and took the pill, placing a light hand on her stomach and closing her eyes a moment. When she opened them, she blushed and glanced away.

"We have target two," Joy said.

Charlie grinned.

Sara smiled back.

"Have you been married long?" Charlie asked.

The blushed deepened and her hand rose to her stomach again. An awful suspicion took hold of him. If she was pregnant, he couldn't take her this way, the stress could cause a miscarriage. She'd never forgive him if she lost a baby. They'd need a new plan to hold them both until she safely delivered.

"Not long, no." She turned away, placing both hands on the rail.

"Are you expecting?" he asked bluntly, and Joy gasped.

Sara blushed so hotly he imagined he could feel the heat of it. Her head lowered and she didn't answer.

"I only ask because of the medication. If you're seasick, I can get you something that won't hurt you."

Sara turned back, a shy smile on her face. "We aren't expecting yet. We want to be. My father..." She trailed off, appearing to remember she was speaking with a stranger and shrugged. "The pills are for my hands. Sometimes they hurt."

"I can imagine." Charlie glared at the scars on her hands, dizzy with relief. She wasn't expecting Oz's child. He could safely remove her from here tonight.

She blushed again. "We were in an accident; I don't remember it at all. I don't remember anything really, just Zachary. I remember loving him. Our hands and faces were cut up very badly by the windshield. My father has us seeing specialists and a doctor travels with us. The pain isn't bad, they just tingle at times."

"When was this?"

She turned toward him again and took a step closer.

"Have we met before? Your voice is familiar." She glanced at his hands and blushed.

Does she have a memory of me somewhere, locked in her head?

Sara took another step closer. He smiled at her and the pulse in her neck pounded. It was all he could do to resist placing his hand on it.

She set the glass of wine on the railing and wiped her palms on her skirt.

"Sara..."

She began to sweat as her pupils dilated. One hand rose and reached to him.

"My name is Beth," she said faintly.

"You are my Sara," he said and touched her hand. A sigh he barely heard came from her lips as she fainted at his feet. He scooped her up as his magic surrounded her and he jumped over the side of the ship, landing in a small rowboat beside Hawk and breaking the No-See-Um the boat was hidden under but no one on board the yacht appeared to notice.

"Target one acquired!" Fierce exultation filled his voice.

"You bastards!" Oz struggled in Marcus's grip "Don't hurt her! My father-in-law will give you whatever you want. I'll do anything! Please, I'm begging you! Let Beth go!"

"Calm down. We won't hurt either of you!" Charlie hugged Oz to him. "We won't hurt you," he repeated softly and let Oz take Sara from him.

Oz hunched away from him, clutching Sara awkwardly to his chest, his tear-filled eyes glaring at his captors.

"Hawk," Charlie said, and Oz batted at Hawk as he reached forward with the syringe.

Oz screamed a breathless sound as his grip on Sara relaxed and he tumbled to the side.

Marcus grabbed him, turning his glowing blue eyes to Charlie.

"Her too," Charlie said, and he hugged Sara tightly as Hawk injected her. His magic was ecstatic, and he wanted nothing more than to hold her and feel her breath.

"Chief," Marcus said and nudged his arm.

Charlie wiped his teary eyes, he hadn't even realized he'd begun to cry, and Spell-Stole her heal. The red line crossing her brow grew lighter.

"They need more than we have," Marcus said angrily. The heal he casted had no noticeable result.

"We knew they would," Hawk said reassuringly as he wrapped Oz in a blanket.

"We're in position," Stasia said impatiently, and Charlie was overcome with a fierce desire to fight.

"Marcus, get them to Todd. Hawk, you're with me." He placed Sara at Marcus's feet, summoned his sword into his hand, and leaped for the rail, screaming his attack cry. Rick, Mike, and Marcus echoed him, and Charlie laughed as he casted Waylay and stabbed the startled guard at the rail. He let the body fall and leapt again, straight up to the rail above him, pulling himself over as the guard on this deck fired.

Men and woman screamed, and a burst of gunfire rent the air from the other side of the ship.

Charlie ran forward and ripped the guard's arm off, throwing it and the gun over the side as he hacked off the guard's head. A flaming arrow streaked by his face and the resultant explosion blew out the wide windows and sent small pieces of shrapnel among the gathered men and women who screamed, pushing and shoving each other and trampling their dead and injured in their haste to escape.

Charlie crashed through the remains of the glass and swung as a flurry of arrows cut into the screaming crowd. Another smaller explosion started a fire at the podium and smoke mixed with the magic, obscuring the life-sized portraits of his naked wife and Oz.

He yanked a framed copy of Sara's dissertation off the wall and beat the man who cowered beneath it to death with it. The woman beside him whimpered and held up her hands.

"Please—"

He ripped out her neck. Blood doused him in a warm torrent. He leaped to the next screaming woman.

The magic hated these people. They were the Enemy and Charlie agreed. He had no mercy as he hacked his way through the crowd.

"Stasia?"

"I've got him," she said, and Charlie screamed his attack again, leaving the corpses to the growing fire and jumping back to the second deck.

"Liniar is dead and so is the butcher," Joy said angrily. "They were killed by the guards."

"He should've suffered!" Stasia snarled.

"Liz, how are their vitals?" Charlie wiped his bloody face on his sleeve as he ran to Stasia's position.

"All good but I'll feel better when I'm with them."

"Ha! I won't feel better until Tomas's severed head is at my feet!"

"Charlie, he's her father…" If she doesn't remember, and you kill him, what then? If she does remember— oh god, if you have any mercy make her forget the last months," Liz prayed suddenly. "If she does remember, she can decide for herself."

"That's cruel, crueler than my deciding it. She'd never choose that, except in the heat of anger. You propose I let her kill him and then live with the guilt? God, Liz!" He held up his hand, halting the restless movements of the magic wielders who crouched beside the door to a stateroom. Glowing blue eyes followed his movements as he paced around them with quick, short strides.

Liz said, "You can't kill her father."

"Watch me!" he snarled as he kicked in the door to Tomas's stateroom.

Tomas fired, the bullets lodging in Charlie's chest plate but doing no damage. He didn't even feel them. Tomas retreated, still firing as Charlie stalked forward.

Stasia glided past him. Her expression was fierce and she clutched a bloody dagger in each hand.

Charlie let her take position without comment. She was letting him choose the manner of Tomas's death.

The gun clicked empty, and Tomas dropped it, backing from Charlie until his back hit the wall, watching with wide eyes as

Charlie strode to the computer consoles on the desk.

"See this, Liz? This is what Sara is worth to her father!" Bids filled the screen, a blind auction, Sara and Oz's worth broken down into categories, eggs, semen, and time shares. He smashed the monitors to pieces.

"Sara—"

"Might have mercy, but I have none. And is it fair to ask her? To make her decide?"

Rick entered followed by Brenda who yanked Rick back with Protective Companion and grasped his arm hard.

Stasia left Tomas and ran to Rick, becoming visible.

Tomas goggled at her with a mixture of dread and greed.

"It's all clear, Chief," Joy said. But he'd known it already. He felt the magic's satisfaction and the ship was perfectly silent now.

"I do love Sara," Tomas said but he sputtered to a halt as Charlie jumped forward. The two men stared at each other a moment.

Tomas said, "I handled it badly. I know that now. It was cruel and didn't need to be, but I didn't know it until too late. We can work together. Let me have my Meredith back and I'll give you—"

A sharp report of gunfire and Tomas's surprised face coincided with Charlie's scream as he lunged forward.

Charlie screamed again, this in time in rage as his sword connected to Tomas's already dead body.

He hacked the corpse to pieces, and still panting in rage, turned to his brother.

Rick dropped the smoking gun as he said, "I did it for you. His blood can't be on your hands."

Charlie gazed down at his bloody hands and shrieked. He wanted to kill him. He needed to kill him.

Joy leapt forward and hugged him.

"Let it go. It's over. He's dead." She continued talking but he couldn't hear her over the blood pounding in his head. The room wavered, growing darker and brighter, making him dizzy with the changes. He staggered, taking Joy to the floor with him. Hawk grabbed his arm and pulled him up.

"They're all dead," Hawk said in satisfaction. "Every damned one of the sick bastards."

Charlie let Hawk pull him from the room.

"Burn it, Lee."

Manny said, "Pulling the plug."

A series of rippling explosions sounded from beneath them and Hawk tugged him faster.

They leapt off the rail, floating to the water and hovering inches above it from Brenda's Ascension spell. Lee began to cast. Glowing balls of fire raced from her fingertips, blowing through the ship with satisfying crashes.

"We have incoming," Gina warned.

"Keep casting," Charlie said, and Hawk began shooting. Flame flickered off the water and black smoke rose in thick plumes as the boat sank. Lights in the distance grew closer.

"Chief?" Gina asked worriedly.

"We should go," Joy whispered and took his arm, pulling him easily while ascended. He willed Ascension off and sank into the water, stealing Hawk's air bubble and propelling himself downward to hack at the sinking boat.

The water slowed Lee's fireballs but didn't dampen the strength of the impacts.

"Let him," Stasia said and grasped a rough edge and yanked.

Mike charged, leaving a wake of small bubbles from the strength of the spell's propulsion, and he yelled his attack while he punched and kicked at the boat.

Charlie lost track of time as he hit the boat, spending his rage on the useless destruction. He knew it was a waste of time and could lead to discovery but was unable to stop. He needed the boat broken, shattered beyond repair or recognition.

"Charlie," Liz said, and he jerked in surprise to find her beside him. She hugged him quickly. Manny swam beside him and handed him a detonator.

The resultant explosion blew him ten feet backward, tumbling him through the water. He wished he could do it again and stayed to watch the pieces drift to the ocean floor.

Brilliant yellow light encased Sara and Oz who lay on the deck of the *Rheal Lucky,*

which had just arrived. Both were still sedated and unaware.

The scars marring their faces and hands faded within seconds, but the Scouts kept casting until the lightning appeared.

Charlie hunkered beside them, his gaze intent as the lightning lingered.

"It's working," Liz said unnecessarily.

The lightning surrounding Sara and Oz dissipated five minutes later. Charlie smoothed her hair and kissed her cheek before picking her up. He placed her in their bed and backed away to check on Oz and let Liz examine her.

Marcus had placed Oz in the rear cabin and sat at the foot of his bed with the remainder of the magic rods at his feet. Brenda and Lee glanced to the door but continued to settle Oz, covering him with a light blanket and combing out his damp hair.

"There's enough in the ship. Use all you need," Charlie said.

Brenda gestured to the bandage Lee had wrapped around his forearm. "Their healed, Chief. It hasn't absorbed.

"Keep checking and use Soothe on Marcus, then you, then Lee, and then Oz for the next few hours."

"Yes, sir," Brenda said as Marcus said, "I will."

Charlie nodded acknowledgment. Soothe would help but his warriors needed to release their rage.

"We'll go spar in a bit," he promised.

Marcus nodded as Charlie clasped Oz's hand a moment, feeling the pulse in his wrist.

On the next Spell-Steal cooldown he stole Soothe from Brenda and cast it on himself.

Rage still surged through him. He wanted to hit something, to hit until his fists were bloody, to stomp on his enemies' dead bodies and hear their bones break. He wanted them to suffer, to scream in agony and fear, to beg for help, for pity, for mercy, for death. He shook with rage. Finally, he went to the rail and screamed his berserk cry.

A far-off echo of the raid screamed it back. The raid circled them, keeping watch, making sure they were safe.

But there was no safety anywhere for them. All their security and precautions had been gotten through like smoke because Sara had trusted. *God, please don't let her remember*, he begged as he fell to his knees. She wouldn't be able to bear that Oz had suffered because she'd let her father into her office and left him unattended.

"Please God, don't let her remember that." Charlie knelt on the deck of his boat begging God aloud. "Please, God, don't let Oz remember a thing of his captivity, not one thing, please."

He screamed his battle cry again. From across the water the raid echoed him. Mike, Marcus, and Rick echoed him from below deck. Charlie clenched his hands into fists to stop them from trembling and went to check on his warriors.

- 23 -

THE GIFT OF FORGETFULNESS

"Well?" he asked anxiously three days later as he pushed into his cabin.

Sara still slept peaceful. No sign of the biopsy Liz had just preformed remained. Even her hair had been freshly washed. She wore one of his t-shirts and he could almost fool himself into believing everything would be okay now.

"It looks good, Charlie. Regeneration is almost complete. I have no idea if their memories will return or not…" Liz trailed off and took his hand.

"When?"

"One more night. Let them wake in the morning."

"What will I say to her?"

"Truth is always best."

He released Liz's hand to sit beside Sara and stroke her bright hair. Not one scar remained. She was as perfect as Joy.

"Joy doesn't remember her death," he said thoughtfully.

"They were never dead. The injuries— the circumstance aren't the same."

"No, I meant, the magic can make you forget." He waved his hand through the blue cloud that still covered Sara. "The magic can make us perceive things that aren't there and hide things that are."

"I agree magic *could* make someone forget, but we have no way to ask it."

"It understands pain and it hates it."

"I don't like the sound of that..."

Charlie flashed her what he intended to be a reassuring smile.

She sighed hard and sat beside him to take his hand again.

He said, "The magic is perfectly happy now. It doesn't even mind our worry; it wants us to worry over her." A gust of magic billowed past Charlie to settle atop of Sara.

Small flecks broke off, darting for the door but they became too insubstantial for him to see within seconds.

Magic wound through the lower deck of the *Rheal Lucky*, lingering on all the casters before returning to Oz and Sara.

“I can’t imagine... It won’t understand…” She cleared her throat and started again. “Even if you could forget her, would you truly want to lose those memories?”

Charlie smiled crookedly. “That isn’t what I meant either. But, no, I’d never willingly give up one second of my time with her.” He leaned down to kiss Sara’s brow. “She isn’t strong enough.” He shook his head. “No, not strong, she’s plenty strong. Not callous enough…” he shook his head again, unable to articulate what he meant. “Her mental pain will terrify the magic. I’m going to ask it to make her forget and not just for my sake, for its.”

“You could destroy all of her memories completely.

“I know.

“It might not work, or it might but not as you intend. She could forget her time with you and remember the time with him.”

"I know, Liz!" he snapped and took a deep trembling breath. "I can't say I'm okay with that but it's better than her remembering the fear of captivity.

"You'll remember…"

"It makes me furious. Not a mental pain that the magic minds," he said wryly.

Liz winced.

"Gather the others and have Marcus bring Oz. It's going to be a long day."

Charlie sat cross-legged on the deck, lifting his face to the sun and called his magic out, trying to teach it to erase a memory.

"Forget," he whispered and imagined Sara waking and crying. He remembered the pain she'd felt when kissing Mike in their magic and imposed Oz's face on him.

"Pain," he chanted while remembering her terror and the magic agreed it was pain. "Joy, think of the gunshot that killed you and the fading into the dark and your happiness to awake to Drew.

He rose to crouch before Brenda and take her hands.

"I know the lightning hurts and I'm sorry to ask this…"

"I'll do anything I can. I love them too."

"I know you do," he whispered and hugged her tightly.

She was as sickened and worried as he.

"Stasia?"

"I'm trying," she said absently.

She sat on the deck with her eyes closed, focusing on changing what her See the Future spell showed her.

Charlie left her to commune with her magic.

"It won't work," Rick whispered.

"I'm not trying to change the past or the future, just communicate. Rogues see clear visions. And it has to be the magic showing them so it must see them too."

"That's a big leap," Rick said.

"It's all I've got."

Rick shook his head. "No. You've got her back and she's safe. It will be hard, but she *is* safe and that's what counts.

"I can't let her remember how terrified she was."

Rick paled and waved him away, going to Stasia, saying over his shoulder, "You're right. They should never remember. Stasia, picture casting the spell and what we want her to forget fading to black."

Stasia shuddered and opened her eyes, ducking her head from Charlie's gaze, half turning away, her dark hair falling forward to hide her expression. But he knew it mirrored his own. The horror of it left his stomach twisting and a cold sweat on his brow.

Rick continued, "Let it feel how much you don't want to see it." His voice broke and he cleared his throat. "I want to unsee it too," he whispered and kissed Stasia's brow.

"See what?' Charlie asked.

"I'll never tell you," Rick said so firmly that Charlie believed him, but he knew. She'd known what they'd do to her. He scrambled to the side where he vomited until dry heaves wracked him.

Joy moaned softly and the magic around her pulsed.

"Forget," she whispered, begging the universe.

Charlie collapsed to cry, huddled against the rail, then angrily wiped the tears from his face and crawled to Joy. His magic hummed beneath his skin. It was trying to understand, and his self-pity wasn't helping.

The hum grew and faded as the magic twined about them.

"I think it's learning," Stasia said hopefully as she jumped to her feet to pace. "That's twice now it saw what I wanted instead of showing me the *Rheal Lucky*. She glanced at her HUD. Three minutes and I'll try again. Joy, you try too. Give us all the magic."

Brenda laid her hand against the metal mast pole and the cloud around her grew deeper. She strode into the swirling cloud to place her hands on the rail and the cloud doubled in size. She walked the ship, stopping to touch the metal fittings, drawing out the magic that Sara had placed there in her fight for dominance.

Sparks grew and bloomed into skeins of lightning that flickered between them with painful zaps. The whirling magic gained speed until a vortex strong enough to lift their hair encircled them and the lightning manifested, slamming into Sara then leaping to Brenda.

Stasia grasped Brenda's hand, "Now, Joy!"

The two rogues cast See-the-Future. The lightning flared brighter.

"Forget!" Charlie pleaded as he fell to his knees beside Sara. He cried out, giddy with excitement as the lightning leapt to Oz.

"Forget," they chanted and lifted their clasped hands to the sky.

"Everyone, picture them slumping in that park and waking here!" Charlie yelled, imagining it as hard as he could.

Heat radiated from the lightning and the pulsing picked up in speed. It dissipated with a blinding flash and soundless explosion that knocked them over.

Charlie rose on his hands and knees to examine Sara and Oz, then sat shakily to cradle his throbbing head.

"Thank you," he said sincerely.

"Let's make them more comfortable," Hawk said and went below to get an air mattress.

Liz and Gina brought them food that no one ate. The sun had set, and the stars lit the deck with a silvery glow. The sun would return in a few more hours and Sara and Oz would wake. The Scouts remained on deck.

No one wants to leave them or maybe my joy in their company is keeping them with me, he thought ruefully.

Stasia dozed in Rick's arms, and Lee slept with her head in Marcus's lap. Charlie wasn't sure if Brenda slept or not. She hadn't moved in a few hours, but he knew Mike was awake. The warriors anger felt like sunshine on his face, and he peered over his shoulder to see if Hawk and Todd had managed to get any sleep.

Both rangers reclined on chaise lounges behind Sara and Oz. Liz had brought potted ferns and palms with her and they now encircled them.

Tank picked his head up. His blue eyes glowed slightly as he scanned the deck before lowering his head to his paws again. Charlie rose to ruffle his ears.

"He's happy," Hawk whispered. "He senses the tension, but he isn't alarmed. He missed them." Hawk's voice broke and he stopped talking to wipe his eyes.

"Oz—"

Oz stirred and Hawk jumped to his feet to lean over him.

Footsteps sounded on the stairs and Liz poked her head from the hatch. "He's waking. My monitor just beeped. Keep nice and calm and remember we might be scary to them. Give them a few minutes before throwing the truth at them."

"Our truth," Charlie said gruffly.

Liz nodded and squatted to lay her hand on Oz's cheek.

Oz moaned softly and rolled to his side. He pushed himself up, shaking his head and lifting a hand to push his hair back.

"Jesus, what the hell… Sara," he gasped and reached for her.

Charlie inhaled sharply, and Oz swung his gaze to him.

"What happened? I feel like shit. Is Sara okay?"

"You know who I am?" Hope made the words tremble, and Oz cocked an eyebrow.

"Are you okay? You don't look so good, Chief." He reached to his wrist and frowned.

Stasia laughed and slapped her hands to her mouth.

"What the hell is wrong with you guys and where's my—" Oz's eyes narrowed and he glared down at Sara. "Goddamned Tomas. We were in the park. That man he met..." Oz's brow furrowed, and Charlie held his breath. He could feel the sudden tension in the air as Oz pondered.

"They drugged us?"

"Yes."

"And took us?"

"Yes, but we got you back." The satisfaction he felt from saying that built and he triumphantly screamed his attack cry, shocking all of them and himself. Magic billowed about them in a sudden storm, bring their feelings of joyous relief with it.

"Get a grip," Oz said, and Charlie burst into tears.

He hugged Oz tightly while Oz awkwardly patted his back.

"You're freaking me out, here," Oz whispered.

"I know. I'm so sorry." And he was sorry, but he couldn't make himself release him.

Stasia sobbed once and hugged him too. Hawk was already patting his back Charlie realized, and he laughed through his tears.

"Took a while to find us, *huh*?" Oz said and he pushed Charlie away to hug Stasia and clasp Hawk's hand. "Thanks." He frowned and released Stasia to lean over Sara. "How long?"

The murmurs behind them died and Charlie sat back on his heels.

"How long?" Oz asked insistently.

"She'll wake soon," Liz murmured.

"How long, Liz?" Oz asked.

"Ninety-eight days, sixteen hours and twelve minutes," Hawk said.

Oz turned to him as Liz said, "No, leave her alone, Charlie. You'll scare her to death if she doesn't know you..."

Charlie reluctantly sat back on his heels, letting his reaching hands fall to his side.

"Doesn't know you? Were we dead?" Oz asked, and Charlie shuddered from the strength of Oz's fear.

"No!" he said emphatically. "You're perfectly fine!"

Stasia was crying hard now, sobbing on Oz's shoulder.

"I'm okay," Oz said as he hugged her.

Charlie closed his eyes, not wanting to see the fear on Oz's face, but he felt it. He wasn't okay.

"He'll need a minute," Liz said reassuringly, and Charlie turned to her. She was frowning at her HUD. Everyone was just as anxious as he.

"We all need a minute," he said and took deep, slow breaths trying to calm himself.

Joy laughed shakily and knelt beside him, taking his hand and placing their clasped hands on Oz's knee. She laughed and released him to hug Oz.

"I'm so happy to see you!"

Charlie laughed too, feeling her happiness and peals of semi-hysterical laughter rang over the decks as the Scouts enthusiastically hugged Oz, welcoming him back.

Charlie eased aside to let them pass, crouching beside Sara, being as careful of the others to keep his magic from touching her. He knew he should sit back, that looming over her as she woke could be frightening but he couldn't pull himself away. A glance at his HUD confirmed she could wake any time. Normal sleep rhythms had replaced the slower rhythms of a drugged sleep and the

Scouts were making enough noise to wake the dead.

His flippant thought made him cringe, his internal spike of worry transmitting through the magic and dampening their joy.

Sara woke suddenly with a scream that shocked him. She thrashed free from the covers, panting hard and lifting a trembling hand to her head, and Charlie sobbed with relief. He'd felt her fear and confusion to wake on the deck of the ship.

"Charlie," she said and reached for him. Her fear spiked when he began to cry, and he grabbed her so roughly she squawked.

"You're okay," he said, laughing and crying as he kissed her.

She wasn't okay, he was scaring her, or maybe it was the wildness of the magic that swooped about them or the crying Scouts. He didn't know what she was scared and worried about, but he felt her as clearly as he ever had, and she knew him. Her love was a tonic, and he wanted to bask in it. He didn't care if it was for him or Oz or sunny days or the damned dogs. She felt love and that was enough. He grabbed Oz from Stasia and hugged him too, crushing them both to his chest. Charlie knew his hysterical response to their awakening was causing them distress, but he couldn't help it. He needed to touch them both and to have them touch him.

When Sara kissed his neck, he burst into tears again. Oz clutched in one arm, Sara the other, he rocked them both, hiding his face in Sara's hair. Stasia and Hawk crowded around, patting their backs and rubbing their hair. Joy moved up, then Marcus, then Mike and Lee and Todd until they were all touching.

"So, we died then..." Oz said in a small voice.

"We aren't talking about it." Charlie shook his head and tightened his grip. "You aren't thinking about it or dwelling on it." He took a deep breath, debating a minute over what to say. He couldn't bear the thought of her mourning her dead father. She needed to know he was a bad man. "Sara, your father is dead. He was responsible for taking you. But you're both safe now."

He pressed his lips to her pulse that thudded in her neck. Shocked and bewildered, she clung to him.

"My father?" she asked breathlessly.

"Yes, I'm sorry, but he was a bad man, a crazy man. It hurts, I know, and I'm so sorry." Charlie hugged her tighter as her distress mounted.

"He was truly crazy, Sara," Liz said unexpectedly. "He was ill, brain lesions, nothing that happened was your fault or responsibility."

"The fact that you're saying that means I did something to cause this," Sara said in a sad, scared voice.

Charlie released Oz to frame Sara's face in his hands. "No, you did what any of us would do. You met your father for lunch. What he did was his choice, crazy or not. You're not him, and you won't become like him."

"How long were we missing?"

Hawk told her and she turned white.

"We've been dead for months?" Sara's voice rose shrilly.

"No, you've been sedated for months." Charlie winced; his lie was apparent to everyone.

Oz jumped to his feet and began to pace. Sara was thinking hard, the familiar feel of her concentration was comforting but it worried him also. He prayed she wouldn't remember.

Oz squatted in front of Charlie. "No, we haven't been. We'd be weak and ill even with heals, and we aren't. I can feel the lie, and I know you mean well, but tell us the truth."

"No." Charlie pressed his lips together. "I'll never do that, and you'll never ask again."

Oz jerked back, his face paling as Charlie attempted to use his commanding voice on him purposefully.

Charlie said, "We just found you and brought you back here and healed you. Those missing months are missing to spare us all pain. Everyone suffered with your loss. The magic needs to forget and so do we."

"We can't just forget it, Chief." Oz took Charlie's hand, his eyes beseeching him. "For Christ's sake, we were gone months and we're tan and fit! What the hell happened that you want us to forget so badly? It must be pretty awful. Do you want us to imagine horrors?"

Charlie stared at him, not knowing what to say. Oz would pursue this and might be able to persuade his magic to show him or investigate and uncover the truth. With all his soul, he never wanted Oz to remember what they'd done to him— or the feel of Sara's skin.

"You and Sara were lovers," Liz said softly, "Not by choice. Tomas wanted an heir from you, Sara, and he forced you both."

Charlie put his face on Sara's neck and breathed deeply of her familiar scent. Her pulse pounded as hard as his.

Oz paled, swayed, and sat abruptly. "Yes, we should never remember that. God, Sara, I'm so sorry." He turned stricken eyes to Charlie. "Chief—"

"No, we'll never speak of it. There is nothing to forgive," Charlie said. "I love you. You're my brother. It wasn't you. You'll never remember any of it."

Sara shook in his arms, so ashamed that tears of sympathy filled his eyes. Sad, confused, and afraid, her grip on him lightened and she attempted to pull away. He tightened his grasp. "Sara and I both still love you. That will never change. There's no need to feel guilt or shame, either of you!" The magic brought him feelings of protectiveness from all of them. Love, dismay, and small tingles of embarrassment was mixed with a fierce need to protect them.

Oz rose and turned his back. His gait stiff, he stalked to the railing and clenched it.

"Go to him..." Charlie whispered.

She followed Oz, humiliated and ashamed but appearing calm. The rest of them withdrew their magic and left quietly. Charlie stood behind them, unspeaking. Oz gripped the rail of the boat so hard his knuckles turned white.

"You made the magic make us forget," he said without turning to face Charlie.

"I begged it to," Charlie agreed.

Without warning Oz was violently ill. Sara reached for him, and he shrank from her. Her inner turmoil was a pain in Charlie's gut, but he was grateful that they remembered nothing. This pain he embraced.

"What happened wasn't you, and it wasn't her," Charlie said firmly, willing her to believe.

"How could I do that to her," Oz asked in a voice that shook with self-disgust.

"Stop it!" Charlie grasped his shoulder and shook him. "I made you forget on purpose. Who would it help to remember details? You and I both know neither of you would willingly do that. Does it matter what they did to force you?" He glared at Oz, shaking his head when he opened his mouth. "Believe me when I say they forced you."

"Right, Sara held me down and forced herself on me," Oz said bitterly. He was quiet a moment and then vomited again.

"Would you rather they'd tortured her to death? God, Oz, it wasn't a fate worse than death! I don't want her to remember you, not because you were awful to her— she never stopped loving you. When we came for you, you were begging them to spare her, and she was clinging to you. She loved you then, and she loves you now. Please, can't we put this behind us? Can we forget? Can I have my wife and best friend back? I don't want you to be sad or guilty, either of you." Charlie stood with an arm around each of them as they stared out to sea, thinking their own thoughts.

They stood together until the sun rose, bathing the deck in a soft pink radiance. Charlie didn't need the magic to know how horrified Oz was. Sara felt bad but it was nothing to the terror she'd felt, and his relief and joy were so strong it made him giddy. He laughed softly as he kissed her temple, wincing when she trembled but his momentary dismay was no match for the overriding joy of feeling her love for him.

"I—" Oz shook his head and scurried for the stairs.

Sara whispered. "I believe you. I must've done it, but I don't remember doing it. I'm sorry I hurt you."

"Sara, I thought you were dead. I wasn't hurt, I was relieved. I was and am furious that your father did what he did. Not at you or Oz— at him. I'm comforted by the thought you weren't alone. I'm grateful it was Oz who loves you and not a stranger."

She shuddered violently. "Oh God, Charlie, what if it wasn't only him? What if I'm pregnant?"

"You aren't. Liz checked. It wouldn't have mattered anyways," he continued hurriedly least she sense his lie. "Not about the child, I mean. I'll love any child you give me. I'd hate for your sake, but for my own, your children will be mine."

They stood silently again. Her emotions were in a roil that were impossible to sort. He didn't want to sort them or even sense any except the love she felt when he kissed her warm hair.

He said, "I'm so sorry, sweetheart. Oz loves you. He would've been as kind and gentle as he could be. It's okay to still love him."

"How can you still want me?" she asked bitterly.

He laughed. "You know I do. Nothing's changed for me. If you need time, that's okay. I can wait forever. Feel what you feel, sweetheart. I'm not going anywhere."

She threw herself into his arms and kissed him passionately. "I want you, only you. I don't remember. It never happened."

He returned her kiss and ran his hands under her shirt onto her bare back. His relief that she still felt the same for him was enormous. She still loved and desired him. He let his magic loose around her. He didn't want to miss any of her feelings. He wanted to be sure her shivers were passion, not fear. He went slowly.

She lay on his chest afterward, lazily rubbing her hands over him, feeling his heartbeat slow as he relaxed. "It's only been two days for me since we've made love. I remember it clearly. This is the longest we've been apart for you; I'm willing to make up for lost time. She pushed herself up and kissed him deeply. He smiled against her neck.

- 24 -

THE MAGIC DOESN'T LIE

Rick paced in a small hotel room on the shore of the isle of Molokai as he called his father.

"They don't remember anything. Burn that file! Don't open it! Burn it to ashes!"

"What will you all do now?" John asked worriedly.

Rick was silent a moment. "Major Nelson betrayed us, Dad. We need to find him and question him to be sure he was acting alone. We need to question them all."

"What are you going to do, break into the White House and force the president to confess?" John asked sarcastically.

"Exactly."

John sighed. “Son, look— you can’t do that. Let me rephrase that— you shouldn’t do that. Question him, by all means, but make an appointment and do it in a civilized manner.” His father sighed again. “He has no reason to be involved. They were his enemies too. Well, Liniar was anyway.”

“I think the major more than knew. I think he actively helped. My spell-bracelet was replaced, leaving me unable to summon them. Sara had just checked them all that week and refilled them.”

“Maybe she missed one.”

“Dad, it was only days ago for her. She remembers filling them. She remembers having a stack of new ones to fill.”

“Maybe you got one of those by mistake?”

“I don’t see how I could. Sara had them. They weren’t in our lockers.” Rick was quiet a moment. “I have to go ask her if they were there when she left Tomas in the room alone.”

“Rick, your mother and I are concerned for all of you. Don’t do anything in the heat of anger. This isn’t about revenge. It can’t be. I agree you need to be safe, but don’t burn your bridges here. You had a great working relationship with the government. Do you really want to lose that?"

"We can survive without them and find a new place. We don't need them at all. If they had any hand in this, we're done with them forever," Rick said.

"And the rest of us; all of America, are you done with that too?"

Rick laughed a short, angry bark of laughter. "If America is so corrupt that it'll stand behind this kind of backstabbing in its ranks, then to hell with it!"

"You'll go public then?"

"I can't say what we'll do until we find out who else knew."

"Tell Charlie and Sara they're welcome to come here and stay with us while she recovers."

"She's fine. Charlie isn't. For her it was just a day, thank God. She and Oz are acting like it never happened. Charlie is so angry all of us feel it."

"That doesn't seem healthy to me, son—pretending it didn't happen. Anger is a more reasonable response."

"I agree, but what do I say to her? I'm so happy she doesn't remember any of that. I'm okay with her pretending it didn't happen."

"Where do they think they were the entire time? How are you explaining the amnesia?"

"Obviously, they know time passed. They know we asked the magic to remove their memories like it did for Joy when she died."

"They think they were dead?" John's voice dropped into a disapproving register.

Rick cleared his throat. "They were told part of the truth. Liz told them they were lovers, that they were forced to be to conceive a child. They both agree they want no memories of that."

"Rick... It isn't a lie, but it isn't exactly true either. I can't imagine the harm this is doing to them."

"Dad, believe me when I say it has got to be less harmful than the truth." Rick paused a moment. "We're going to ask the magic to erase all our memories. Everyone who saw the pictures and recordings. As soon as we clear this up, we want to forget."

"You're sure that's wise?"

"I'm sure I can't stand to hear Stasia cry every night or to have nightmares that make her sick to her stomach. She's lost twenty pounds. She's a wreck. Drew and Joy aren't much better. We need to forget this, Dad."

"You do what's right. Take care of them."

"I will." Rick hung up and turned to Agent Lewis. "You've been a good friend to all of us. What should we do?"

"Your dad is right. Call— make that appointment and ask your questions."

The problem is we don't trust them now, so how can we believe the answers?"

"Major Nelson was wrong, one hundred percent wrong both legally and morally, but that doesn't make them all wrong. I'm certain those weren't orders. He'll be court martialed."

"How do we know they weren't orders?" Rick paced the small hotel room. "Did you see what they did?"

"No. I was informed by Mr. Taylor."

"If they can stand by while we're tortured to protect their secrets or the economy or for any damn reason... Do you see why we have to know?"

"I do. The president will too. Please, call him and talk this out. Tell Charlie to talk with him."

He's in no shape to speak with anyone. It's ironic, but Sara and Oz are both doing better than he is. I'll go with a few Scouts. Tell the president I'll meet with him in two days."

"I have to stay here and oversee this mess, but I'll make sure you get your meeting. Rick, we really do want to work this out."

Rick turned away and stalked to the window overlooking the parking lot. "Let them go. Don't try to follow us. Any action on your part will be perceived as hostile. Give us some time."

"You're all officially on leave. They can go where they like."

"Thank you." Rick nodded and strode from the room.

That night on board the *Rheal Lucky* Team Valor held a meeting. Rick, Joy, Todd, Lee, Marcus, Brenda, and Mike sat on the benches on deck. Charlie stood with his hands on his hips before them.

"We're officially on leave. We should split into small groups until we know for sure what's going on." Charlie examined them, satisfied with their angry faces. "If they did this on purpose, they could decide to go for broke and kill us all." Charlie pulled Sara closer to him; her hand trembled in his, but it was still pure joy to touch her.

"Stasia, Joy, Drew, Rick, and Lee will go to the capitol and talk to the president. Stasia, stay invisible and with the president. Keep in contact with the rest of your party."

"No, I'm going too," Oz said. "I can be the mage and attend the meeting."

"Absolutely not!" Charlie held up his hand when Oz started to interrupt. "No, I mean it. No! You and I, Sara, Hawk, Brenda, and Mike are staying on this boat. Lee will be their mage. She can use the security equipment. I need you near me. I'm sorry, but I do." Charlie let his magic touch Oz. "Please, Oz," he whispered.

Oz nodded unhappily. Hawk moved close enough to sling an arm around Oz's shoulder.

"Guthrie, Sam, and Gina will follow us in the other boat."

"Toric will take Gamma and go into hiding." Charlie pulled Sara into his lap, putting one arm around her waist. Her trembling hands had turned into shivers. He got up and sat as close as he could to Oz so his magic could cover them both. Sara took one of Oz's hands in hers, and Charlie kissed her temple. He was trying to encourage their natural reactions to each other. They were stiff and awkward, uncomfortable interacting, afraid both to hurt each other or him with a casual remark or touch that proved to be upsetting.

Charlie put his arm around Oz's shoulder, clasping Hawk too and hugged them a moment. "Stasia and Joy will have to search all of their offices. After you search Pierce's office and home and anywhere else you think he might have information, I want Joy, Drew, and Marcus to go to Iraq and search the general's things. No one goes anywhere without backup."

Charlie turned to Oz. "We need the magic indicator built into the spell-bracelet and it needs to be tamperproof. And tamper proof doors and desk drawers. Sara's father was able to replace the full spell bracelets with empty ones way too easily." He kissed her temple again. "That anger is for him, not you.

You shouldn't have to be wary of your own father. We'll improve our security. We'll improve it so much that Stasia and Joy can't get through it." Charlie examined their faces again. "Sedatives are a blessing and weakness for us. We need to figure that out. That has to be one of our priorities. As soon as we get this mess straightened out and can gather in a group, we'll attempt to teach our magic to help us with it."

"I don't understand why we didn't escape," Oz said in bewilderment. "We must have had opportunities to."

"You did." Stasia took his hand, leaning on his shoulder. "We aren't talking about anything that happened. You just have to trust us. We'll make better plans, get more guards, have better security. This won't happen again— to any of us."

"I'm sorry. I want to let this go, I really do, but we had good security with microchips and wristcomps. Two guards were with us, one hanging back able to summon us. You say they didn't know about our magic that it was just about getting a super smart child. I don't understand how we couldn't get away from them with all of that," Oz said plaintively.

Sara started to cry. Her tears dampened Charlie's neck as she sobbed. Her angst made his stomach clench in a tight knot.

"It was me, Oz. Obviously, I told my father too much. They don't want me to blame myself or you to hate me but I'm the only way he could've known about the microchip. I don't remember saying anything about it to him other than I had good security who could find me anywhere. I must've though."

"Stop! Both of you!" Charlie shouted angrily. "We aren't talking about this! How many times do I have to say that? Jesus, Sara, let it go! I don't want you to remember. Oz, please trust me. I don't want either of you to remember. Sara was careless with her father; she left him in her office alone. Sweetheart, no one blames you for that. You had no reason to think he'd do anything bad. We all thought he was sucking up for business reasons. We knew he didn't have your best interests at heart. We all thought that and none of us changed our security. It isn't your fault. For the love of God, let this go please!"

Oz nodded and patted Sara's back. He rose and nudged Hawk over until he was next to Charlie. Charlie laughed bitterly. "I need like five rangers around me. I'm sorry my anger is upsetting you all." He took a deep breath, and then released it slowly trying to calm himself. "We have one last thing to discuss and it's going to suck. Do any of you have any doubts about any of our remaining team members?"

Rick grimaced. "Sam, but only because he was there when they were taken. He's never done or said a thing that would make me distrust him. I was there and failed as well. Most likely he's trustworthy."

Charlie pinched the bridge of his nose. His brother had been suffering and he'd done nothing to help him, too caught up in his own misery to give a damn what anyone else was feeling.

"I should have said this sooner, Rick, much sooner, but I never blamed you. I'm sorry..."

Rick cleared his throat gruffly and Stasia clasped his hands hard in hers.

She said, "We all feel bad for our mistakes. God, I made so many of them!"

Rick's eyes filled with tears and he ducked his head to press her hands to his lips.

Charlie said, "You and me both. God, if only I'd gone with her..." He cleared his throat, shaking his head. "I know that's stupid, as stupid as you feeling bad for not sticking to Tomas like glue. We all believed his drugged ravings."

Tomas had told him the literal truth and even though he'd known the man had no affection for Sara, he couldn't conceive that anyone would treat their own child so despicably. It had never entered his mind what Tomas had planned even when he'd said it right to his face.

Brenda said, "We all need to forgive ourselves and each other and move on. Charlie is right. We need to improve our security. We should question Sam in the magic."

Charlie nodded his agreement. He'd make time later to speak with his brother. "Anyone else?"

"Toric," Brenda said slowly.

"Toric," Charlie repeated in surprise, rising an eyebrow. He kissed Sara's head that was still tucked under his chin. "He loves her. He wouldn't hurt her."

"Exactly, he does love her," Brenda said unhappily. "I hate saying this. I like him, but he *does* want her. If someone said they had a plan that would give her to him..."

Charlie closed his eyes to rub them. "Toric would've never agreed to do that to either of them."

Mike said, "But what if he didn't know that's what they would do? What if they'd said something different?"

"Okay, Sam and Toric. Call them, Joy. We'll ask them surrounded by our magic. They won't get away with a lie."

"We'll hurt their feelings," Stasia said softly. She glanced at Sara crying and Oz sitting so close to Hawk their shoulders were touching and her face hardened. "We need to know. Call them, Joy."

"Does anyone have anything to add?" Charlie asked.

"Guthrie, and Captain Sanders," Rick said after a moment. "They're our officers, and we need to know we can trust them. I have no reason not to, but we should be sure.

"Liz," Joy whispered, glancing at Sara apologetically. "She's in charge of our medical care. If they turn her, we're doomed."

"Liz would never have done that to me, not ever," Sara said in a quavering voice.

Charlie kissed her temple and rubbed her back a moment as he murmured reassurances in her ear. The darkness the thought of Liz betraying them invoked in her scared him.

"We'll question everyone." Charlie stood and held out his hands, waiting until their magic touched him. "I didn't know where Sara or Oz where until five days ago. I had nothing to do with their abduction. Does anyone have anything to ask me?"

He sat and Stasia stood. She said when she'd found out and that she'd had nothing to do with it. They all stood, one-by-one, and Charlie didn't detect the least bit of uneasiness from them. He called for the Scouts to gather.

Stasia hadn't been wrong, the Scouts were offended, Charlie thought as eyed them milling on the deck as Joy explained what they planned to ask them.

Toric glared and marched over when he caught his eye. “Charlie, you need to get over this. I’ve always been honest with you. Have I ever acted dishonorably with anyone? For crying out loud, I’m not a rapist! Do I want her? Yes! I know I’ll never have her. I can be her friend and that will be enough. I’ve wanted others in the past I couldn’t have. I’ll get over it.”

Toric waved his arms as he paced in their magic. “This magic is uncomfortably intimate at times. I’d love to be able to lie to you all and say she doesn’t mean a thing to me, but you would know it was a lie.” He squatted on his heels and ran a hand over Sara’s hair.

She shuddered and tried to get closer to Charlie. Her fear was clear to everyone and made the deck spring into focus in the way that told Charlie his eyes had begun to glow.

Toric backed away from her, holding out his hands. “You don’t need to be afraid of me. I’d never hurt you on purpose, not ever. Trying to take you from him would hurt you, I know that. I’d still like to be your friend. We were friends once. I’ll find someone someday— you don’t need to feel bad for me.”

Toric sighed in exasperation. "I don't know what those feelings are for. Are they for me or for this situation?" He shrugged and stood. "I feel your fear, your confusion—the guilt, sadness, and shame. I'm sorry if I'm causing any of that. I'm angry that Charlie thinks so badly of me, I'm not angry at you."

"We had to be sure, Toric." Stasia stood and took his hand. "I'm sorry, but we did. We've all answered the same questions. It isn't personal."

He shrugged. "I get it; I'm not one of you. Will you question the major this way when we catch him?"

"You *are* one of us." Sara wiped her eyes and left Charlie's side. On tiptoe she hugged him. "The love is for you," she whispered. "I never doubted you, but Charlie needed to know. The guilt and fear is for what Charlie thinks. I don't want him to doubt my love for him, especially now that I've been unfaithful."

"You weren't. He knows that," Toric whispered and hugged her hard, then stepped away.

Charlie eyed them thoughtfully. "I never thought of that. We should question them all with the magic."

Rick put his hand on his brother's shoulder and pulled him away from the others. "We'll go. They can't be there." He glanced at Sara and Oz. "It wouldn't take all of us. We'll take Hawk and leave you Todd. Hawk has stronger magic; it should be enough to tell the truth from a lie."

"It's such a risk for all of you," Charlie whispered worriedly.

"Give us Brenda and Mike too. We could clear the entire White House with them."

Charlie returned to Sara. "Brenda and Mike will go as well. Go fully suited up, no skin showing with your eyes covered— be prepared. Everyone steals Hawk's air-bubble. I have enough rage to fill a million bracelets. Wear both kinds. If they do attack you, it'll likely be by sedatives, not bullets, but take nothing for granted."

"Let's finish questioning everyone and get on our way," Rick said.

Everyone was honest. When it was Guthrie's turn, Charlie asked him if he had orders to kill them.

"Yes, but not like you're thinking. I attended a meeting where they discussed getting rid of the magic permanently if it became a threat to the United States. I agreed I'd sedate you if in my personal opinion there was such a threat, but I told them I wouldn't follow that order blindly." Guthrie held out his hands. "I've sedated you and ordered you sedated, but I'd never harm one of you for any reason except if I thought you were going to harm an innocent person."

Charlie nodded. "We know they had plans in place and agree they're necessary. We don't agree with their assessment that we're a threat."

"I don't think you are either, and I don't think they believe you are. I think Major Nelson did and acted rashly. I read the reports he did. I wonder if he read the reports Sara or Pierce wrote? The reports he read were accurate but much more pessimistic. War over the new engines is possible but unlikely. Progress is hard and there's bound to be some turmoil as people adjust but war over that doesn't make sense. War is more likely if the world learned of you, I'll admit that, but Major Nelson wasn't acting on that scenario. None of us can tell the future. He shouldn't have done what he did for any reason." Guthrie shrugged helplessly. "I love you guys. I'm sorry he ruined our trust."

"We're questioning everyone," Sara assured him. He nodded and sat down. Sara stared after him. "That's not true you know. The rogues can tell the future."

Guthrie frowned and shrugged. Sara pursed her lips as her brow furrowed. Charlie eyed her thoughtfully. Her sudden intense concentration was slightly worrying but she didn't react to him. He was already so worried she problay hadn't sensed a change, he thought, smiling ruefully when she reacted to his spike of grim amusement.

Liz stood and said the same thing Guthrie had.

Charlie smiled grimly. "Okay, so we're all on the same page now. Go find out if we're safe. If they won't join the raid, don't push it just leave. We'll have our answer."

"Where will we go?" Rick asked.

"England," Sara said unexpectedly. "We'll go to England and talk with the queen. We need a country. A strong one with a good justice system. Somewhere we can help reach its full potential."

"Sara and I've discussed this in the past. England is the best choice," Oz said.

"Before you pack your Macintoshes, let's speak with the president," Guthrie said.

The meeting broke up, everyone going their separate ways. At the prow of the ship, Sara stood shivering as the Scouts got into motorboats. He knew she was afraid but wasn't sure if it were for the Scouts safety or of what they would learn. He supposed it was both.

He stood behind her, relaxing when she leaned against him, her fear changing to the contentment she always felt when she touched him. But his relaxation was short lived.

Someone below deck laughed and she jumped. A spike on anxiety rapidly became embarrassment and shame that he hated with all of his soul.

Her worry when his anger spiked made his anger spike higher. He put an arm around her, and she flinched. Another wave of shame and guilt that she knew he felt turned to embarrassed dismay with a black tinge of fear. And it was growing worse, not better. They weren't in a loop but a spiral.

"I'm sorry," she said, barely above a whisper.

His anger grew, feeding her shame and guilt. Fear was now obscuring her other emotions and making all of his muscles tense. His magic hummed unhappily within him.

"If you say that again, I *will* be angry with you," he said in a calm voice. "My feelings for you haven't changed at all. Not even a little bit, I swear it. I'm angry, I'm beyond angry, but it isn't for you or Oz.

"We agreed to trust each other, remember? We agreed that if we said a feeling wasn't intended for each other we'd believe it. If you say your guilt and fear isn't for me, I'll believe you."

She said nothing. Awash in guilt and fear, she trembled against him.

He sighed. "I don't know if we should talk about this or let it go. I hate to ask this, but are you afraid of me?"

"I'm afraid this is too much to forgive and you'll leave," she mumbled into his chest.

He sighed again. “There’s nothing to forgive, nothing! How many times do I need to say that before you believe me? I’ll never leave you, never ever!” He kissed the top of her head. Her guilt felt like acid on his soul. *Maybe the guilt was because she wanted Oz now,* he thought suddenly. He spoke slowly in forced calm, “Do you want me to? Do you want me to release you from our vow?”

“I only want you. I wish Oz hadn’t asked or Liz answered.”

“We could ask the magic to make you forget again. It might be able to,” Charlie said.

“Will you forget too?” Hope flared as she leaned back to see his face.

He groaned softly. “I can’t. To take care of you, I need to remember. If I forget, I won’t look as hard. I’ll trust where maybe I shouldn’t. I won’t be as careful as I should be with you or push for better security.” He groaned again. “God, Sara, I want to forget, believe me, I do. I just can’t leave your protection to someone else. There’s no one I trust to see you safe as much as me.”

“Then, no, I don’t want to forget either. I would hate if you knew such an awful thing about me, and I didn't know it. That I couldn't try to make amends or make you feel better." She stiffened in his arms as she felt his guilt.

He tried to think of anything else. "I feel guilty you're suffering for me. Please, let's not talk about this." He hadn't lied, but it was close. "Rhea and Lucky are at Paul's house. Abby is looking after them. I didn't want to leave them alone in the lab with just the hired guards.

She stiffened, knowing he'd lied. "Abby didn't mind?"

He heaved a hard sigh. "Not at all. Hawk has been flying to Vermont whenever he gets the chance. Tank has been staying with Abby sometimes too. I was thinking of giving them to her," he admitted, and his guilt eased. Her expression lightened as her worry eased and she kissed his neck.

"What about school. Did you miss all of that time?" she asked in sudden worry.

He laughed, the laugh growing when she felt offended. "You have to stop worrying about that. I wouldn't care if I flunked out." He sighed in exasperation at her alarm. "I didn't flunk out, and I'm not AWOL. I finished the term and went to the *Truman* and oversaw the installations. Stasia was excused from her summer tour. She and Joy were searching. Hawk was supposedly on duty in Iraq, but he was in— he was searching for you."

"When is your leave up?"

"Sara, we don't need to worry about it. I'm staying with you!"

"I'm not worried," she lied. "I'm interested."

"Monday— I need to be back on Monday, but I don't give a damn! Hell, we might be in England Monday."

Sara stood quietly, staring out to sea. "Let's raise the sails and go fast," she said suddenly. "I want to forget all of this and have fun on our boat."

Charlie laughed in relief and called Sam who was following them in a motorboat. He hollered down the ladder that they were raising the sails.

Sara shrieked with laughter as the spray shot up on the leeward side. Charlie called out directions and she raised and lowered sails as they raced through the water. Marcus, Todd, and Oz joined them, and they all got soaked. Laughter rang out over the water as the boat rode the edge of the waves, racing ahead of Sam.

Charlie told Sam not to worry; he could catch up with them later. Sara and Oz were laughing— it was enough.

They lowered the sails at dusk and turned the engine back on. Marcus took the helm after his two-minute shower.

Sara took out pasta sauce that she'd made months ago from the freezer and put the pasta on to boil while she waited her turn for the shower. Charlie came out wrapped in a towel and headed to their cabin. She left the pasta with instructions to Todd and followed him.

He laughed when she started undressing, dropping her wet clothes in a pile and pulled his towel off to hug him.

"You're a popsicle." He rubbed her back, trying to warm her. "Everyone's awake right outside this door," he whispered as she started kissing his neck with clear intentions.

"Then you shouldn't walk around in just a towel," she whispered back and kept kissing him.

He laughed again and returned her kiss, his rage temporarily subsumed by lust.

- 25 -

COVER UP

Rick and Stasia picked a hotel at random. Stasia called her mother to check-in as she had every day. “Liz is headed back to the lab and should be there tonight or tomorrow. I’ll let you know as soon as we find out anything. Mom, if I call and say run, or if you don’t hear from me in a day, you know what to do, right?”

“I know,” Camila said unhappily. “I can’t believe this is happening, none of this.”

“We’ll get through it. I love you, Mom.”

“I love you too. Is Sebastian with you?”

“No, I’m with Rick. We thought it best to separate for the night. He’s with Guthrie.”

“And you’re sure we can trust him?”

"Positive. The magic doesn't lie; I wish we'd questioned the major with it after the stasis incident."

"I still can't believe he was involved."

"It breaks my heart," Stasia admitted. "We all trusted him."

"Stay safe," her mother said and waited for her son to call.

Hawk called his mother while Guthrie called Agent Lewis.

"We have a handle on this mess down here," Agent Lewis said. "None of you were ever here. We've come up with a plausible story about their disappearance that doesn't involve any of this mess."

"What's the story for the, as you say, the mess?"

"Money and drugs. There was enough heroine and opium in the house to fund a third world country. Agents will look and find nothing much except a trail that leads to Nicaragua. There's nothing to connect their disappearance with the deaths except the timing.

"The servants saw them."

"One and we've handled her, and no, we didn't kill her. We bought her off. If she wants to stay bought, she'll cooperate. And I really think she'd have lied for free. She did like Sara and Oz, and when we told her Tomas was drugging them to sell breeding rights it horrified her."

"She believed that?"

"Everyone at the house knew Tomas was desperate for a child and had brought in women as potential surrogates for the brain damaged couple."

"Then they'll realize it was Sara and Oz.

"No way. Sara and Oz are perfectly healthy. The shamblers were decidedly unhealthy.

"The shamblers?"

"What the guards called them. The help thought Tomas had harvested Sara's eggs and was using comatose surrogates— look, none of that matters. Trust me that I've got it covered. There's bound to be some bad publicity about him over this, but it shouldn't lead to the exposure of their secrets. I've called Mr. Martin. I'm sure there will be inheritance issues."

"Oh god, I didn't think of that. What will we do about that?"

"I have no idea. I'll text Charlie and see what he thinks."

"Shit, there'll have to be a funeral as well. God damn it!" Guthrie yelled furiously. "She shouldn't have to attend that!"

"She won't." Hawk laid a hand on Guthrie's arm. "Lee can go as her. We should leave it up to her though. She might want to go. She doesn't remember a thing he did."

"God damn that man's soul to Hell!"

"I'm sure it's roasting there right now," Hawk agreed.

"I better text Charlie."

"I'll call him and tell him the cover story," Lewis said. "They'll need to have it in place soon."

Lewis called Charlie. "You were never in Hawaii. You're returning from Cuba. Sara and Oz were being held in a house there while Liniar tried to extort the government. They were unharmed, just held. Your security found them and rescued them. You arrived after it was all done to take your fiancé home. Luckily, you weren't far as you were visiting your mother who's made a remarkable recovery.

"Tragically, Sara's father was killed in a drug deal gone bad. There will be rumors that Sara's disappearance panicked him into looking for a surrogate mother for his child. I think we can muddy the waters enough to confuse even those who'd been offered, *um*—"

Charlie stopped growling, not even aware he'd started until Lewis paused.

Lewis continued, "Very few people actually saw them in Hawaii and most of them are dead. Tomas's medical records will be leaked and exaggerated stories of his confusion spread. But their own duplicity should keep them quiet if they knew the truth.

Anger roiled within Charlie. "You'll tell me if you find anyone else was involved?"

"Probably not."

"They deserved to die!"

"I'm not arguing that. Trading in human flesh is despicable. But you rampaging around is sure to lead to leaks we can't cover up. And we need time, Charlie. We're still learning and planning. I think you could hide and escape, but the world will panic. The longer we can put that off, the better.

"I've read their reports." He glanced at Sara who slept peacefully beside him. His rage was exhausting her and energizing him, keeping him wakeful, or maybe he was just unwilling to close his eyes and rest. He shrugged off his distraction and snapped. "Save us all the effort and just tell us what you know— when you know it. Not when it's convenient for you. My rogues will be looking and I'm not going to take it well if you're keeping her enemies safe from me.

"Liz reports you're having a hard time controlling your anger."

Charlie shrugged. "I control it just fine. I just have so much of it."

Lewis winced. "Keep in mind not everyone invited to that, *um*, party partook. Being invited shouldn't—"

"If they were told she was for sale and did nothing to help her, they're just as guilty!"

Charlie slashed his hand through the air to end the call. His anger was disturbing her sleep *or maybe it was me yelling*, he thought ruefully as he stoked her hair. She murmured his name but relaxed again into a deeper sleep. He was just dozing off when his phone chimed, the soft sound transmitted through the sticky com he wore constantly now.

A flick of his fingers accepted the call.

A miniature image of Guthrie appeared before him. "I just wanted to make sure you'd been told the official stories."

Charlie eased from the bed and pulled the light sheet over Sara before tiptoeing from the room.

"Yeah, I just spoke with Agent Lewis."

"Did he tell you the president will be commenting tonight in a special bulletin that the designers of the new engines were retrieved safe and sound from Cuba by U.S. Marines? He'll also say that while their loss would be tragic, it would in no way slow production as the plans are already available."

"It's so plausible I almost believe it myself."

"I've spoken with Mr. Martin. He's looking into the will. Find out what she wants to do about a funeral."

"Let him rot."

"She—"

"I know!" Charlie shouted and a second later Todd ran down the stairs. Charlie waved him away and waited until he'd returned to the deck to say. "We'll do whatever she wants."

"Try to get some sleep," Guthrie said.

Charlie disconnected and returned to his bed where he lay unmoving, staring at the dark ceiling until Sara woke.

- 26-

COMMANDER IN CHIEF

The guard at the gate of the White House called for security when the Scout's stepped from the vehicles. Ten secret service agents approached and waved the guard away.

"This way, sir, ma'am." Their eyes darted over the armor and weapons, and hands hovered over sheathed guns, but no one tried to disarm them or stop them.

"We'd been warned you were an intimidating bunch," the lead man whispered as he held the door for Rick. "It must be the swords. You're scaring the piss from my men." He gave Toric a small salute, the academy ring on his finger winking in the light. "*Semper Fidelis.*"

Toric nodded acknowledgment but didn't return the salute. He and Andre were the only two in uniform, dress blues and greens. Everyone else wore full armor, including facemasks and sunglasses. Even Tank wore armor with his name and Scout patch beneath an American flag embroidered on the right shoulder of his bulletproof vest.

Rick knew letting such heavily armed and armored personnel into the president's presence was unprecedented and had debated leaving the swords, but trust was a two-way street. If they didn't trust them enough to face them with weapons, he didn't trust them enough to face them unarmed.

He'd been a bit worried his aura would cause problems, but the agents didn't seem unduly panicked. He assumed they were all retired Marines, chosen so a warrior's aura wouldn't panic them.

They were directed to a small conference room where Pierce Taylor, Captain Sanders and General Campbell waited. Rick didn't have to signal, his team automatically spread out.

"Take a seat, please," Sanders said as they entered and took up positions. "You can take off your cover."

No one sat or removed their face masks or eye protection. Sanders frowned and stood. "I asked politely, but it was an order."

Rick held up his hand to stop Guthrie from speaking. "Have you seen the footage Stasia recovered?"

Sanders looked confused. "No, I was told about it, of course—"

Rick interrupted. "I assume you have it on the laptop there?" Rick gestured to the laptop and files before Campbell.

Sanders glanced at the general who nodded.

"We're going to wait in the hallway. You're going to watch that footage. Then you're going to think about the fact that our commanding officer did that. Come and get us when you're done." They quietly filed out.

The captain's surprised gaze followed the general as he left with them, leaving Pierce and Sanders alone in the room.

"Have you seen it?" Sanders asked.

"No, just read the report like you. It sounded horrible though." Pierce turned on the laptop and they watched the footage.

Sanders shut it off at the same point Rick had. They sat quietly a moment. "Let them stand where they want," he finally said as he rose to invite them back in.

Everyone stood unspeaking until the president arrived. President Carmichael took a seat beside the general.

"I know you're here for assurances that Major Nelson wasn't ordered to do what he did," the president said immediately. "I did *not* give that order."

"Mr. President, I invite you to join my raid," Rick said.

The president eyed him thoughtfully. "I accept," he said after a tense moment, and shoulders relax. "I assume you have something magical to show me or tell me?"

"Mr. Taylor, General Campbell, I invite you to join my raid," Rick said.

As soon as Pierce accepted, the room filled with magic.

Rick said, "Did you order Major Nelson, or anyone else, to abduct Sara or Oz? Did you know about it? Did you help in any way? Did you know where they were? Are these the only copies of what happened to them? Do you intend to kill any of us? Do you intend to incarcerate any of us?"

When they'd all answered the questions, Rick removed his headgear and sat. Brenda and Mike sat on either side of him. Hawk remained standing in the back of the room, one hand resting lightly on his gun, the other on Tank's head. Lee hesitated then stood beside Hawk, her finger hovering over the icon that would send the message to attack.

"Do you have any questions for us?" Rick asked.

"So many that I don't know where to start," the president said, a small smile on his lips. "You can recall your magic; I'll believe what you tell me. My first question is purely personal. Liz has sent me reports, of course, but how are they doing?"

"Very well." Rick leaned back slightly in his chair. "They'll be better once they get my report."

The president frowned thoughtfully. "You really believed I'd ordered that?"

"No, but I can hardly believe Major Nelson left them there, and he admitted it to me. Can you blame us for being cautious?"

"No, I assume you had a plan if I'd done it?"

"Yes, we would've left immediately, using whatever force was necessary."

"And gone where?"

"England to approach the queen and ask for protection for Sara and Oz to work there."

"So, you're no longer a loyal soldier of the United States?"

Rick laughed bitterly. "Would you be loyal to that? We trusted him. He commands us and sold them out! He let that happen!"

"Is our working relationship ruined beyond repair?" the president asked.

"I don't know, is it?" Rick rose an eyebrow and leaned farther back, clutching the edge of the table lightly.

The president was silent a moment. "I have no use for soldiers who can't or won't follow orders, but that being said, these are exceptional circumstances. I can't expect you to follow blindly to a hideous fate. I assume you trust we don't intend that now?"

Rick nodded.

"And you're prepared to follow all lawful orders from your superior officers?"

Rick hesitated. "I'd like to say yes, but we aren't normal people anymore. The magic has needs we have to fulfill. Right now, Sara can heal Marines because we're Marines. We could resign, I'm sure she could still heal us, but you'd lose a lot. And we're all proud of being Marines and of our place in the Core. We want to stay, but we have conditions. I understand that normally that would be unacceptable. If it is, we'll all quit as soon as we can."

Campbell frowned. "What are the conditions?"

"All people who join the raid in any capacity must answer those questions to the magic. We'll never again trust blindly. If any of us or all of us go crazy and wreak havoc, we'll be contained if at all possible, not killed. We'll do our best to hide the existence of magic but we won't accept being murdered to preserve the secret. If Sara runs through town glowing blue and smiting buildings we contain her, we don't kill her."

"Is that all?" Campbell asked, still frowning.

"No, all copies of what happened to them are to be destroyed immediately; no notes, memos, pictures or recordings are to remain. They're never told. It's never mentioned or alluded to. No one speaks of it again."

"They really don't remember anything?" A small, relieved smile lit the president's face.

"Nothing— and we want to keep it that way. We're going to ask the magic to make us forget as well."

"I'm so glad they have no memory of that. My heart aches for them," the president said.

"They have no memory, but they know bad things happened that we aren't telling. Sara has nightmares again. God, Stasia has screaming nightmares from it."

"I'm very sorry," the president said to the air behind Rick.

Rick snorted back a laugh.

"So you'll return to your duty?" Campbell asked.

"I can't speak for Charlie, but the rest of us will. He's furious. He's beyond furious."

The general stood and paced a moment. "The Scouts are allowed special privileges and more leeway than any other soldier—don't let it blind you to your oath, to your duty. We won't tolerate insubordination! Am I clear?"

"Yes, sir!" they chorused.

He nodded. "I order you to remain quietly seated." He tapped his wristcomp to make a call. "Send him in," he said in a resigned tone.

Major Nelson entered. He wore his dress uniform and saluted crisply.

The roomed gained the deadly stillness of a panther about to pounce

The president spoke calmly, "He turned himself in and asked to speak with you. I ask that you use the magic to discern the truth."

The magic filled the room in a rolling boil of static and sparks. Agitation was both seen and felt in a wild cacophony that settled down to rage and sadness.

Nelson licked his lips. He was facing a room full of trained killers who wanted him dead, and he knew it, Rick thought in satisfaction.

Nelson said, "I never knew where they were. I received that file telling the outcome of what happened to them a month ago. I was approached on our first visit to Singapore and offered a deal. They'd send me assurances of their wellbeing and make sure that the both of them were happy and cared for if I would misdirect the investigation."

It took effort to remain seated and not reach for his sword. Rick was surprised he was able to resist attacking when the raids' anger was so clear to him, but the magic wasn't pushing for him to kill the man. It was own hatred he felt. His magic was perfectly calm.

Nelson continued, "I agreed after they showed me the reports on the probable outcome of Oz's invention if he was allowed to continue. I *did* think they were safe. I also thought I'd be able to find them and assure myself of that. Charlie was hurt but functioning. The raid was fine. I had no idea they intended to hurt them again or of the breeding scheme. I really thought if we brought them back Charlie would go crazy and harm them. You know I'm telling the truth. I was looking for a safe place to stash them myself. Yes, I knew for a month they were recovering, but I also knew they were unaware of who they were— and they were together. I was about to go to the general when Brenda came. Everything I'm saying is true."

"How many times was Sara raped in that month do you suppose?" Rick asked thoughtfully.

The major winced. "It wasn't like that. They do love each other."

"How about if we carve your brain out and tell you you're in love with a gorilla or an aids-ridden whore? You'd think you were in love until you recovered enough of your frontal lobe to know better. Does that sound fun? Then we'll do it again, but this time we'll tell you you're in love with your mother. It's okay though because you won't recognize her. Maybe to add to the fun you could become pregnant, gain awareness, have your hands cut up, be tied down or locked up, have your baby stolen, and have no idea what happens to it, then have your brain cut out again and do it over and over until you die. That sounds safe and happy to me. I think you should try it!"

"I had no idea!" Nelson yelled.

"If she'd been your daughter or wife, would you have left her there? You're afraid of her, of them, but mostly her. Are you afraid she'll change you?"

Nelson didn't answer.

"I don't get it. You wanted to be one of us. What changed your mind?"

"She controls you all," Nelson said softly.

Rick frowned. "No, she doesn't."

Nelson laughed bitterly. "Then why are you all so upset, so crazy to find her? You're all obsessed."

"We love her, you moron!" Stasia yelled, becoming visible behind Rick's chair. "We love her," she repeated more calmly. "How do you not see the great gift they have? Not just the healing, but their compassion, their drive to give the healing to others. They spend their time trying to help others. We aren't their slaves— we love them. God, how can you not see what amazing people they are?"

"I see how she calls and Charlie runs to her. I see how Toric wants her. I see you, Hawk. I see Marcus. I don't want that. That doesn't mean I meant her any harm.

"Charlie runs to her because he loves her. She goes to him the same way," Rick said in disgust. "You're worried because you play a warrior too. She hasn't attacked me yet. I haven't left Stasia. I haven't even thought of Sara in a sexual way. You won't become her love slave. You could've just quit the raid. Charlie will kill you for what you did."

Nelson laughed bitterly. "My point exactly. He's obsessed with her."

"I'm obsessed with Stasia. Do you feel the need to make her disappear?" He waited for a response. When he didn't get one, he laughed bitterly. "Your logic doesn't hold. If I'm a warrior and obsessed with someone else, then Sara didn't enslave me. I love her for herself. She's my brother's wife, my family. You're a coward."

"It isn't cowardly to not want to be at someone's beck and call, under their complete control. All this is irrelevant anyway. Charlie is angry because I didn't inform him of the recovery. I didn't inform him of the extent of the damage either. If I'd told him, it wouldn't have helped find them. One week. I knew where they were for one week! Does our past friendship mean so little I can't get one week's grace from you? I was about to call the general. I didn't know what to do. Am I afraid to become addicted to her? Yes! Is that why I did it? No! I was deciding what to do. I feel your anger. Can't you feel my remorse? If Brenda hadn't come, I would've called the general and reported what I knew. We still would've found her."

"We found them within one day of gaining the information you hid from us. We trusted you," Rick said. "You were our friend. We looked up to you. How could we trust you again? We forgave you once already."

Nelson snorted. "I'm your commanding officer. I get to decide, not you."

Rick jerked away fighting the impulse to summon his sword into his hand.

2He said, "When you shot Charlie, were you trying to kill Sara?"

Nelson glared at him, his face turning red. "I thought we settled this?"

Rick turned to the general. "How can you ask us to follow him?"

"I'm not asking," the general said.

Rick growled, so angry words failed him.

"I'm not ordering either," the general said tiredly. "He'll be reassigned." He turned to the major. "Were you trying to kill Sara?"

Nelson exhaled heavily, dropping his eyes to his hands. "I suppose I was. I knew it would kill her, and I could've sedated her. I did hope it would just remove the magic and leave her alive, but I knew it was deadly." He slashed his hand through the air. "That wasn't about Sara, but her magic. I don't want her dead just not so aggressive magically. You all forget that she isn't a girl. She's an alien in a girl's body, and she's trying to reproduce for reasons we don't know!"

"Remove him from the raid," the general said. "Major, I'm disappointed. You were a tremendous asset. You should've come to me about this earlier if you felt she was such a threat. Report to Baghdad base. I'll decide what to do with you."

Campbell turned to Rick. "He won't be court martialed. His orders gave him leeway to act under his own discretion and we can't afford to hold a trial."

Campbell took a small box from his pocket and handed it to Guthrie. "I'm sorry your promotion has this cloud hanging over it. The situation had nothing to do with the promotion except for the actual time. We've been planning this, but they need officers they can trust right now. Command Sergeant Major Guthrie, you'll report to Captain Sanders. I'll be looking for a new major for your group. Third Lieutenant Glenn Howard will assume command until then."

He turned to Rick. "I understand that your brother is very angry over what happened to his wife and Oz. But he'll have to control it. I'll met out discipline. He will *not* approach the major or in any way contact him."

Campbell turned back to Nelson. "You aren't getting off scotfree here. You didn't break any orders, but by your own word you did attempt to murder Sara Mitchel when she was in your care. That's a very serious offense. You've put us in a very difficult position. You know enough to really harm us."

"Excuse me, General," Rick said softly. "Maybe we could make him forget. We could ask the magic to go back to his first sight of Sara until now. He'd have nothing to say. You could assign him to some obscure area where people don't know him."

"He'd know he was missing four years," Campbell said doubtfully as the major said, "You can't do that! I won't say anything."

"Tell him he was in an accident or something. He'll believe whatever you say." Rick smiled ironically at the major. "Sucks, don't it."

Stasia laughed a sharp bark of laughter. "Make him forget us all. Assign him to the ass end of nowhere and let him wonder why his career halted."

"You can't do that! Taking my memories away, that would be cruel!"

"God, you're a hypocrite!" Stasia spun away from him.

"Me?" Nelson yelled. "You wanted to kill her too just for the thought of her stealing your boyfriend. I was trying to protect the world from them!"

Stasia paled. Rick glared at the major and took her hand. He said, "Stasia, I invite you to join this raid. Joy, I invite you to join my raid."

"Forget," Brenda chanted with her eyes closed. Blue magic began to swirl around her. It grew denser and gained speed, the other caster's magic joining it, whirling in a vortex around her in seconds.

Nelson headed to the door.

Guthrie shot him with his tranquilizer gun as Rick leapt across the table.

Rick grabbed him and dropped him on the table. The magic whirling around Brenda began to give off sparks.

"Forget," Stasia whispered and clasped Joy's hand.

Lightning blew through the window impacting Brenda then leaping to Joy and Stasia before sliding over the major. It disappeared a minute later with a whoosh of air that fluttered their hair and Brenda slumped.

"You okay," Mike whispered as he pulled her up.

Rick glanced at his HUD, checking vitals, then leaned down to feel for Nelson's pulse

Brenda nodded to Mike and said, "I don't know if it worked or not. Wouldn't it be ironic if he changes into a warrior instead?"

"Ironically terrible," Rick said as they all stared at the major's unmoving body. Rick sighed unhappily. "I really liked him. I'll miss him."

"We could recruit him again," Toric said, "I mean, he wouldn't remember a damned thing. Sara is way better at handling the magic now. He'd have no need to be afraid of her."

"Yeah, I don't think Charlie would go for that," Hawk said.

"I won't go for that. I don't trust him anymore," Stasia said.

"We wanted to forget as well. We won't remember not trusting him," Rick said.

Stasia frowned unhappily. She turned away from the major's body and hid her face in Rick's chest. "We can't forget. We need to stay vigilant." A shudder traveled her.

Rick leaned down and kissed her. "We have time to decide. It's only been a week." He glared at the major, Stasia's pain filled him with an urge to hit the man but he knew it wouldn't end in a simple fight. It would be Nelson's death on his hands, and he hastily looked away before he could lose control. He turned to the general. "I know Charlie has to report to his ship on Monday, but Sara will need him here for her father's funeral. Lee could pretend to be him on the ship."

"No, I'll see that he can stay with her here as long as she needs." Campbell assured him. "I want you all here. Everyone is to speak with Doctor Gotlieb until he releases you." He rubbed his eyes tiredly. "I'll deal with Major Nelson."

"Oz is redoing all of our security. We'll need time to organize that before we can be reassigned anywhere." Rick glanced at Mike then away flushing. He didn't even like to contemplate how panicked Sara's magic would become if she ever remembered. He was glad her magic loved Mike better than him, but he doubted two warriors would be enough for it. It had been harder than he liked to admit to himself to leave her, and he knew Mike felt it too.

Stasia gave him a worried glance and he smiled ruefully as he withdrew his magic. *She has two warriors with her*, he told himself forcefully, annoyed that his musings had stirred his magic.

He said, "Sara might need Mike or Todd or Joy. Please make them available to her."

"The entire raid will be assigned as their security until we get this worked out. I realize none of you are just going to bounce back from this," the general assured him. "More guards will be assigned to both the house and lab," he added.

Rick nodded thankfully. "Frankly, we aren't fit for any missions right now. We're all exhausted and sick from worry. The magic is stressed and unhappy with us. We need peace."

"Go and rest. Talk to Doctor Gotlieb. Report for work on Monday," Campbell said.

Rick rubbed his forehead and turned to Pierce. "Who do I talk to about her father's body?"

"Me, call me. We can have it shipped wherever she likes," he said.

Rick nodded.

"Dismissed," Campbell said softly.

They stood and saluted, pulled down their face masks, and left.

The same Secret Service agents escorted them out.

The president took a deep breath. "I think we can be grateful the magic can tell the truth from a lie."

Campbell frowned. "Their discipline is slack. They ignore protocol when it suits them. Hayes was the lowest ranking officer here and he took over as if the chain of command didn't exist.

"He's a warrior and it's what they do. Besides, this was personal, not professional. They saw this as a personal attack," Pierce said.

"Yes," the general agreed unhappily.

"Who knows how far back this sent our reputation with them. I want the magic happier," the president said emphatically. "Do whatever we have to do to make it happy. If the magic needs them to sit in the sunshine all day, do it! We're learning too much— it's too valuable for us to lose it."

The general said, "Major Nelson was correct in a way. We aren't dealing with men and women. They've been changed into other than human. I'm not quite convinced it's alien manipulation though."

The president waved his hand and rubbed his forehead.

Pierce said, "I've read the same reports you have, and I agree what they perceive as other could be their subconscious desires, but the struggle to hold it back is real. Whether the needs they fight are their own, a sort of split personality, or truly the needs of another being is almost impossible to say. Does Sara want Rick on an unconscious level? Does she pick men who admire her, or does she force their admiration? Is she really just fighting herself? Charlie tells us he fights his impulses, what he describes as the magic's push to kill threats. And he does so relatively easily by telling himself it isn't a threat. Is that him telling his subconscious or him telling a separate being that trusts him utterly?"

The president said, "We've had this discussion *ad nauseum*. You all know I believe it's an entirely different entity and a young one that's learning. Unlike Major Nelson, I don't think we're dealing with a being that intends to subjugate humans but with one who was just born. Although, I admit, I could be wrong, but I think we'll find out when she has her thirty. If it stops there and the push to reproduce fades, we'll have our answer. And meanwhile, we learn." He shrugged lightly. "It isn't like we know how to destroy the magic anyway. Killing a host just leads to more hosts. Our best option is to continue as we are. Keep them under control and use them."

"While we learn, it learns." Campbell flicked at glance at Nelson's unconscious form. "As a weapon it isn't working out so well."

"There's more to be gained than using them as weapons." The president smiled ruefully. "They've worked very well as hostage rescue. Putting them at risk is dangerous, we know that now. We need to be very careful how we use them. Joy should never have been sent alone to Libya. Major Nelson screwed up there as well."

He sighed, rubbing his temples and leaning back in his chair. "We learn so much from our mistakes. But we can't afford to keep making them. Sara and Oz are impetuous. They're young and need time to develop wisdom. We need to guide them better, keep them focused. They have an idea and run with it until another idea sidetracks them. It's partially our fault, their ideas are so intriguing that we hurry them. We need to slow them down. They're producing new technology so fast that we can't assimilate it.

We haven't had time to study the ramifications. And we need time. Let's give them time as well. Let them sit in the sun. It hurts no one. We need to know how long the magic can go without needing to reproduce. Unless we can keep them all calm and unhurt, we'll never find that out."

"I'll keep a closer eye on all of them," the general said.

"I'll have Special Agent in Charge Lewis keep in closer contact as well," Pierce said.

The president stood. "Thank you both for coming." He gestured to Nelson's body. "My men will help you out."

- 27 -

OWN YOUR ANGER

Rick called his father and told him what they'd found out and what they'd tried to do to the major. "I still need to tell Charlie. He'll want to go kill him, Dad. Being a warrior... I can't explain it; the protectiveness you feel for those you love— people in your care. You feel your rage more, it makes you powerful, but it also demands action. He's full of rage and will need an outlet for it."

"Can't he use target dummies?"

"Yes, he can spend the rage he has, but it will regenerate quickly. I don't know how to stop that, how to make him less angry about what happened."

"I don't know either," his father admitted. "I hate to suggest it; it's unfair to both of them, but maybe if you said Sara needed him calm?"

Rick laughed bitterly. "She does need him calm. It enrages him more; every flinch makes him angrier. They're both trying so hard, Dad. She feels his rage. He feels her fear. It's a vicious circle."

"They need therapy."

"They'll get it; well, he will anyway. It's mandatory for all of us. They can't order Sara or Oz." Rick groaned in frustration. "Her father will need to be buried. She has no memory of what he did. Charlie does, and it's sure to infuriate the hell out of him when she goes and is upset. You really need to be there, Dad."

"I will be. Your mother and I will go and offer her what comfort we can."

"Does Mom know?"

"I told her what Sara believes. I'm not sure I did the right thing."

"Don't let her make Sara feel bad about any of it."

"She would never; she realizes it wasn't their choice."

Rick was silent a moment. “There could be pictures or live witnesses of Sara and Oz together and happy. I haven’t mentioned that to Charlie. I’m sure he must’ve thought of it himself. I don’t think we should tell Mom what really happened unless those pictures surface. It would kill Sara if Mom thought badly of her.”

“And if Sara sees them?”

“I don’t know,” Rick admitted.

His father sighed. “I know you’re all trying to protect them, but this lie is getting complicated already.”

“It’s the best we can do, Dad. Even if she sees them, that lie is better than the truth.”

John Hayes was silent a moment. “Will you forget?”

“God, we want to, we really do, but we can’t afford to. We need to be vigilant.” Rick cleared his throat. “We can make you forget,” he offered.

“No, I’ll bear it for my son’s sake. I need to remember to understand if you ask me for help.”

“I love you, Dad.”

“I love you too, son.”

Rick hung up to call his little brother.

"So, he gets away with everything, and he doesn't even have to remember what he did," Charlie said bitterly.

Rick said nothing. He didn't know what to say.

Charlie said, "Shit, I'll talk to Sara and see what she wants to do about her goddamn father!"

Rick could practically feel the fury over the phone. "You need to spend some rage. You're going to scare her. You know she feels it too."

"God damn it, I know that!" Charlie was silent a moment. "How, Rick? You tell me how not to be angry about all this."

"Spend it. Spend the rage. Leave room for love."

"I'll call you when we have funeral plans." Charlie hung up. *Thank God she was napping,* he thought and rubbed his throbbing head.

Stress was exhausting her. His rage was energizing him and tiring her. *Thank God we have Todd*, he thought as Todd glanced up from the book in his lap when he peeked into their bedroom.

She slept better if Todd was nearby. Todd was a giant, ranger, teddy bear. Charlie winced. They were using Todd unfairly, not that he'd complained at all. He was very kind to Sara and him. *God, he was lucky to have such good friends.*

He placed his glowing on Todd's cheek for a second, letting him feel his affection and gratitude.

Todd's eyes lit with a blue glow, but he kept his magic contained, nodding and flushing slightly. Charlie left him guarding his wife and returned to the top deck where he stared out to sea as he tried to control his anger.

He was calmer by the time Sara woke but she still flinched from his anger. He waited until after she'd eaten supper to talk about her father.

She looked away, ducking her head to hide her face but she couldn't hide her guilty fear from him. "I don't want to go. I don't want to talk to his friends."

"Then we won't go," Charlie said and clasped her hands that were twining nervously in her lap.

"If I don't go what will people say?"

"Who cares?"

She frowned, her worry and fear buffeting him, but he knew it was his anger that made her cry.

She stopped quickly, taking hard breaths, and feeling so guilty it brought tears to his eyes.

"Hawk said Lee would go as you," Charlie offered.

"I don't want to, but I think I have to go. Tara will go. If I don't, she'll get mad." Sara turned away again. "Charlie, I'm sorry," she said in a small voice as she started to cry again. "I don't think I could stand it if she started rumors about me. It would be true now." She cried harder. "Please, don't be so mad at me. Lee can be you or make Mike you. You don't have to go."

"I'm not mad at you," he sighed resignedly, "I'm tired of telling you that. I'm really not mad at you. Of course, I'll go with you. I think I hate Tara. I didn't before. I found her annoying, but I didn't hate her." He pulled Sara into a hug. "We'll go and leave quickly." He kissed her cheek. "I'll call Rick. He can make arraignments. He's there and won't mind. We'll fly home and bury your father Friday."

"I'm sorry," she said again in a small voice. He sighed in exasperation. "Go talk to Todd. Tell him we have to fly back. Figure out where to sail us to and get us all tickets home. We'll hire someone to get the boat home for us. I'll call Rick."

He waited until she went below deck to call his brother back. "Can you arrange the funeral for Friday? We're coming home. She's afraid Tara will carry through on her threat to make her look bad and the idea of it terrifies her now. God, the guilt she feels... Don't say it! I know she doesn't need to feel my anger. We both know Tara is a vindictive bitch. She would do it if the mood strikes her. We need to stop her. Please, Rick, help me stop her."

"I don't know how to. Let me think about it and talk to the others, and for the love of god, Charlie, burn off some of that rage!"

Charlie wanted to scream and curse, instead he quietly ended the call.

He found Sara in their cabin. "I need to run and get rid of some of this. I'm going ashore. Sam will pick me up and bring me back. Will you be okay here a while?"

She smiled at him, the smile a lie he felt in his soul. "I'm fine. Go beat up some trees and feel better."

He nodded and left, whispering to Todd, "Stay near her, please."

"You don't need to ask. I'll watch out for her."

Charlie ran along the deserted shore and beat up the trees. He'd taken one of his swords and swung wildly, hacking trees to pieces. His rage scared her. Even with Todd there, knowing he was here and hitting nothing except trees, her fear was mounting. He tried to calm himself. Everyone who'd hurt her was dead. She and Oz were safe. Both were dealing with everything remarkably well. She loved him. Nothing had changed for her. Her feelings for him were the same. If he could master his rage, her fear and worry would lessen.

More than anything in the world, he wanted her to be happy. If he couldn't have happy, he'd settle for calm.

But he didn't know how to stop being so angry when he thought of what they'd done to her and Oz. For another hour he hacked the trees. Branches and leaves flew. He dropped his sword and used his fists, breaking the bones and cutting himself but the sharp stabs of pain disappeared so quickly he barely felt it.

As fast as he spent it, the rage regenerated. His magic could heal these small wounds indefinitely. With no real foe to fight, he'd never be able to spend the rage he was generating.

He closed his eyes, pressing his forehead against a tree to catch his breath, wishing Nelson were in front of him. He wanted to beat him bloody, his betrayal hurt. Charlie had thought he was a friend and trusted him with Sara's life. *What a fool I'd been to trust anyone else with her life, never mind someone who'd already tried to kill her once.*

Anger surged and he realized he was angry at himself the most. He'd known Nelson was a danger to her. He'd known and let him lead the search, had let him stop him from forcibly questioning Tomas. He'd known her father meant to use her. The man had never shown a spec of interest or caring, and he'd let him try to manipulate her.

This was his fault. When she'd needed him so desperately, he'd failed her. When they'd finally found clues, he'd almost failed her again. They'd arrived the day they were moving her by blind luck. One more day and she would've been gone again, who knows where. Nelson had almost lost her for him again, and it would have been his fault for trusting him.

So close, it had been so close.

He turned and slid limply down the tree. The lies he'd told were piling up. Liz hadn't preformed a pregnancy test. Sara could very well be pregnant. On the yacht, she'd said she wasn't, so he could probably fool her into believing the baby was his. She couldn't be too far gone. He hoped she wasn't. He didn't want to explain the lie. But he didn't want her to worry about it, let her think Liz had tested. The thought of her making love to Oz, of Oz touching her warm skin, skin no one had ever felt except him, hurt so badly he moaned with the pain of it.

"Fuck," he screamed and swung in such a rage he lost track of time and place only regaining himself when he stumbled to his knees in the shredded foliage too exhausted to stand.

He sat in the pile of hacked limbs and thought about the lies he'd told and decided he could live with them all. The truth was much worse. He could lie to himself too. If she could pretend it hadn't happened, he would too.

The smell of fresh cut wood drifting over him was somehow soothing. He tipped his head back against a tree and took deep breaths, closing his eyes and consciously slowing his breathing. For her, he could be calm. Already she was much less worried. Never again would he entrust her safety to another. Every security procedure he would vet himself. No one he didn't interview personally would guard her. By some miracle he'd gotten a second chance to keep her safe. He vowed to himself he wouldn't blow it this time. He headed back to her before she could start to worry again.

Todd would make dinner. It was his night to cook. Charlie could sit with Sara and Oz. They could spend one last night on the boat before heading home. One last night to sit together trying to heal before they had to face the circus that would be her father's funeral and the reporters who were sure to hound them over the abduction.

Liz waited by the small boat that had brought him to shore. She rose and dusted off her pants, smiling ruefully.

"I didn't know you were waiting," Charlie said.

She offered him a brown pill bottle. "A mild sedative. Aura suppression 2.0. Before you ask, we didn't have it available until last week or I'd have given it to you so you could leave the base. The first version wouldn't have worked but this one is much stronger. It shouldn't make you sleep although it will likely make you tired. I'm hoping it helps you control the rage too. You look calmer though."

He shrugged and sheathed his sword.

"Sara's taken one and she says it helps calm her magic." She closed his hand around the bottle and kissed his cheek. "There'll be lots of people at the airports and while I could summon you back to the campus, Sara will need you. Take the pills, Charlie. They should help dampen your aura enough that you don't cause riots."

Charlie opened the bottle and shook out a small pill. It was larger than the other pills she'd given him and a creamy yellow.

"They work fast," Liz said. "You can take up to three an hour."

"I thought she was just feeling better."

"She is," Liz said. "She can still sense you. The pills just help her relax. These aren't traditional antidepressants but something we've formulated specifically to mute the magic's push. I was afraid you'd get caught in a loop. You're both very stressed. Give yourselves some time to recover."

Charlie took the pills. Maybe now he'd be able to sleep.

- 28 -

BURYING THE PAST

They traveled home together on a private plane flown by Todd. Reporters lurked at the airport when they landed. A line of armed Marines held them out of range of Charlie's aura, although Charlie thought it probably wasn't necessary. The pills did help, and he was more worried than angry anyway.

They were big news. The police had to clear the way so they could leave. An armed Marine escort followed.

Sara and Oz were white from the strain. A rented limousine driven by Joy took them straight home. News vans crowded the street outside of their house. Someone had hung tarps to block the view of the yard and partially rebuilt house. Reporters yelled questions as they hurried inside the garage. Stasia and Hawk were there already with Rick.

"This is a nightmare" Sara said. "We need more security for the funeral."

"We'll have it," Brenda assured her.

Sara paced the small space. "Hawk, would you mind going to get Lucky and Rhea? It doesn't feel like home without them." When he nodded, she added hurriedly. "Don't go alone."

Hawk kissed her cheek and left.

She called Abby.

"Sara, I'm so glad you're back. How are you?"

"I'm fine," Sara said.

Charlie frowned and turned away. He had to leave the room while Sara told Abby the public version of events. Her angst didn't show in her voice or outward demeanor, but she felt so bad it made him feel sick.

"I'm glad to be home. I've asked Hawk to get Lucky and Rhea. I've missed them so much. I can't thank you enough for taking care of them while we were..." She trailed off.

"Thank you," she repeated as Charlie slammed the door.

He returned ten minutes later. To his surprise the girls still spoke. She'd calmed enough he'd thought she'd hung up.

Sara's glance flicked to him and she immediately felt guilty and ashamed. It made him sad which made her sorry.

"I have to go, Abby. Thanks again."

"I'm so glad you're both back safe and sound. We were happy to have them. My family will miss them, and I'll miss Hawk coming to visit them."

Sara laughed. "I admit it was a good excuse, but I'm sure he'll think of another."

Abby giggled. "I hope so. I only have a few more weeks of plebe summer to get through. Then one week at home. I'll be at school with all of you and able to see him more."

"I forgot you were in school now," Sara admitted. "How do you have your phone?"

"Hawk called the school and said you'd be calling me and they let me have it. Everyone here was very worried."

Charlie took another pill and began making sandwiches, concentrating on the small task and Sara eased, speaking normally to Abby without the inner turmoil.

"Being at school with Hawk will be hard, take my word for it. It's incredibly frustrating not to be able to touch or hold hands or anything in public. You can visit the lab whenever you like though. It's private there, and he has his own office. I'll cover for you."

Abby giggled again.

"It's the least I can do for you for taking care of my pets. Thank your parents for me, will you?"

"I will, Sara. If there's anything I can do for you, don't hesitate to ask. I know Paul considers you both his good friends. I hope we become good friends as well."

"You already are." Sara said goodbye to Abby then ordered her Valory to have fruit and flowers delivered to Abby's parents with a thank you note.

She returned to the kitchen and sat heavily on the bench seat. "What do I need to do for the funeral. I've never done that before. I don't remember my mother's."

Rick kissed the top of her head. "Nothing, it's all been done. Go to the church at ten. Sit there for forty minutes or so. That's it. A memorial is being held in Florida for his business associates to attend. Notices have been sent and flowers arranged. His body will be sent to Florida for burial. It's all arranged, Sara."

"Thank you."

Charlie frowned, not liking how dull her aura was.

Rick handed Charlie a small brown bottle. "Take one every hour. It's a mild sedative that will hopefully keep you calm enough your aura won't cause a riot. I've taken them and it does help. I feel sort of disconnected, but I can still cast although it takes longer."

Charlie waved his pill bottle at his brother and flopped to his sofa to watch Sara pace the small room while waiting for Hawk to return.

Oz headed next door to his trailer. Stasia and Rick followed him, and Sara sighed in relief, then glanced at Charlie and felt guilty. She put her head down on her folded arms on the counter.

"Go to bed, sweetheart. I'll bring them in," Charlie said.

She shook her head and waited. Happy relief buffeted him, waking him from a light doze when Hawk returned. Rhea danced around Sara happily and then played with Tank. Tank was overjoyed to have his playmate back. Sara laughed at their antics and felt truly happy, which made Charlie laugh too. Lucky purred and butted her head against her hand, demanding attention. Much more relaxed, Sara said goodnight to everyone and went to the tiny bedroom with Lucky held to her chest.

"Let Rhea stay with Tank, she'll come in when she's ready," Sara said to Charlie as he called the dog. She rubbed Rhea's ears again and told her to go play. The smile on her face matched her inner happiness as she stared after Rhea running back to Tank. And for the first time since they'd retrieved them, Charlie fell asleep normally and slept all night.

Charlie's parents arrived the next day. Sara flushed red when his mother hugged her and told her how glad she was to have her back. Charlie knew she was mortified with embarrassment and sick with guilty nerves.

She sat beside him on the small couch with her head down.

He tried to keep the talk light, asking his father about work, and Sara eagerly joined the change in conversation. He had a hard time focusing on the small talk. The pills made him sleepy, but he took another. She'd never face Tomas alone again. For a moment his anger surged and then he remembered Tomas was dead. He rubbed his forehead, yawning deeply,

"Will Tara be attending," Mary asked, and Sara's surge of anxiety pushed through the fog surrounding him.

It made Charlie sad how strained and awkward she felt with his parents. He needed to do something about Tara.

Sara and his mother went to Oz's trailer to help Camila prepare dinner for everyone.

As soon as the door closed behind them, Charlie turned to his father.

"I have no idea what to do about Tara. Just the thought of seeing her scares her. Should I tell Tara not to go?"

"Joy's handling it," Rick whispered as he glanced to the door.

"Handling it how?" John whispered back, his eyes narrowing.

"Tara must have a million dirty secrets." Rick turned his glowing blue eyes on his father. "She went to find some. If she can't find anything, Stasia will lie her head off about Tara. We can make bad stuff up too. We won't let her hurt Sara."

His father frowned unhappily. "All these secrets and lies, this isn't good."

"It wouldn't be my first choice," Charlie murmured quietly. "If she leaves Sara alone, I'll leave her alone. If she wants war, we'll give it to her."

The women returned from next door.

"Camila shooed us out. The kitchen is too small..." Mary trailed off as the men straightened and leaned away from each other.

When John looked away flushing, Sara murmured an excuse and fled to her room, crying, deeply humiliated.

"Smooth, Dad," Charlie said sarcastically and followed his wife.

"I need another pill," Rick muttered.

John closed his eyes and took a deep breath. Mary gently patted his shoulder.

"We'll get through this in time. She feels bad. We all do. She's embarrassed even though she doesn't remember it. In time, she'll realize we don't hold it against her."

"We're all embarrassed," John murmured.

The closing door cut of his mother's reply. He held his wife while she tried to hide her embarrassment. She was thinking hard, and he let her be, letting the familiar feel lull him to sleep.

The next morning Sara emerged from the bedroom wearing a plain, high-neck, long-sleeved dress with black gloves. Her hair was back, braided tightly into a bun, not a wisp escaping, and her blue eyes were swollen and red from crying. Charlie followed in his dress uniform. He'd given up telling her she didn't need to feel bad. He wished he could make her forget her damned father completely. That she might be feeling bad about that asshole's death angered him so much it scared her. He said nothing and took two pills.

She clutched him, laying her face on his chest and cried again but her fear eased, his touch easing her, which lessened his anger. They were stuck in a damned loop. He couldn't wait for this day to end.

His parents borrowed the bedroom to change, and they headed to the funeral. Reporters and photographers lined the street outside the church. Sara ducked her head and leaned into Charlie's side, clutching his hand. Charlie glowered, happy for once his aura moved people involuntarily out of his way. The pills seemed to be working. No one screamed and ran. Rick and Stasia walked behind them, also in uniform. Oz walked with Charlie's parents. Camila and Liz came together. Guthrie, Drew, Marcus, Harrison, Hawk, Toric, Amy, and Paul followed, all in uniform. Joy remained stealthed beside Sara. The rest of the raid wore plain clothes and spread out in the crowd.

They settled into the front pews on the left. Tara and her entourage followed and sat in the pews on the right. Flowers filled the church, sent from Tomas's business acquaintances and employees. Charlie found the smell cloying.

Every word the minister spoke raised Sara's distress and his anger. Caught in a loop again she began to shake against his side. Charlie nudged his father who handed him his sunglasses and the pill bottle. He turned to Sara and put his lips on her neck.

"I love you. Ignore my anger, none is for you. This is for you," he whispered as he kissed her neck and concentrated on the warmth that flowed through his entire body from the small touch. Suddenly, she was crying in his arms, burrowed against his chest. The pastor paused as people stared, then cleared his throat and continued.

In a moment Sara sat back in her seat and used the tissues Mary handed her. The rest of the service passed in a haze for Charlie.

He kept both her hands in his. Behind his sunglasses his eyes were closed as he envisioned making love to his wife. Not the physical act, the mental one, the connectedness and contentment she brought to him. The hands in his relaxed as love echoed between them.

When the service ended, Tara came over to her. "I'm sorry about your father," she said civilly.

"Thank you," Sara murmured. Her body tensed against Charlie. This time Charlie's anger made her relax against him.

Tara paused, seemingly at a loss for words. She wiped her sweating brow and turned as if to go then straightened and turned back. She finally patted Sara's gloved hand and scurried away.

Sara sighed in relief. Her relief grew when the Scouts surrounded her. Reporters had again gathered outside of the half-rebuilt house. They swarmed the street and hollered for interviews.

"Back off!" Charlie snapped and almost laughed when the closest reporters scrambled away. He held the garage door for Sara and waited until everyone was inside before following.

She was already in bed wearing one of his sweatshirts, clutching Lucky. Neither of them spoke. He sat beside her until she dozed off. The cat peered at him from half-closed eyes, yawned, and went back to sleep.

Charlie tucked her in and went back outside where the raid had gathered. They spoke of work and tried to make small talk, but Charlie knew his anger was upsetting everyone.

"Ironic, isn't it."

"What is?" Brenda asked and took his arm.

"I'm angrier now."

"You were too sad to be angry earlier," she said and patted his clenched hands with her free one. "It's okay to be angry. Don't fight it so hard and just feel what you feel. You're as guilty as Sara of trying to make yourself feel things you don't."

Charlie glanced to the door as it opened, and Sara stepped into the yard.

He hated how embarrassed she was and the guilt that immediately followed it.

"You're going to strain something trying to hold it in," Brenda said, and Oz snorted with laughter. His laughter faded when Sara joined them. It didn't take magic to tell she was nervous. Oz was flushed now and frowning at his feet.

"You all need to loosen up a little," Brenda said. "We're all friends here and no one is judging. If you want to rage— rage. Go beat the target dummies." She released Charlie's arm to turn to Sara. "If you want to mope around being all embarrassed over something you don't even remember, go ahead, but if you're trying to hold back anger at your father because he was your father, don't bother. Biology only gives you so much. My dad was an ass. I didn't hate him, but I didn't mourn him either. Does that make me a bad person?"

She shook her head and waved her hands at the academy grounds. "How can you be so smart and so stupid? You don't owe that man a thing." A thoughtful expression crossed Brenda's face. "Charlie didn't kill him. It isn't your fault he's dead. Did you know Liniar's own bodyguard shot him?"

"Brenda," Charlie said warningly, and she waved him off without even glancing at him. He grabbed her arm hard.

Brenda said, "They were stealing the drugs. We interrupted them. Tomas would've been next. Or maybe not. They all knew he was diseased so might have left his shit alone. But my point is he was a bad man surrounded by bad people."

Charlie released his tight grip as Sara's guilt eased.

"And, yeah, we're dangerous but Tomas knew that when he messed with us."

"Mess with the bull, you get the horns," Manny said, and Sara laughed. She slapped her hands over her mouth, looking horrified, and Charlie laughed over her guilty amusement.

He said, "I swear I didn't kill him. I would have, but I didn't."

He shot a quick grateful glance to Rick and mouthed thank you to Brenda when Sara hugged him. Her guilt fluctuated, morphing too fast for him to nail down what she was thinking about before settling into determination.

She pushed away to see his face when she said, "I did feel bad. Like I'd brought this to him, but he did choose it. I didn't make him do any of things he did. And he was sick—but I'm glad it wasn't you who killed him. And, yes, it does make me feel guilty that I give a damn. I know he was an ass. I didn't love him, but I wanted to."

She flushed and turned to Brenda. "I hate thinking everyone is wondering about Oz and me—"

"*Pfft*, that's actually kind of boring. No offense, Oz. Your hot and all, but if I'm imagining sex it isn't you with Sara." She winked at Rick, and Mike exclaimed indignantly, making Sara giggle.

Brenda continued, "If I'm imaging how they'd do it, I have to admit my thoughts go to Joy and Drew. She's so damned tiny..."

Drew laughed and Joy punched him on the arm.

"I'll show you how," she said, and she grabbed Drew's arm, twisting and spinning sideways to throw him over her shoulder. He landed on the ground with Joy kneeling on his chest.

Sara's laughter was tonic to Charlie's anger, and he laughed too as Joy kissed Drew then flipped backward to land on her feet.

"I suppose the rest will have to be left to your imagination," she said and turned to eye Rick who held up his hands and waved her away. "Now, me. I appreciate Rick's charms or Harrison. Where'd he get to anyway?"

The Scouts continued to joke, flirting and insulting each other in good-natured camaraderie. Sara relaxed and enjoyed their company and Charlie forgot his anger, laughing with Stasia as they teased Oz about the female plebes who pestered him.

When they finally broke up for the night he was relaxed and not even dreading returning to his post. Sara was looking forward to it, had questioned Brenda eagerly about the instillation, flirting with her eyes and enjoying the lust echoing between them. Her grin when he took her hand made his heart swell with tenderness.

"I'm the luckiest man alive," he whispered with heartfelt sincerity as he bent to kiss her lips.

He huffed a laugh and Sara drew away to examine him.

"What?" She asked suspiciously.

"I was just thinking Major Nelson was worried about engines. Even after all this time and everything he knows about us, he still doesn't see that we're more dangerous than any invention you could make."

The reports Nelson had read had been accurate. They all knew war was coming. The world wouldn't meekly accept them, he was certain of that. But he had no intention of being meek.

"Study hard," she said as she hugged him tightly.

"No one will ever hurt you again." He kissed her temple. "When war comes, we'll be ready."

THE END

Upcoming Book

VALOR 7

A VOW UNBROKEN

Vows are nothing to take lightly, especially when enforced by magic…

In just a few more months, Charlie will finally be a lieutenant in the Marines and able to embrace his true nature, but while everything appears to be going well, he can't seem to get a handle on his anger— or his jealousy.

Magic complicates everything…

www.ingramcontent.com/pod-product-compliance
Lightning Source LLC
La Vergne TN
LVHW050911080826
845145LV00001B/54

* 9 7 8 1 9 4 7 1 2 2 4 3 7 *